DESTINATION UNKNOWN

Book three of the Earth's Angels Trilogy

y Beth Worsdell

Cover designed by GermanCreative

Beth Worsdell
Visit my website at www.bethworsdellauthor.com

Printed in the United States of America
First Printing: August 2020
Beth Worsdell Publishing.

Dedicated

A big thank you to all my supporters and readers for your unwavering encouragement. It's been an honor to have you share my publishing journey. Special thanks to my sisters, Emma and Emily, my amazing mum, Lin and close friends, who have been o honest with their feedback.

My husband, Ian and my kids have been my ggest supporters and inspiration.

I would also like to say a massive thank you everyone who has been kind enough to leave hoest reviews for my Earth's Angels Trilogy. I truly ppreciate you taking the time to read and review my ork.

"Believe in yourself, even when it feels like no one else does."

QUOTE BY BETH WORSDELL.

CHAPTER 1

We have all been through hell and back. It was bad enough that our planet started to die, but when the ancient angels arrived, we were suddenly full of hope. Unfortunately, that hope, along with our planet, was soon destroyed by the Marilians. We thought we had the advantage with the ancient angels, elders, and dragons on our side.

However, not only did we lose more of our friends at the hands of those Marilian monsters, but now our whole remaining race is homeless. We have a plan though, and that plan involves the angels helping us to find a new home for all of us.

*****

We left the large meeting room on the angels' main craft, feeling a little more in control now that a loose plan was put into place. Tracey, Akhenaten, Luiza, and Shawn joined us as we were exiting the room, and I was going to enjoy catching up with them. Our kids had already left and were heading back to our rooms to relax.

"Thank you for the training you gave us and the kids," I told Shawn and Luiza as we walked through the busy control center. "You made a massive difference. We couldn't have fought like we did without your help."

Both of them smiled. They were very humble people, James and I liked them a lot, but with all the shooting lessons and target practice they'd been doing with everyone, we hadn't had the chance to really get to know them.

"It was our pleasure," Shawn said with another smile. "To be honest with you, we both really enjoyed it. Your Abigail and April are quite the sharp shooters!" He laughed.

"Yeah, they enjoyed reminding our boys of their mad shooting skills." James chuckled as we began our walk down the long pearlescent corridor.

"Are you nervous about adopting the three orphans, Tracey?" Luiza asked.

Tracey walked hand in hand with Akhenaten and she shrugged her shoulders.

"Nah, not really," she said nonchalantly. "I had two twin terrors before the end came, so trust me, these three are going to be a piece of cake. Plus, I have my own personal angel who happens to have the patience of a saint." She giggled.

"Give those kids two months and they'll be swearing like sailors just like their new mama." I chuckled.

Tracey gave me a fake scolding look, making me laugh even more.

"Hey, I can be saint-like too, you know. I had code words when my kids were little, so they didn't hear me swear. Only John, and our close friends and family knew what they meant," she said proudly.

"Such as what?" I asked, now feeling very curious.

Her resounding cheeky smile told me that this was going to be good.

"Well, let me see. There was, son of a goat, bar steward, mother ducker, and my all-time favorite, focus," she said proudly.

"How on earth does focus substitute a swear word?" I asked.

"Easy," she said with a grin. "Fudge Off Coz U Stupid, F...O...C...U...S... See!"

"OMG! Tracey you are so funny," I told her as we all started laughing.

"I'm going to remember that little gem," I told my husband.

We chatted as we walked, and before long Shawn and Luiza were saying goodbye. They were going to help the angels with the orphaned kids who needed pairing with new parents.

"We'll see you soon when we bring the kids over to you," Luiza told Tracey and Akhenaten as they waved goodbye and left down another corridor.

Before long Tracey and her angel had left too, and it was just the two of us.

"I'm really pleased for Tracey, not only about her getting together with Akhenaten, but also with her becoming a mom again. Having three new kids to look after is going to help her heal. Every time they smile, laugh or do something sweet," I told James just as we arrived at our rooms.

Our own kids were indeed relaxing when we walked in. The boys were reading books about architecture and the girls were all playing a card game on the floor. It was such a wonderful sight, especially as they were no longer glued to their cell phones or on their gaming consoles.

"Where did the cards and books come from?" James asked when we walked in.

"Holly," April and Abigail said in unison.

Antony looked up from his book with a smile.

"She brought all our stuff from our cabin at the cruiser just in case. Plus, a lot more books on practical stuff like filtering water, building bridges and even medical books," he said with a grin.

"And she brought books that we like too," Abigail said.

"As well as games," April added with a smile of her own.

I grinned at our family's content faces. They finally looked at ease and totally relaxed.

"We're very lucky that your sister is so thoughtful and practical," I told them.

We spent the rest of the day enjoying the kids' company. Christine had the odd teary moment when she thought of her dad which was to be expected, and Anthony was a pillar of strength for her, giving her hugs and a shoulder to cry on every time she needed it. It was nice to know that she felt comfortable and secure enough to be vulnerable in front of us.

Apart from the kids and families being relocated, there was nothing else happening on the craft, so we made the most of our lazy day together. I had a feeling that with our 'to do list' written, we were going to be fairly busy during our journey. As I sat next to my husband in our seating area, feeling our baby move and kick, it was lovely to watch our family enjoying each other's company.

Every now and then I would look out of the small circular window in our room and watch the vast amount of stars go by. I wondered how long it would take to get to the Angels' planet, Anunaki, and what it would look like. A loud tap at our archway entrance to our rooms broke me from my thoughts. When James asked whomever it was to come in, I rose from my seat.

It was Tracey, Akhenaten, and their three new children. Tracey's face showed how delighted she was to have a family again. They had three young girls with them, and they were beautiful, all hiding behind their new parents. The smallest little girl used her hand to slide her tight curly hair out of her eyes, so she could peer around Tracey's legs.

I think we all smiled at Tracey's new daughter, as she looked at us all with big brown eyes. She was watching our girls playing cards on the floor and I had a feeling that she wanted to play. The girls obviously thought so too.

"Would you like to play with us?" Abigail asked her gently.

The little girl nodded her head as her sisters peered around Tracey and Akhenaten.

"Come on then," Abigail told her with a big smile.

The next thing we knew, all three of the young girls rushed forward to play. At first, they were very shy with our kids, but as they played, they got braver and braver. They regularly looked over to Tracey and Akhenaten, so we could tell that they had already started bonding. As James and I sat with Tracey and her angel, there was another tap at our entrance and Hulaz walked in with food and drinks for everyone.

"Hulaz, did my growling stomach send you a message through my com?" I asked her humorously.

She smiled as she glided in and placed the tray on the table between us.

"I believe if your stomach could have done so, it would have, Mel," she replied. "I heard your stomach growling from the other side of our craft," she added with a smirk.

Tracey and my whole family burst into laughter, while the little girls and Akhenaten looked confused.

"Damn, you're becoming one funny angel, Hulaz," Tracey said between giggles.

"Thank you, Tracey, I believe I am learning from the best," Hulaz said as she dipped her head to us.

At that point, I was laughing just as hard as everyone else.

"We will be bringing you all food on a regular basis. We are also supplying food in the room next to the medical room," Hulaz said as our laughter died down.

"That's new," James said, sounding as surprised as we all were.

"Your body clocks, as you call them, will be disrupted for a while. As you no longer have a sun to guide your sense of time, you may be hungry at different times," Hulaz explained.

"I think it's a great idea Hulaz," I told her, selfishly thinking about my cravings in the middle of the night. '*Poor James*' I thought. "Would you like to join us?"

"I am afraid I cannot. I will see you all again soon," she said, dipping her head in respect before gliding out.

Tracey created a little picnic for the girls, so they didn't have to stop playing. As we all are together and while the girls were distracted, Tracey told us about the girls' circumstances and how they ended up alone. She explained to us that their father died protecting the farm they had lived on.

The girl's parents were homestead people, and their mother had stores of preserved food, which had kept them going. Unfortunately, people from the nearest town had become desperate when the end came, and they began to travel to the houses further out looking for supplies.

It sounded like their father had put up a good fight, but they were outnumbered, and the girls were young. Their mother had no choice but to drive away with her girls when her husband had been killed.

Their mother had been in the battle against the Marilians, and she'd been caught by the fire coming down from one of their ships. The angels weren't able to get to her in time before she perished.

As I listened to the girl's story, I was glad that they didn't have any memories of what had happened to their father. I was also heartbroken for them because they had lost their mother. It was a small consolation that she died a heroine, trying to save our planet.

Charlotte was seven years old; Rachel was nine, and Bethany was eleven years old, and I hoped that they would remember their mother well.

The rest of the day and evening was full of light-hearted talk and games with the kids. Tracey's new daughters became more confident and chattier as the hours passed. One by one, they came back to their new parents and cuddled up as they became tired. When they decided to call it a night, Akhenaten had to carry Bethany and Rachel, and Tracey carried the youngest. It wasn't long before we all decided to call it a night too. We were still mentally drained from everything that had happened.

I cuddled up to my husband, wrapping my arms around his tapered waist and enjoyed feeling his body heat warming me through and through. '*Can I remember what it was like to have a waist?*' I asked myself. It wouldn't be long before I would need help washing my feet and was no longer able to see them, that's if I carried our new daughter like I carried our other children.

With my previous pregnancies I ended up looking like Buddha; you couldn't tell where my boobs ended, and my bump started. I let sleep take me as I became sleepy and warm. My sleep was full of dreams and possibilities, of different planets and moons.

When I woke up the next morning remembering all the different things I'd dreamed about, I felt truly positive and raring to go. Breakfast was already waiting for us on the table, and I helped myself to coffee and fruit. While waiting for everyone else to wake up, Christik reached out to me via her com.

‘*Good morning Mel, would you be able to help us heal some people today*?’ she asked.

‘Sure.’ I told her, feeling glad to help, ‘I’ll meet you there after we’ve all had breakfast.’

When the kids woke up, they looked like walking zombies. None of them had slept well. As we ate our breakfast, the kids told James and I about their horrible dreams and my heart went out to them. I knew it would take them a long time to come to terms with what they’d had to do and what they had seen. I was grateful that they were openly talking about it.

I walked alone to the holding room where the encapsulated people were kept. James and the kids had decided to go with Christine to identify her dad's body and support her while she decided whether she wanted him buried or cremated. I wasn’t sure if it was a good idea, especially after all their bad dreams, but they were determined to go.

There were going to be a few weeks of funerals and wakes on the angel’s craft, but at least people had the choice about what they wanted for their loved ones.

Christik and her parents were waiting for me when I arrived, with Harrik, Zanika and Hulaz. I could understand why they would want healing angels there; Anthony had started bleeding from his wounds quite badly once he was out of his containment.

The angels obviously wanted to be able to work fast so there wasn't any suffering. There were still rows and rows of encapsulated people in the bright white holding room. The blue capsules were keeping them alive, and they were also keeping the change at bay.

The elders, angels, and I worked tirelessly for a good few hours. There were so many different kinds of injuries to deal with once they were out of their bubbles. From deep body slashes on necks, chests and stomachs from the Marilians talons, to terrible burns from either the Marilians using the fire themselves or their ships weapons.

I had never seen burn injuries like that before, and to be honest, it was stomach churning. Some of the Marilian victims had burns that were so bad, their skin had literally melted. All of them had one thing in common: they had all started to go through the change. The plus side was that the change had made them lose their memories of being attacked, so at least they wouldn't have nightmares about it.

Every time I felt utterly drained, either Christik or one of her parents would give me a boost with their power. We really did make quite the team. As soon as we healed a person and they were ok to go to their new room or family, one of the angels would flit them to where they needed to go. The majority of them were thrilled to still be alive, and between us we received plenty of hugs. That was the easy part. The next part, healing the Marilians and changing them back to whatever they were originally, was going to be harder.

James kept me updated on how they were doing with Christine and the other grieving survivors. It seemed that they were all on an emotional roller-coaster. My husband sent me images through our com on what they were seeing, and it was awful. If our children hadn't been in the actual battle and had seen it all first hand, I wouldn't have let them go. But they had already seen it and they were doing an amazing job by helping the other survivors find their lost loved ones.

James and the kids got back to our rooms first, and they were already stuffing their faces when I got back.

"Are you going to leave anything for me?" I asked as I walked in.

"Depends on how quickly to get over here," James said teasingly.

Christine was very quiet during our meal hardly eating anything, but picking at her food instead. I couldn't imagine what she was feeling.

"How did it go, Christine?" I asked her gently

"It was ok, I guess," she said hesitantly. "It was tough seeing my dad all cut up like that again. I don't think I can picture my dad looking normal ever again, but at least I can plant his ashes like Tracey did for John."

As her eyes began to well up with tears, a single tear rolled down her cheeks. Anthony wrapped his arm around her shoulders, pulling her close and she snuggled into his large frame.

"Please let us know what we can do to help you, darling," I told her.

We were so utterly drained that we wilted very rapidly after eating. After freshening up we fell into our beds and were asleep very quickly. I spent the night tossing and turning, worrying that the kids were going to have nightmares again. Every time I heard the slightest noise, I thought it was the kids, but it was mainly James turning or farting in his sleep.

Just as I began to fall into a deeper sleep, a blood-curdling scream had me leaping out of bed. I rushed over to the barrier between our rooms with James scrambling after me, and when the barrier vanished and the light came on, we could see Christine sitting up in her bed shaking like a leaf with Anthony trying to comfort her. Her whole body was trembling as tears streamed down her face. Poor Anthony looked at us with pain in his eyes. He wanted to help her, but he clearly felt helpless.

"Let's take a walk down to the angel's canteen. We can get a drink and talk," I told them as Christine looked at all the kids faces, who were all looking at her with sympathy.

Christine looked up with grateful eyes.

"I'm sorry I woke you all," she tried to say through sobs.

"You don't need to apologize, my darling," I told her gently. "I'm sure most of us will be waking you up over the next few weeks."

Before long, we were making our way down to the canteen. None of the kids were ready to go back to sleep, and as we strolled down the long corridor, the kids began discussing their dreams. The canteen was surprisingly full of people and children. There were so many, young and old, who were crying and sobbing at their loss while being comforted by friends, remaining family members, or angels.

When we entered, we were given knowing looks of sympathy and understanding. There were many familiar faces there too, including Tracey, Akhenaten, and their girls. Both Tracey and Akhenaten were talking gently to their three new daughters, and because we didn't want to intrude, we took seats around a large empty wooden table.

"I'll get us some drinks," James said before walking away with both of our boys following him.

Christine sat between me and Abigail, and I reached over taking her hand in mine. "Would you like something to eat?"

The poor girl looked uncomfortably embarrassed when she looked up, and I could see the pain in her light blue eyes.

"I don't think I could stomach anything to eat right now," she said quietly.

"Were you dreaming about your dad getting hurt?" I asked gently.

Christine nodded her head. "I was dreaming about the whole battle," she answered as her voice trembled with emotion. "My mind replayed the whole thing. When I dreamt of my dad being slaughtered, it was like I was there again," she said, her voice nearly a whisper. "I didn't realize I screamed out loud, I'm really sorry," she added.

Without realizing, I started to stroke her hand trying to comfort her in some small way.

"You honestly don't need to be sorry, Christine," I assured her. "Sometimes our mind cries out for help and comfort when we don't realize ourselves that we need it."

Christine gave me a grateful smile just as James and the boys came back with our much-needed drinks. When James placed a steaming hot coffee in front of me, I could have kissed him. I'd always been one of those people who could drink coffee right up to bedtime and still fall asleep right away, which was something James envied.

"I hope the angels have got plenty of coffee to keep you going," he said with a smile.

"What will we do if our plants and trees won't grow on our new planet?" Harrison asked curiously.

We all stopped drinking to ponder his question, because not only would we be affected by it, but so would our animals too.

"I suppose we'll have to keep looking for a suitable planet for all our plants and creatures," James told him with a thoughtful look. "It wouldn't be right for us to survive and not our animals. They wouldn't be able to adjust as easily as us on a new world, and we don't want them suffering."

We spent a couple of hours in the canteen discussing our possible future and new home. None of us seemed too worried, knowing that the angels weren't going to leave us stranded somewhere that wasn't suitable.

As we talked about the possibilities, which was a welcome distraction for Christine, people left the canteen and more arrived. It was very clear that this was what it was going to be like for a while. The angels could heal wounds—soothe emotions through their power and touch, but they couldn't purposefully take memories away or heal our grief, as much as they would like too.

Christine appeared much calmer on our way back to our rooms. We were so tired that our walk back was slower, and our footsteps were definitely heavier. We fell into our beds without even saying goodnight again, even James and I rolled over without saying a word.

CHAPTER 2

James and I woke to the sound of our kids doing their version of talking quietly. Unfortunately, the more they talked the louder they got. It was wonderful to hear them all sounding more cheerful than the night before, and I could tell that they were stuffing their faces from the sounds of crunching.

"Good morning, my tribe," I said as I struggled to get out of our bed.

I seriously felt like I needed a big crane to hoist me off the comfortable mattress, but James kindly decided to help me up by pushing my widening backside.

"Thank you, husband of mine," I said as I began to stretch out my back by tilting back slightly.

"That's what I'm here for, my lady," he said with a cheeky smirk.

When I looked at our kids sitting at the table with their breakfast, they were rolling their eyes. The morning meal was a short affair with James and I trying to eat something, anything, before the kids demolished the lot. As we sat eating, my mind wandered. It felt strange to wake up and not have things to do, such as shooting practice or battle preparations. I was seriously wondering what to do with myself, and I knew it wouldn't be long before our kids would be bored too.

"I'm going to speak with Christik and the elders today," I told James and the kids. "We need to get things back to some sort of normality. Otherwise everyone's going to get bored and frustrated. Plus, all the kids still need their education."

"I think you're right babe," James said, nodding his head. "Being busy will help everyone focus on something positive too."

The kids subconsciously nodded in agreement while finishing the last pieces of fruit.

"I'd like to get back to my studies and painting!" Abigail exclaimed with a beaming smile.

"What about you guys?" I asked the boys, April, and Christine, "What would you like to do?"

Christine looked at Antony before giving her answer. "I'd like to design houses for us to live in, ready for when we get to our new home. I really enjoyed working with my dad, and I want to use the skills my dad taught me," she explained honestly.

I couldn't stop myself from smiling at her with pride, and I knew her dad would have been extremely proud of her too.

"Anthony, what about you?" I asked our eldest son.

He smiled at his girlfriend before looking at James and me. "Harrison and I were talking about it last night while the girls were getting ready for bed. We'd like to carry on learning about all the green energy that the angels use, and also help Christine to design environmentally friendly homes."

"Well, Holly certainly saved you all plenty of books and materials for you to use," I told them. "April, what would you like to do or focus on?"

Our new daughter straightened herself up in her comfy chair and pulled her shoulders back confidently. "I want to work with all the animals on board the ship," she said.

"Then you can work with me and the angels honey," James told her warmly. "I still want to be a vet, so maybe we can work together."

A huge smile spread across April's angelic face and her eyes immediately lit up. "I would love that, Dad, thank you," she told him, her happiness and excitement clear in her soft voice.

"What are you going to do, Mom?" Anthony asked.

My kids knew I wasn't the kind of woman who could just do nothing, and I had always been the same since I was a young child.

"I'm going to help organize schooling for all the kids, and then I'm going to sort out the Marilians the angels captured," I explained. "I don't know how many there are, but I'm sure we can get them all changed back into what they were originally."

After finishing our meal, James left with April to go down to where the animals were all kept. I could tell April was really excited about working with the animals, because she wasn't walking out of our suite, she was positively bouncing with happiness. Before they left, James made sure that he took his basic veterinary books with them, so he could start teaching April what he'd learned so far.

Our boys and Christine had asked Christik if they could use one of the smaller meeting rooms for their work, and she couldn't have been more helpful. As soon as they had arrived, Anthony reached through his com to tell me that the angel had arranged for papers and pencils, as well as shelves for their books and refreshments. I knew they were going to make the most of having the room to themselves to work, and I was looking forward to seeing what they came up with.

After reaching out to her previous volunteer teachers, Abigail decided she would walk with me in the direction of the large meeting room. She was going to meet her teachers at the new canteen room, as there were plenty of tables and chairs for the kids. Abigail wasn't the only child who had already reached out to the teachers. It seemed that many parents and kids alike had wanted to get back to normal.

"Are you looking forward to getting creative again and learning from your tutors?" I asked her as we walked down the long pearlescent corridor.

Her beaming smile said it all.

"I really am Mom," she said. "I did like the combat training, even though I wouldn't have chosen to do all those things normally. I am glad I take care of myself now," she added.

"I know what you mean, darling. I wouldn't have chosen to learn those things either," I told her honestly. "At least we have extra skills now."

"Like riding dragons?" Abigail grinned

"Yes, like riding dragons." I laughed. "You never know when dragon riding is going to be useful," I tried to say in a mock serious tone, Abigail laughed as we carried on walking.

Before long, we had reached the canteen and Abigail gave me a hug before she dashed off into the large room. I knew that I'd have to come back and get her later in the day, because she'd be enjoying herself so much. More adults and children were walking towards the canteen as I left to meet Christik and the elders; the kids all looked excited and the adults looked relieved.

It reminded me of my own kids on their first days of school. Anthony hadn't wanted to go, and he didn't feel ready at all. The twins were excited on their first day, but were devastated that they wouldn't be in the same class together. As for Holly, she took to school like a duck takes to water. At home time she'd be sad to leave and during the long summer holidays, for her, it felt like punishment not being able to go.

The memories made me smile and I hoped that once we were settled on our new planet, we would be able to set up schools quickly for the kids, so they could still learn and have that structure. As soon as I thought about living on a new planet, butterflies fluttered in my stomach and I felt my baby girl wriggling, almost as if she felt them too.

I arrived at the main control room and all the angels were occupied at their consoles busily working. Those who noticed me dipped their heads in respect and smiled warmly. As I walked through the large room, I glanced at the massive glass window at the front of the craft.

We were traveling so fast, the stars and planets were a blur of flashes as we zoomed past them. I forced myself to look away, knowing that I could easily stand there like an idiot watching the universe pass us by.

The elders and Christik were all talking around the large wooden table as I approached the meeting room, and the doors opened before me. There were beautiful smiles from Evest, Lindaz and the other elders; Mikaz, Eliz, Ronak and Nical, who had arrived with them. I gave them a bright smile before dipping my head in respect. I was surprised to see all the elders in the meeting room, only expecting Christik's parents to be present.

"Hello, Mel," Christik said warmly. "The elders are here to help us today."

I shouldn't have been surprised that Christik had picked up on my thoughts straight away.

"I didn't think we'd need that much power," I said, surprised, hoping I didn't come across rude.

Christik grinned as my cheeks began to turn a darkening shade of pink.

"I do not think that you realize how many Marilians we have captured, Mel," Evest said from across the table. "Do not forget, the Marilians invaded your whole planet, not just your country. We captured hundreds of them, and they are aboard all of our main crafts."

"I can't change hundreds of them!" I squeaked, knowing how exhausting that would be.

"That is why we are going to help you, Mel," Ronak said kindly. "We will magnify your baby's power, so you can change many Marilians at the same time."

"Well ok then," I told them. "I'm game if you are."

All of them smiled at me, not because they understood what I'd said, but because they could feel my uncertainty and determination to get the job done.

"The Marilians are being held at the back of our hangar. We did not have any larger holding rooms for them," Christik told me. "Come, we will go there now."

The elders rose from their seats and they led the way out of the meeting room and into the main control room. I felt tiny walking beside the tall gliding elders and Christik as we passed through the large room. This time the angels in the room didn't just dip their heads, they pretty much bowed to the elders as we made our way to the exit. I could feel the reverence and respect from all the angels, and I could understand why.

It was nice walking with the elders and Christik and I was relieved that we weren't flitting down to the hangar. The silence from the elders was regularly broken with hellos from other human survivors going about their business or just talking a walk.

The elders didn't feel the need for small talk which made a refreshing change, especially as I had so much going on in my mind. The uncertainty of our future and having no home was starting to get to me, and I was also feeling very hormonal.

When we finally reached the large hangar, I couldn't even see the Marilians that were supposed to be in there, mainly because the hangar was so big and was filled with all the smaller crafts. Evest and Lindaz led the way through the crafts and when we finally passed through them my breath hitched in my chest. All along the back wall were dozens of Marilians, all restrained in silver metal vines with the large gold discs above their heads and under their large hairy feet.

Even though the Marilians had all started off as various races from worlds all over the universe, they all looked the same. They had long, coarse dark brown hair covering their muscular bodies, vicious looking faces that appeared part sloth, with small ears set at the backs of their heads. Their wolf-like muzzles were fully equipped with super sharp pointed teeth, and their long metal talons were as sharp as razor blades.

The Marilians blood-red eyes made my own blood run cold, and my heart began to hammer in my chest. Hairs on the back of my neck started to prickle and stand up, matching the hairs on my arms that were standing to attention on the goosebumps I suddenly had. I could feel their frustration and their desire to kill or turn me, and it struck me that they weren't having those feelings towards Christik and the elders.

“Can you feel what they’re feeling?” I asked my angel friends. “It’s as if you don't exist.”

Lindaz, who was standing next to me, took my hand in hers letting her power run through my body, settling my nerves and calming my racing heart.

“We believe they are not driven to hurt us because they sense that they are unable to hurt, kill, or change us,” Lindaz explained.

“That's why they are all homing in on me?” I asked with wide eyes.

“Yes,” she answered honestly.

“Well, the sooner we change them the better I’ll feel!”

As we moved towards the Marilian monsters,

their feelings of aggression towards me escalated, and they began to fight against their restraining metal vines. I trusted the angels and their restraining techniques, but the sight of the Marilians struggling and fighting against their bonds had me on hyper alert. I suddenly wished that I had Qiu the dragon with me for moral support and protection, just in case.

While we moved closer, the elders and Christik started to fan out behind me, all moving into position. Whereas before, when I was helping our human survivors after the battle, Christik and her parents gave me power boosts, this time they were going to do things differently. I stopped in front of the struggling, defiant Marilians with their blood-red eyes all on me, just far enough away so that my baby girl's power could reach them all.

One by one, the elders and Christik all placed a hand on my body. I could feel them gently making contact with my arms and shoulders. Christik was the last to place her hand between my shoulder blades before she spoke next to my ear.

"Trust your baby and your own instinct, Mel, you will both feel what you need to do," she said softly.

I took a long, deep and slow breath, letting myself feel and absorb the angels' power flowing through my nervous body through their light touch.

They made me feel powerful, and within moments, I felt as though I had the power within me to do anything. Opening my eyes, I scanned the rows of Marilians before me and I raised my hands, aiming my palms at the evil monsters.

The power from my baby girl was building in the center of my body, and as soon as it began to feel too much for me, it burst from my hands in a flash of brilliant shimmering white streams, branching out to each individual Marilian.

The power hit them with full force in their faces, and as soon as contact was made, the white power spread over their bodies as if coating them. Their faces turned from pure aggression and hatred, to a look that made them seem completely spaced out. We could see them visibly relax within their bonds, slumping against the metal vines that were keeping them in place. Seeing them so subdued made me relax, especially as I could feel that none of them wanted to kill or change me anymore.

For a moment I wasn't sure what I was seeing, it was as if their faces and bodies were going out of focus. At first, I thought it may have been my eyes, because of the power that was coursing through my body. I concentrated and I noticed subtle changes beginning to occur.

There were so many of them that I decided to

focus on just one. I stared at the closest Marilian in front of me, and I could see the dark thick hair absorbing back into its body. The small ears set back on its head became smooth and they began to grow upwards and outwards, its muzzle started to smooth and elongate more, as the creature before me began to appear more bat-like in appearance.

I couldn't take my eyes away from the changing creature and in my peripheral vision, I was noticing various colors appearing, some brighter than others. The Marilian before me was not looking like a Marilian any longer. The razor-sharp talons were disappearing into pale orange hands, which then grew into three stubby fingers with red tips. My eyes scanned over the new alien before me, and it was quite a sight.

The creature definitely had bat-like ears, but on the sides of its bright orange and green tinged head were what looked like large gills for breathing. When I looked down its lean muscular body, down to its hands and feet, I noticed that the alien had pale, sheer webbing in between its fingers and long bulbous toes. I was fascinated with the new creature in front of me, and I knew that it obviously lived underwater or some other kind of fluid. '*This was going to get very interesting*' I thought to myself.

The power flowing through and out of me started to feel different. Looking at my outstretched hands, I saw the power changing color from the bright white to a pale blue, getting darker with every second that passed. I knew straight away why it was changing. Most of the aliens in the hangar wouldn't be able to survive the oxygen rich environment that the angels had provided for us. Our power was beginning to coat them all in the blue fluid capsules, holding them in stasis. It wasn't long before all of the aliens were encased inside the blue capsules, and I could feel the power inside me starting to wane.

The blue power streams coming from my palms lessened until it finally stopped, and I was happy that I didn't feel exhausted like before. I lowered my hands as the elders and Christik removed theirs from my body.

"Would you like to take a closer look at them?" Christik asked as she waved her arm at the rows of encapsulated aliens.

I felt somewhat hesitant walking up to the aliens to stare at them, like they were in a zoo or freak show. Christik obviously picked up on my uncomfortable emotions.

"Do not feel uneasy, Mel, they cannot see you or feel your presence while they are contained," she assured.

I was the only one in the hangar who was in

awe and intrigued by the various aliens that were lined up. The elders and Christik had encountered and worked with aliens from all over the universe, so nothing surprised them. I smiled at Christik's reass-uring words and then tentatively walked towards the alien that I had been watching.

The silver metal vines were no longer restr-aining the alien, but rather holding it in place as it floated inside the blue fluid bubble. Its dark green eyes were open, but they appeared glazed and unsee-ing. As I looked closer at the alien's skin, I noticed that it wasn't smooth like I first thought, it appeared snake-like, with a visible and delicate scale pattern of various shades of orange. Even though the alien was extremely strange to me, it was quite a beautiful creature in its own way.

I looked away and began to slowly walk alo-ng the first row of aliens and one of them caught my eye. It was floating in the middle of the blue fluid capsule and it looked like a large, elaborate jellyfish. It had the same domed shape as the jellyfish that we'd seen when we'd taken our kids to the Sea Life center in Long Beach, but this was a lot bigger and it was covered in various fluorescent colors. Even within the blue fluid, its colors were vibrant and glowing. I turned to Christik and the elders in sur-prise.

"This one looks a lot like the jellyfish that were on our planet!" I exclaimed.

"That is because they are related," Christik told me, "when the Marilians attacked their planet Cidari, they took much of the Jeli's water and what they did not take, they made uninhabitable for this race. We were forced to relocate the Jeli to your planet while we repaired theirs."

"But why were there still jellyfish on Earth?" I asked.

"Some of the Jeli race did not wish to leave," Lindaz said softly. "Just like our son did not," she added with a weak smile.

As I stood looking at Lindaz, I wondered how many other aliens there'd been on Earth that we didn't know about.

CHAPTER 3

I took a moment to take in what Lindaz had told me, and her angelic face looked quite bemused as she picked up on my feelings of surprise and curiosity. I wanted to look at the rest of the aliens even more, especially knowing that there might be others that I might recognize.

Smiling at Lindaz, I carried on looking through the capsules to check out the aliens, and my goodness, they came in so many different shapes, sizes, and colors. There were creatures of all colors with long fur, wings, horns, scales, and some that had multiple heads. My eyes were nearly popping out of my head at the sight of some of them. Many were so big that they had moved the other capsules around them.

When I walked up to one of the larger aliens at the back of the rows, I think my jaw may have dropped to my boobs. There in front of me was a woolly mammoth with the biggest tusks I'd ever se-en, but it wasn't brown fur that covered its massive body, it was thick, shaggy silvery-grey fur.

"These were on earth when the dinosaurs we-re around," I said to no one in particular. "I saw photos of them in books when I was in school."

"Yes, they were another race we saved," Ev-est said. "Unfortunately, their planet was completely destroyed, so they stayed on Earth until we could find them another planet to inhabit."

"Don't tell me, some of them didn't want to leave," I said with a smile.

Evest smiled back with humor dancing in his colorful peacock eyes.

"Exactly, Mel."

"I can't wait to tell James and the kids that woolly mammoths were actually aliens." I laughed. "I'm sure they're not going to believe me."

"You are more than welcome to bring them down here, so they can see the Mammot for them-selves," Christik said kindly.

"That's what they're called, Mammot?"

"Yes," Christik said with another smile. "Many names were changed over time. Your language changed and developed very quickly over the centuries."

Just as I was pondering over the new information, thinking of the slang words that were invented since I was a child, my stomach gave a loud growl. It was as if it was telling the whole hangar it was hungry. I was so embarrassed that I could feel my cheeks instantly burning, so I knew that they were bright red.

"I think now is the time to eat," Christik declared with a grin.

I honestly didn't want to leave, and Christik and the elders knew it.

"We still have work to do," I said through my embarrassment.

"That we do, Mel," Evest replied as he held out both of his palms.

I looked at the elders outstretched hands, without a clue as to what he was doing, then in a flash of white power a mini feast was appearing in his hands on a stone platter. Just enough food for all of us. My expression must have been a happy one, because all of the elders and Christik smiled back in response. I helped myself to what I could fit in my hands and began to eat, my stomach grumbling loudly in gratitude.

"Thank you," I told Evest warmly.

As Christik used her power to make a small table and some chairs appear, I slowly carried on, walking along the long rows of aliens with Lindaz walking beside me. After a few more minutes, Lindaz pointed to a capsule just ahead of us.

"This creature is called a Jagu and I do believe that they visited your planet when your race was evolving well. I understand that the Jagu had quite an impact on your ancient Egyptians."

"Can it breathe oxygen then?" I asked as we walked right up to it.

"Yes, it can," Lindaz replied.

I walked up to the encapsulated Jagu and it was extremely cat like. It was taller than James, so I guessed around a height of six foot five, and its body was muscular but slender. It was definitely male, from the male tackle that was hanging just above the apex of its thighs. I made myself look upwards and the Jagu's face was feline in appearance, with the same kind of muzzle and nose as a big cat, such as a lion or puma. Although he had more human-like eyebrows and no whiskers like an earth cat would have. His whole body was jet black, and it looked as smooth as silk. When I looked at the top of its head, there was a mass of long, dark grey braids growing from behind its large, pointy cat-like ears.

"If the Jagu were interacting with the ancient Egyptians, then they must have been friendly," I said, as I studied the elegant figure before me.

"Yes, they are friendly," Lindaz said. "In fact, they had such a good relationship with the ancient Egyptians that the Egyptians became cat worshippers after the Jagu left your planet," she added.

"I can't believe there's so much that we didn't know," I uttered, feeling flabbergasted. "Can we release the Jagu from the capsule? It seems unfair to keep him contained if he can survive on board."

I knew there was no point asking for the Mammot to be released—its sheer size made it impossible.

"I'm sure there's a lot we could learn from the Jagu, especially about our own race."

Lindaz smiled at my words and my feelings of compassion towards the alien.

"We can release him. Your kindness never ceases to impress me, Mel," she replied. "You have the power to release him," Lindaz said as she waved her arm at the Jagu.

Standing in front of the Jagu, I felt my baby moving inside me as her power began to build. Lindaz lightly placed her hand on my shoulder, letting me use her power too. Raising my hands with my palms facing the blue fluid capsule, I let my instincts take over once more. It felt easier this time, and I didn't think it was just because Lindaz was helping me. It was as if my body and my baby were completely in sync and it was beginning to feel effortless. The fluid surrounding the Jagu acted the same as with the humans I'd healed, and it began to ripple rapidly and turn to miniature waves.

This process seemed faster than before, and as the waves moved along the fluid's bubbling surface, I waited for it to reach for me. I felt it change before the first turbulent wave protruded from the bubble, feeling cool as it touched the sensitive skin of my palms. As my body started absorbing the blue fluid energy, I could feel it soaking into every fiber of my being and before long the bubble thinned, then it was gone. Bright, emerald green cat eyes were suddenly blinking at me in confusion, flitting from me to Lindaz and back again.

I felt the alarm coming from the Jagu as he realized he was restrained within the silver metal vines, and he began to struggle against them, trying to get out. His eyes started to dart around the hangar as he desperately searched for imminent threats. The elder could obviously feel the Jagu's confusion and alarm. She glided towards him without hesitation, making eye contact with the Jagu and placing her hand gently on his muscular chest. Her other hand went to her throat and it glowed as she changed her dialect.

'*Do not panic, young one,*' I heard in my head, as she spoke to the Jagu in a language that sounded as lovely to my ears as the French dialect. '*You are safe and the Marilians are no longer a threat to you.*"

The Jagu's demeanor changed immediately, and he relaxed at her words and the calming power that flowed through him. His metal vine restraints melted from his body at the same time as his fighting instincts, pooling at his bare feet within the gold metal disc he stood on.

'*Where am I?*' I heard in my mind as Lindaz translated.

'*You are on board our craft, young one, let me help you understand us both before I explain everything to you,*' Lindaz told him. '*Please step down*'.

The Jagu stepped from the gold disc, allowing the top disc to slowly drop and meet the bottom one, before making contact with the floor. He nodded his head to Lindaz, and she raised her other hand with her palm upturned. Within a split second of white light, she held two communication bands, just like James and the other men wore. Another burst of light from her power, and the Jagu was suddenly wearing clothes.

His attire looked Egyptian in style. He wore a pure white, wrap-around skirt with a strange looking woven belt around his waist, and around his neck, resting along his shoulders, was a decorative collar adorned with colorful glass or gems. I wasn't sure which. He looked down at himself and a smile appeared on his striking, feline face.

'*Please hold out your arms*' she asked him kindly before she removed her other hand from his chest.

The male Jagu did as requested and with a new confidence he held out both arms to the elder. Very gently Lindaz slipped both of the bands onto the Jagu's wrists with ease, and we watched as the bands seemed to melt and absorb into his silky black skin. I could barely make out the hieroglyphs between the bands, but his raised eyebrows gave me the impression that he'd recognized them.

"Thank you," he said to Lindaz with a smile. "Are any more of my tribe here?"

"We have only you so far, young one, but we still have many more to heal. What is your given name?" Lindaz asked as the Jagu looked at us both in turn.

"I am Orchi of the Arbari tribe," he declared with the same pride in his words as his new demeanor.

I was seriously impressed with the Jagu warrior, I knew straight away that James and the kids would be too.

"It's a great pleasure to meet you, Orchi," I told him, holding out my hand for a hand-shake. '*What the hell am I thinking*' I instantly told myself. '*Only humans shake hands for, fricks sake*'.

I chided myself for being a complete idiot, but my hand was already outstretched, and I wasn't sure what to do. Luckily Orchi took my hand in his, raising it to his face as I watched completely stunned. I wasn't sure what to expect. Orchi surprised me by placing his nose to the top of my hand and sniffing it. '*What the hell*' popped into my head, but I was too surprised and too polite to say anything.

"You are good inside," he said, and I could feel that he meant it as a real compliment.

"Thank you," I said politely as my cheeks began to heat. "I'm Mel."

Orchi released my hand and then he placed his own hand on the center of his chest.

"My honor," Orchi replied as the other elders and Christik came to join us.

After introductions, Christik took Orchi to what would be his new room, with the promise that the elders would let him know if any other Jagu were found. I was left with the elders in the hangar, wondering what we were going to do next. Evest glided over and stood next to me, looking at the aliens closest to us.

"Are you ready for the next group?"

When I turned to look at the elder, he had a smirk on his face and a little more sparkle in his peacock eyes.

"Yes, I believe I am," I said, with a little smirk of my own.

There was a little shimmer from his body, and all of a sudden, the golden angels that I'd seen before at Cubanaz, the underwater city and at Stonehenge, were all standing next to the encapsulated aliens. Each of the angels placed their hands on the capsules they were next to, and in a blink of an eye they vanished. In the next moment they were back again, but this time they brought more unchanged Marilians.

I stood there with my mouth agape for the next hour, watching the golden angels remove and replace the aliens for Marilians. I actually felt worn out just watching them work, even though they made the process look effortless.

A strong male voice in my head broke me from my almost trance like state.

'*How's it going baby*?' James asked, sounding very cheerful.

I reached for the communication device at the top of my breasts. I was so used to having the necklace shaped device on that I always forgot it was there until I needed to use it.

'*It's going really well baby, you wouldn't believe all the different aliens that I've seen so far,*' I told him. '*Talk about us humans living in ignorant bliss. I think it would have blown our minds to know how many other races there were in the universe. Have you and April finished with the animals*?' I asked.

'*Yeah, we're just putting some books away for tomorrow, what about you*?' James asked.

'*We aren't done by a long way. Why don't you and April join us down here in the hangar?*' I suggested, knowing that both my husband and daughter would jump at the chance.

'*We'll be right down,*' he said quickly.

James and April arrived in less than five minutes, appearing out of thin air with Harrik holding onto their forearms. Both my husband and newly adopted daughter were shivering slightly from flitting. As the last of the aliens were taken by the golden angels and the last batch of Marilians arrived, James and April both stood with wide eyes and their mouths open, showing me what I'd looked like hours earlier.

"Damn, there's so many to change," James

said looking at me in surprise.

"These are the second batch," I told him with a grin. "We've already changed this amount, there must be lots of them on all the main crafts."

Finally noticing the elders in the hangar, James and April dipped their heads in respect and said hello, before moving closer to the encapsulated Marilians.

"You may need to move back slightly, James, April; we will be changing the Marilians in one go," Evest told them warmly.

James and April didn't need telling again, they trusted the elders' judgement.

"Are you ready, Mel?" Evest asked, as he and the other elders began to place their gentle hands on my upper body once again.

"Yes."

The elders and I went through the whole process once again, this time with our little audience. I couldn't see James's and April's faces, as I was concentrating on healing the Marilians, but I could feel their amazement at what we were doing. When the Marilians were changed back to their original races, James and April stood in a stunned silence. As soon as it was over, and the elders removed their hands, James and April didn't hesitate to come over to join me.

"That was amazing, Mel!" James said with a look of awe written on his handsome features.

"You're a bad-ass, Mom!" April declared, making the elders smile at her.

"Do you want to go and have a look?" I asked.

Both of them nodded their heads eagerly.

"If you spot any cat like aliens then let us know. They're called the Jagu and we've already released one, called Orchi," I told them.

"Really?" James said with surprise. "You've released an alien on board the craft with families on here?"

"Don't worry, James. You need to trust me babe. The Jagu visited Earth a long time ago and they're friendly," I said curtly.

My husband held up both of his hands, as if in defeat.

"You can meet him later and see for yourself," I assured him.

'*Damn, I'm feeling moody*' I thought, as I watched James and April looking through the capsules at the aliens.

We stayed down in the hangar for quite a while, while James and April studied the aliens and discussed their various differences with the elders, and what kind of planet they may have come from. I was starting to feel tired, but I didn't have the heart to hurry them along. Both of them were in their element, studying the creatures and enjoying each other's company. I knew and understood that having a father in her life was new to April, and I felt like she had a lot to make up for. Every now and then April would look over to me, as if checking that I was alright. I smiled at her in reassurance.

"Shall we have some refreshments and a sit down?" Lindaz asked, as if reading my mind.

I smiled at the elder in gratitude and she quickly glided away, leading me to the waiting chairs and table that were now ladened with fresh drinks and fruits. My mind was full of thoughts of aliens and planets, as if my brain was trying to process all the new information and grasp the fact that we humans were just one of millions of races in the universe. It was mind blowing.

"We are not far from the Jagu's planet. It may be a suitable planet for your race, if the Jagu do not mind sharing it," Lindaz said.

I swear it was uncanny how the angels felt our feelings and read our minds. Her words had me intrigued immediately.

"You think that's a possibility?" I asked, trying not to get my hopes up.

"It is a possibility. However, there are many

things to take into consideration. The Jagu are tribal and are very territorial over their lands, but they are also a highly intelligent race. They may see benefits in having another race living on their world," Lindaz explained.

"I suppose there's only one way to find out and that's to ask them," I replied with a sigh.

"Ask who, what?" James asked with a humongous grin on his face and excitement in his eyes as he walked over with April and the elders in toe.

"To ask the Jagu if we can live on their planet with them," I answered, smiling at my husband, and daughter who was also grinning.

"Ooooh, I see. Don't you think we should meet them first babe?"

"Absolutely, and check out their planet," I told him with a smirk. "We aren't just going to move in babe, and shout, WE ARE HERE!" I added sarcastically.

James looked a little embarrassed. "You're right baby, I'm still in shock from all the aliens. I don't think my brain is working right now."

Right away, I felt like the world's biggest bitch. It wasn't in my nature to snap at people, especially not my husband and kids. I looked at my husband guilty.

"I'm sorry, James. I didn't mean to bite your

head off."

James walked over to me, bending forward and cupping my face in his gentle, but large hands.

"You're allowed to be moody. You're very pregnant and you've had a hard day," he said softly. "How about calling it quits for the day?"

"That's a good idea."

James offered me his hand to help me up from the chair and as soon as I was standing, he wrapped me in his arms and held me for a moment. '*You are amazing, my lady*', I heard in my mind as I felt his love for me. At that moment, I wished that he could feel my love for him too.

We followed the elders out of the hangar, and as we made our way back to our suite, I was feeling guilty for leaving all the aliens in their bubble capsules. I had to remind myself of two things: firstly, they were all in stasis so they weren't aware of anything, and also most of them wouldn't survive if released. I really hoped that we would find some more Jagu's too. I didn't know if Orchi was religious in any way, but I did wonder if he was wishing with all his might that there would be more survivors of his race. As obvious warriors, I imagined that they had put up quite a fight when the Marilians had attacked their planet.

From what I'd already seen while healing the

aliens, there were quite a number of the same race, and it seemed to me that the numbers were reflected on how aggressive or defendable the aliens appeared. The aliens who looked fierce and able to defend themselves with talons, spikes, or sharp teeth were very small in numbers. Whereas the aliens with soft looking bodies with no visible defensive attributes were in much greater numbers, such as the Jeli.

CHAPTER 4

By the time we arrived back at our suite, I felt exhausted in body and mind. When the kids arrived back, I was already fast asleep, not waking until the next day. The next morning when I finally did open my eyes, it was to the sound of laughter. When I looked to see where the laughter had come from, I was shocked to see Orchi sitting with my family around the small table in our lounge-dining area. I knew straight away that they were all taken with him, as I could hear them eagerly asking him questions about his planet.

"That was excellent timing baby, look who's

here," James said with a smile.

To be honest, I was a little embarrassed that Orchi had arrived while I was sleeping, but then I chided myself for being silly, because no one really cared, so why should I.

"It's lovely to see you again, Orchi," I told our Jagu guest genuinely. "How long was I asleep for?" I asked my husband as I rubbed my eyes.

James looked at me with a little smirk and his brows raised on his too-handsome-for-his own-good face. "You slept right through the night, baby."

"What, seriously?"

"There was no waking you Mel. You were dead to the world, excuse the pun," James said with sympathy now on his face. "You needed it!"

"I'll get a quick shower to wake myself up, and then I'll come and sit with you all," I told Orchi and my family.

I took my time, enjoying the feel of the water on my body. By the time I finished, and I'd cleaned my teeth, I felt awake, refreshed and my mouth no longer felt as dry as a camel's ass. My hair felt as soft as silk, and it was getting so long that I was able to tie it back into a knot. Just as I began to slip on the clean dress from the wall opening in the bathroom, a sharp twinge shot from my swollen pregnant belly through to my lower back. '*I must have slept weirdly*'

I thought to myself. I wasn't too worried about it. After already having four kids, I'd felt lots of twinges with all of them in the later stages of my pregnancies. Especially in the last trimester, when they would press against a nerve in my back or hip.

James and the kids were still chatting with Orchi, who seemed to have the patience of a saint, answering their questions in a friendly manner. The Jagu appeared to be enjoying the conversations just as much as my family. I was a little disappointed that I'd missed so much of their conversations. The last thing I wanted to do was to start asking Orchi questions that he'd already been asked.

"Would you like to get something to eat from the canteen, Mel?" James asked as I approached the seating area.

I instantly realized how hungry I was, and I willed my stomach to remain quiet.

"Yes, I'm so hungry right now that I could eat a horse."

Orchi's eyes grew wide in sheer horror, and when I looked at his face, I knew he'd taken my words literally. I had to stop myself from laughing, not wanting to offend the Jagu warrior. I held up both of my hands automatically to stop any further reaction from Orchi.

"It's just a human expression, Orchi, I wouldn't really be able to eat a horse," I assured him with a genuine smile.

The look on his face was so comical that I had to force myself again not to laugh. I could see the kids were trying to stifle giggles too, following my lead.

"Let's get some food," James announced as he rose from his seat, saving me from the situation.

Orchi walked beside James and I as we made our way to the canteen, and the kids walked on ahead all discussing what Orchi had already told them. The corridor was bustling with people either making their way to or from the canteen. When we arrived, the canteen was packed with people, kids and angels all eating and talking. We had become one big community, and it was lovely to witness.

We managed to find a couple of tables towards the back of the cavernous room, and as James and Orchi took seats, the kids and I went to get food and drinks. We came back to the table with enough food for everyone, and when I placed my tray down on the table, my stomach growled loudly in gratitude. '*Typical*' I thought as I took my seat next to James and Orchi.

"How are you settling in, Orchi?" I asked our new friend.

The Jagu warrior came across relaxed and content, which I was pleased about.

"I am settling in well, Mel. I am grateful to you for healing me," he said, as he placed his left hand against his chest. "I am hopeful that there will be more of my race saved."

"Do you have any idea of what's left of your planet and your race?" I asked him.

His sorrowful expression spoke volumes, and I suddenly felt terrible for asking the question.

"I do not know for sure, but we were fighting harder than I believe they thought we would. The Marilians assumed that because we aren't numerous in numbers across our planet, that we could be conquered easily. What they didn't realize is that we live in harmony with our planet and our plant life protects us."

"What do you mean, your plant life protects you?" James asked our guest.

"I mean literally, James. Our planet is covered in vegetation that not only has defensive features, but our plant life has some kind of intelligence. Our planet is sacred to us, we protected our world and our world protected us."

"What's the last thing you remember?" I asked. "I'm sorry if you've already explained to my family," I added.

"We were talking about our time on Earth

while you were sleeping," Orchi said nicely. "The last thing I remember was our jungle attacking the Marilians as they were trying to attack our village. We live in the trees, and our trees create our dwellings within their branches. In return, we protect them from creatures on our planet who would harm them. I do not know how much damage was done to my world. I fell from my dwelling during the attack. I must have been changed as I laid on the ground."

The feeling of loss that I felt from Orchi was so deep that it reminded me of the recent emotions that I felt, when I witnessed Anthony being attacked and partly changed.

"Do you have a family, a wife and children, Orchi?" I asked gently.

The emotional pain on his feline face said it all before he uttered a word.

"I did, but I do not know if I still do."

"We will do our best to try and find out, Orchi," I told him, and I meant it.

James and our kids, as well as Christine, all nodded their heads in determined agreement. We would all do our best for Orchi and for all the other aliens who had lost so much because of the Marilian monsters.

"Agghh!"

My cry of pain came out of my mouth, as

soon as another twinge coursed through my abdomen, and James was kneeling next to me by my next breath.

“What’s wrong, Mel?”

My hands went to my bump as soon as I felt the pain, but as fast as it came, it stopped just as quickly. It took a few moments before I felt like I could speak again.

“I’m ok,” I told my very worried husband. “I think the baby has trapped a nerve that’s all,” I told him. “It's gone now, so don’t worry.”

James didn’t seem very convinced, but he did trust my judgment. Before I knew it, two of the nearest angels quickly glided over. Both of them began using their power to scan my body with their glowing hands. I could sense the alarm coming from our kids, and I hated the fact that they were all suddenly worried about me.

“How are you feeling now, Mel?” one of the angels asked calmly.

“I’m honestly okay now, the pain came and went really quickly. As I just told James, I think the baby pressed on a nerve,” I explained.

“Your baby is developing faster than is normal for your race, Mel. I believe that your baby could be born a lot sooner than we thought,” the second angel said, as his hands glowed against my bump.

What the angel was saying was making a lot of sense. My bump was feeling bigger and heavier than with my other pregnancies, but because I was much older this time, I'd been putting it down to my age rather than the baby. Also, this baby had wings, whereas my other babies obviously didn't.

"Do you have any idea how long I have before she's born?" I asked the male angel, hoping to at least have some kind of time frame.

"I am afraid there is no way of telling, Mel. I would think maybe within two weeks," he answered, but his face didn't show much confidence. "Human babies and human bodies are very unpredictable, Mel."

His words couldn't have been truer. I knew I'd just have to wait and see. The next thing I knew, Christik and Lindaz arrived and were standing next to me at the table.

"Are Mel and the baby well?" she asked the angels.

I could hear and feel her concern for both of us. The two angels removed their glowing hands and stood to face her, dipping their heads to Christik and her mother.

"Both are well, Christik," the female angel told her with confidence before they both glided away to where they'd come from. I didn't even get a chance to say thank you.

"They felt your gratitude, Mel," Lindaz said warmly with a smile on her lovely face. "Do you feel up to healing some more Marilians, or would you like to have some time to rest?" she asked.

Immediately I could feel James's worry and unease, but he knew better than to answer for me. I understood his concern, but I felt okay again. I trusted the angels and their assurance that everything was good with me and the baby. I looked at both Christik and Lindaz with a confident smile on my face.

"Let's do it," I told them. "Orchi needs some company of his own race too."

Christik and Lindaz smiled back at me, then they both looked at James almost apologetically. My husband smirked knowingly before he stood and took me in his arms.

"Please make sure you tell them if you start to feel unwell, baby, or start hurting," he said seriously with his green-blue eyes boring into mine.

"I will, I promise," I told him sincerely.

As soon as James released me, I gave him a kiss and then I grabbed some of the food off the table to take with me.

"I'll see you all later," I told my husband, Orchi and my kids, before nodding to Christik indicating that I was ready to go.

When we arrived at the hangar, I felt rearing to go as I viewed the rows of Marilians lined up ready for us to change. The other elders were waiting for us, and because I knew that there were even more Marilians on the other main crafts, I was keen to get started. With the help of the elders and Christik all sharing their power, we had changed most of the Marilians within a matter of hours. Every time we changed and healed a batch of them, we took the time to check what aliens we had, and I was always surprised.

It never ceased to amaze me that there were so many various aliens. The great thing was that there were many more aliens that were able to breathe oxygen, and we also found seven more Jagu. I knew Orchi would be very happy and also extremely relieved that he wasn't alone. As I stood in front of a young female Jagu, still contained within her blue fluid capsule, I had to admire her beauty and physique. She was just as feline as Orchi, but her features were sleeker and softer in appearance. The Jagu was also more of a dark charcoal grey than black, and her long braids appeared to have streaks of silver in them.

'*Orchi, are you still with James and my children*?' I asked through my com.

'*I am, Mel,*' he answered, with surprise in his

tone.

'*We've found seven of your race so far, would you like to come down to the hangar to help us release them*?' I asked. 'I'*m sure they'll be a lot calmer if they see you with us*,' I added.

'*Yes, Mel, I agree. I will come to you now.*'

I didn't even take a step before Orchi and James were standing next to me, with Harrik between them touching their arms, and they nearly made me jump out of my skin.

"Goddammit, you scared the life out of me!" I told them as I patted my suddenly racing heart.

"My apologies, Mel, I did not mean to flit so close to you," Harrik said with regret.

"Are you okay?" James asked, looking worried.

"I'm good, just give me a minute to calm my nerves."

Once my heart slowed back to its normal pace, I was ready to reunite Orchi with his fellow tribal member. My aim was to get the female Jagu out and clothed as quickly as possible. I could see James diverting his eyes in respect to her nudity, and I could feel Orchi's gratitude for my husband's discretion. The Jagu and my husband seemed to have bonded and I was relieved, as it would make things a lot easier if we visited the Jagu's planet.

"Are you ready?" I asked them.

Orchi and James both nodded their heads. Christik and the elders stood back to let me work. I was expecting to feel less power in my body with all the Marilians that we had changed, but because of the elders sharing their power, I still felt as fresh as a daisy. My instincts took over once more and before we knew it, the blue power fluid was streaming back into my body through my palms with effortless ease. The female Jagu's eyes began to widen in confusion, blinking rapidly, and her very long black eyelashes fluttered as her fight or flight instincts kicked in. '*You are safe*' I heard Orchi tell her in my mind, although I didn't understand the words, he softly said to her. '*We are going to release you, be still*'.

Her eyes were still wide, but she could sense that Orchi was telling the truth and when her eyes settled on the approaching elder and Christik, her whole demeanor began to relax. The female Jagu could feel that they weren't a threat, just as I felt it when I'd first woken from my long sleep. Christik reached the Jagu, and as she raised her palm towards the silvery vines surrounding the young female's body, she gave her a reassuring smile. As soon as the vines melted from her form, the Jagu fell forward, landing into Orchi's quickly responding arms.

With a wave of Christik's hand, the female

was wearing clothes and they looked just as Egyptian as Orchi's. She wore a thin, white dress with a more feminine tied belt, and she also wore a similar beaded collar around her neck that rested on her slim athletic shoulders. Next, Christik held out her palms and in a small burst of white light, a female communication device appeared. The angel held out the communication necklace to Orchi, and because he'd seen mine and the other women's, he didn't hesitate to take it and offer it to the female Jagu. Her eyes flitted to my neckline where my com necklace rested against my skin, then back to Orchi's proffered hands.

'*This will help you to communicate with everyone*' Orchi explained. The Jagu dipped her head slightly and then she lowered her head to Orchi, allowing him to slip the hieroglyph adorned device around her neck. When she lifted her head, her hand went straight to the com and she lifted it, letting it drop back down under her collar, so it was against her skin. We all watched as it seemed to melt painlessly into her skin.

"My name is Orchi, this is Mel, James, Christik, Lindaz, Evest, Mikaz, Eliz, Ronak, and Nical" Orchi told her as he indicated to us all in turn.

We all dipped our heads to her in respect and smiled at her quizzical looks. She then raised her left hand to her chest and dipped her own head in response.

“My name is Viole of the Zital tribe,” she said with quiet confidence. “Where are we?” She asked, looking straight into Orchi’s eyes.

Orchi explained to Viole where they were and who we all were, which she seemed to accept without question. As soon as she was at ease, we then moved on to the next Jagu to be released. By the time we finished releasing the seventh and last Jagu, we had quite the audience. None of them wanted to leave until the last Jagu was released, and I could feel the strong tribal bond between them. Three of the Jagu had serious wounds when I healed them, which the elders attended to straight away, once they were free from the vines.

All of the Jagu had similar colorings and physical attributes. From their slim muscular frames to their feline features and long thin braids. However, there were slight differences that set them apart, just like with humans. They had various sized ears, noses and other body parts that would make it easier for us to tell who was who.

There were four male Jagu; Ros, Dand, Tuli, Laven, and two other females named Dais and Jasmi. Even though none of them were from the same tribe, they were still friendly and respectful towards each other. They also seemed eager to find out from each other what had happened to the other's tribes and their villages. I turned to Christik and the elders who were all waiting patiently while the Jagu introduced themselves to each other by touching noses and taking in each other's scents.

"How many more batches of Marilians do we have left to change?" I asked them.

Christik smiled knowingly, obviously feeling my desire to get them all healed and get it over with.

"There are two more batches left, Mel. Would you like to heal them today?" She asked with a smirk, knowing what my answer would be before I uttered a word.

"Yes, let's do it." I smirked back to Christik before turning to my husband, who was avidly listening to the Jagu warriors. "Would you like to take the Jagu to the canteen, James? I'm sure they'd like some food and something to drink."

"Sure," he replied quickly with a big grin.

I could tell he'd like any excuse to keep listening and talking with the Jagu, he was just as fascinated with them as I was.

As James began to lead the Jagu out of the hangar, the golden angels started to appear at Christik's request, taking the healed aliens and replacing them with yet more Marilians. Something was telling me that I had to finish and get them all healed as soon as possible, and my instincts were usually right. Within three more hours, all the Marilians had been healed and I began to breathe a sigh of relief. It had been such a long day, but we'd accomplished more than I could have hoped for. Unfortunately, we didn't find any more Jagu.

"I think it's time for you to get something to eat and drink too," Christik said as she glided to my side.

"I think you're right," I told her warmly.

The golden angels flitted quickly to take the last batch of healed aliens, and as they appeared and vanished again with the capsules, I realized that some of the aliens were being left behind. I hadn't noticed before that some of the aliens weren't being taken and I didn't know why.

"The angels aren't taking some of the capsules, Christik," I told my angel friend.

"That is because those aliens are also from planets which may be suitable for your race. We need to communicate with them to find out if their worlds are a possibility," she explained.

A number of the aliens didn't look like land dwelling creatures, and I was more than curious about what kind of planet they could possibly live on.

By the time the elders, Christik, and I arrived at the canteen, after the last of the aliens had left, I was beginning to wilt. James and the Jagu were nowhere to be seen in the massive food hall and neither were my kids. I had no idea what time it was, but my body told me that it was late. As we sat and ate our food, I could sense that the elders and Christik were just as drained as I was, but there was a unified sense of achievement.

CHAPTER 5

There wasn't much talking during my meal with the elders and Christik. We all seemed content to eat in peace and quiet in the near empty canteen. There were only a handful of other people, and like us, they were enjoying their meal in silence. When I'd had enough to eat and drink, Christik walked with me to keep me company.

"When are we going to release the aliens in the hangar?" I asked as we slowly made our way back to my room.

I didn't like the idea of them being stuck in their capsules when there wasn't any need. It wasn't as if any of them were as large as the Mammot.

"The aliens in the hangar do not live like humans, Mel. Some of them live in fluid, just like the Jeli race, while others live in symbiotic harmony with their plants, animals, or another race on their planet," she explained patiently. "We will have to be very careful. We have to have the right environment for them to be released into, so they do not die.

"I understand," I told her.

We enjoyed our walk down the empty corridor, and I waddled to keep pace with Christik's graceful glide. We reached my suite and I couldn't wait to get into my bed and snuggle up to my husband.

"Before you go in, Mel," Christik said as she gently touched my arm, "I believe the animals in our holding room have been pining for you. Could you go and see them tomorrow if you do not mind?"

"I don't mind at all," I told her honestly. "I like spending time with them and so does this little one," I added while softly patting my very pregnant bump. "I'll see you in the morning.

James and the kids were already asleep when I entered our suite. The only noise that I could hear was a soft light snore from my husband. I slid into our bed as gently as I could, snuggling up to my husband's warm body. I fell asleep quickly and my dreams were full of aliens, of all different varieties and in different locations. I was thoroughly enjoying my dreams, right up until another sharp pain ran through my stomach again.

It felt as though it was coming from my back, through to the front of my abdomen and I woke with a start, barely able to catch my breath. Beads of sweat broke out of my forehead as I brought my knee up and clutched my swollen stomach. Luckily for me, James didn't wake up and the angels didn't sense it either. My baby girl moved around slowly, turning her little body, but struggling for room. It was as if she was trying to reassure me that she was okay. After steadying my breathing as the pain dissolved, I laid back down flat on the bed and eventually let sleep take me once more.

Nalik and Holly joined us in the morning for breakfast, and it was lovely catching up with them. Nalik seemed to be permanently glowing and I could feel that it wasn't just the love he felt for Holly, but also his happiness at becoming a father. Holly looked absolutely radiant and she told us enthusiastically about their recent introduction with the Jagu.

"Did you know that their planet is three times bigger than ours was?" Holly asked me, as I tried to quickly chew some lychee. I gulped, not wanting to keep her waiting.

“I didn’t darling,” I answered with a smile. “To be honest, I haven’t had a chance to really find out anything. I’m looking forward to getting to know them and their history”

“The females are amazing warriors, Mom. They’re bad-asses like you,” Abigail said with a grin.

“Mmm, not quite feeling like a bad-ass right now honey,” I told her while rolling my eyes. “I’m going to see the animals this morning at Christik’s request, apparently they are missing us,” I added while patting my ever-growing bump. “Who’d like to come with me?”

“April and I were going to go down there anyway, baby; we’ll come with you,” James said quickly.

Harrison was quick to hold a hand up. “Count me in.”

“We’ve arranged to meet a couple of guys who used to work in construction, but we’ll try and come down afterwards,” Anthony said with a smile. “Christine likes animals and she’d like to see them.”

Christine smiled at our son and his thoughtfulness.

“What about you, young one?” I asked our youngest daughter.

Abigail sighed with disappointment. “I've got

my lessons and I don't want to let anyone down," she answered sadly.

You can come with me later tonight, if you like princess," James told her with a grin, making her face light up immediately.

"We'll come with you later too, Dad," Holly added. "I don't want to over crowd them, and it's probably best if we visit in small groups."

James nodded in agreement.

There were no signs of any angels when we arrived at the animals' holding room, but we could tell that they'd been there recently. Fresh food had been left for all the different animals, from various fruits and nuts to hay and grasses, and the dugongs were happily swimming around in their large natural pool, having just been fed. In less than an hour, we were surrounded by all the animals and they were still rubbing themselves against me and my family when Christik arrived.

"They certainly appear happy to see you all," Christik said with a smile. "It will be good when they can be free once more."

"What about the animals that we all birthed, Christik? They're just going to keep growing in their capsules and then what? We can't release them all on board. Your crafts are big, but not that big," I said, feeling concerned.

“You need not worry, Mel. Come with me.”

We petted the animal’s goodbye and as we left, I could hear their soft noises of distress because I was leaving with the baby that they’d bonded with. I felt terrible having to leave them, but now the Marilians were healed and changed, I knew I would be able to spend more time with them. Christik led us to the room where I’d first woken up and where it all began. We walked through the birthing room, heading to the room which had the wall of encapsulated animals, and a thought popped into my head as my memories of waking in the room resurfaced.

“Christik, why was I the only woman during the five years you were on earth to wake up from the induced sleep?” I asked her.

She stopped, turned and smiled at me with a twinkle in her peacock colored eyes.

“I was wondering when you were going to ask me that question,” she replied, her smile getting bigger. “Both you and James are distantly related to Akhenaten. Your family lines originated in Egypt, so you both have more of our angel blood in you than most of your race.”

My mind was blown by this new information, although it did make a lot of sense.

“So not only did evolution take a leap, but the

greater concentration of angel blood made me wake up and conceive a more angelic baby?" I asked, feeling stunned.

"Exactly, Mel. It obviously took a while for the angel blood to become more dominant in your system, but once it did, you woke from your sleep," Christik explained.

"Well, that does explain everything," James said with a huge grin.

When we walked into the room of encapsulated animals, I was taken aback by the color difference. The massive, thick glass wall containing all the animals was still there and full, but instead of the capsules glowing their usual white shimmer, they were green instead. The actual fluid inside with the baby animals had changed, and they didn't seem to have grown much in size either. As we all walked up to the thick glass wall, we could see all the different baby animals in their neat encapsulated rows, still attached to their umbilical cords and placentas. Every single one of them were glowing in the new green shimmering fluid, which actually made them all look quite ominous. Especially the really wrinkly baby animals and the animals with the big eyes, such as the sharks. The baby bats looked positively creepy in the green light, almost alien like. It was like something out of a horror movie.

"Why are they all in green fluid now?" I asked Christik as she glided beside us at the wall.

"The animals are in the same fluid as they were before. We used our power to change the fluid to stop their growth until we find you a suitable new planet to live on," she explained.

"What if some of the animals can't survive on the new planet, and what are we going to do with all the animal DNA that was collected?" James asked, obviously concerned with the animals' well-being.

Christik didn't seem fazed at all by his questions. She gave one of her reassuring smiles and placed her hand on James's arm.

"You do not need to be concerned, James; follow me."

Christik glided out of the room and she led us out into the long corridor, heading back towards the direction of the animals holding room. Just after the steamed glass doors where the plants and trees were grown, she stopped at a larger archway. The archway looked the same as the others along the corridor, with its darker outer frame and hieroglyphs at the top glowing softly. It didn't have glass doors at the entrance like most of the rooms; instead it had a golden shimmering barrier, set back from the archway entrance. Without hesitation, Christik glided towards it, raising her hand and releasing some of her power. The barrier changed slightly in brightness and Christik lowered her hand, gliding through the barrier as if it wasn't there. One by one, we all followed the angel finding ourselves in a very strange room.

The massive room was white, like most of the rooms that we'd been in on the craft, but this room was full of floor to ceiling thick glass cylinders, that were full of white frosted globes that were floating and moving in a clear liquid. They were the size of an average Christmas tree bauble. In fact, that's exactly what they reminded me of, only they floated around like the inside of a lava lamp. We instantly walked up to the closest glass cylinder and peered inside, my eyes trying to pick and follow just one of the globes to see what was inside it. Whatever it was inside was completely frozen and it looked like it was a creamy liquid at some point.

"What are these?" I asked without taking my eyes off the globe I was studying.

"These are what you would call cryogenic storage units, and those," Christik said, as her hand reached over my shoulder, pointing at the frosted globes, "contain the animal's DNA with dormant cells."

"Why are their cells inside with the DNA?" I asked, still glued to the moving globes.

"I know that one," James interjected.

I pulled my gaze away from the cylinder and looked at my husband, who was looking at me with pride and a grin on his face. I raised my eyebrows in surprise.

"It's because the DNA are just the instructions, but to reproduce a living thing you need live cells as the building blocks."

"That is correct, James," Christik told him warmly.

I was seriously impressed with my husband. He never ceased to amaze me with the knowledge that he absorbed and remembered. I grinned back at James and his beaming face.

"These cryogenic units are powered by green energy, so when you settle on your new planet, any animals that cannot be released straight away can be kept in storage. Any animals that will not survive on your planet will remain with us, until we can find a suitable home for them," Christik explained.

"There aren't any numbers on the globes, Christik. How can you tell which globes are for what animal?" April asked curiously.

Christik held out her hand with her palm facing upwards and in a small burst of white from her power, a round clear device appeared in her hand. She gripped it with her slender fingers, bringing it up to her mouth.

"African elephant," she said, speaking into the device.

She lowered her hand and a hologram image appeared above the device. The image was as clear, as if she actually had a real tiny elephant floating above the device. In the corner of my eye, I caught a glimpse of red, and when I turned in the direction of the red glow, one of the globes was flashing red inside the cylinder and it was starting to float toward the top of the unit.

"Cancel," Christik commanded as she raised the device and the miniature elephant to her mouth again.

The elephant instantly disappeared from above the device, and when I glanced back to the red globe, the color drained away, leaving the original white frosted coating on the outside. Slowly, the globe floated back down to its original place amongst the others, returning to its floating cycle.

"That's so cool," Harrison uttered.

"Well, you certainly have everything covered!" I exclaimed, feeling seriously impressed with everything I'd seen.

James certainly appeared to be a lot happier now that he knew all the animals were being looked after and protected so well. I could feel that all his initial concern had melted away, and was now replaced with satisfaction and excitement.

There was still no sign of Anthony and Christine, so we assumed that they were still busy. Feeling happier, we decided to grab some much-needed lunch from the canteen, while Christik was going to check on the containment for the aliens she wanted to communicate with. She seemed filled with a determination that I knew was her desire to find us a new home as quickly as possible.

The canteen was brimming with people when we arrived, and it was clear that it had become a social meeting room too. Everyone was emotionally healing, some more quickly than others, but healing just the same. The angels healing power was speeding up the process, which was especially helpful to those who were struggling with PTSD and severe grief. We filled our plates with the fresh foods available and sat together at an empty table. We were discussing the animals and the frozen zoo we'd just visited when Orchi and the other Jagu entered the canteen. Those of us that saw them enter smiled in welcome and many dipped their heads in respect. The Jagu dipped their heads in response, placing a hand on their chests in greeting. When Orchi's gaze fell on our family, he instantly walked towards our table and I tried to stand to greet him and his newly formed tribe. He held up a hand to stop me.

"Please, do not get up, Mel. I remember how difficult it was for all of the females in my tribe to move around so close to birthing."

He smiled in genuine sympathy and I appreciated his warmth. I quickly relaxed back in my seat and watched as James and April greeted the Jagu. They were all like old friends already and there were smiles all round.

"Can we join you to eat?" Orchi asked James.

"Sure."

Moments later, after the Jagu had their plates of food and we sat at the table together, April leaned over to me with a smile on her young face.

"I'm going to take my food back to our room, Mom. Abigail and the others are back from visiting the animals," she said eagerly.

"Ok darling, we'll see you back there soon," I told her.

When our new daughter made her quick exit from the canteen, I turned my attention back to our dinner guests.

"How are you all doing?" I asked the Jagu when they were all seated comfortably.

"We still hurt here," Tuli said, placing his hand on the middle of his chest over his heart. "Like you, we have lost many at the hands of the Marilians. We do not know how many survived on our world, or if our world survived at all. We might be homeless like you," he added with true sadness in his voice.

"Let's hope for the best, Tuli. I'm sure we'll find out soon," I told him. "Are you all warriors, or do you have different roles?"

The Jagu seemed to appreciate the change of topic. None of us really wanted to dwell on our losses. As I waited for their reply another painful twinge shot across my bump, but this one was different from the last, and I felt my whole baby bump starting to tighten with a strong contraction. I knew then that my labor had started. There was no point in saying anything to James or the angels, because I knew it was only the beginning of a very long night.

"We are all warriors, but we also have other roles too," Dand said with a smooth masculine voice.

His eyes were bright, fiery orange, and they were almost glowing in contrast against his silky jet-black fur. They were stunning and a little disconcerting.

"I am one of the healers for my tribe," he said with pride. "My parents were both healers too, for my tribe's bodies and minds," he added.

"Laven and I are warriors and tend toour tribes' crops. We make sure that our tribes have enough food for when the cold times come. It is a great responsibility," Jasmi said softly.

All the Jagu had important roles within their own tribes, and I really hoped that they had a world to go home too. We talked for a long time and listened avidly as they described their world and their way of life. They were a very close-knit race who loved to travel and explore. Apparently when they did travel, they did it as a tribe, taking everyone with them. They reminded me of the indigenous people I'd read about, moving across their lands with the seasons and the migration of the buffalo. Living in harmony with their land.

"How did some of you end up visiting our planet Earth?" I asked. "We were told of your connection to our ancient Egyptians."

"It was my ancestors who found themselves on your planet," Orchi explained. "The Marilians are not the only malevolent race in this universe, unfortunately. There is a race called the Sata, who enslave any other race they encounter. They arrive without you knowing and are able to take you in the dead of night without a sound. My tribe woke one morning and some of our tribe were missing. When the Sata arrived on your planet, my ancestors managed to escape. It was the angels who helped them get back to our world."

"How long were your tribe on Earth for?" James asked the Jagu.

"I do not know, James, but I do know it was a long time. The humans they encountered were eager to learn from our ancestors, and our ancestors were keen to learn from them also. They built good relationships," Orchi told us.

I felt another, stronger contraction and knew I should get back to our suite and to try to get comfortable. The angels were able to take the pain away, but I felt that I should have my new baby as naturally as possible, just like I did with our other children.

"I'm really sorry, as much as I could talk and listen to you all evening, I'm afraid I need to go to bed," I told the Jagu. "Are you staying, baby?" I asked my husband with a smile.

"No, I think I'll come with you my lady," he answered with his sexy, cheeky grin.

'*You can forget any idea of shenanigans tonight*' I thought to myself, with an internal chuckle.

"We'll talk again soon, hopefully," I said to the Jagu as I struggled to get myself up off the seat. '*Where's a crane when you need one*' I thought.

The Jagu bade us goodnight and we headed towards the exit. I knew I was starting to waddle like a duck, but I couldn't help it. Our baby girl had dropped into position and I could feel her bearing down in my pelvis.

"Are you ok, baby? You're really walking fu-nny. Is that nerve in your back-playing up again?" James asked, concerned.

Another contraction gripped my bump, and before I could answer, I bent over placing my hand on my knee and tried to slowly breathe through it.

"No, honey, my labor has started," I told him with a smile as the contraction began to subside and my bump relaxed.

"Spank me sideways, we're having a baby! Do you want me to reach out to Harrik and Zanika, or have you already reached out to them?" James asked in a rush of words, not taking a breath.

I couldn't help but grin at his sudden excite-ment and nervousness. He was exactly the same when we had our other children.

"I haven't reached out to anyone, honey. It's way too early and it could be hours before I need assistance. Don't worry, I just need to clean up and get some sleep if possible, before things really get going," I told my frantic husband.

"Do you want me to get one of the angels to flit us back to our room?"

"No, I'll walk," I told him. "It might speed things up—gravity and movement can work wonde-rs," I added with a grin.

CHAPTER 6

We took our time walking down the long corridor to our suite, and luckily, I didn't have any more contractions en-route. The kids were all hanging out in their room, talking about what they'd been up too.

"Should we tell them you're in labor?" James asked quietly with his eyebrows raised.

"No, there's no point. I don't think they'll get any sleep if we tell them, and I don't think we should all have a restless night," I said warmly. "I'll go and get washed up."

I had one more contraction while freshening

up, and I could see and feel my whole bump tighten and get hard as the contraction gripped me, changing from a nice and round to egg shaped. Having had four babies before, I knew that they were nothing compared to what was to come. Having had twins, one of which being a breach birth, I hoped that our new little girl would arrive easily.

As the tightness and pain ebbed away a sudden thought popped into my head: '*Shit, we haven't even discussed names yet*'. I started to think of names that I liked, and another thought came to me. I got dressed and made my way into the lounge area of our suite, where I heard the kids talking to James.

"I've had an idea," I declared to the kids and James, who were all sitting around the small coffee table. "I think we should all decide the name for the new baby together."

The resounding grins from my family made it clear that they loved the idea, and I grinned back at their lit-up faces.

I joined my family and tried to get comfortable the best I could. My labor was still in the early stages, so I knew I could hide my contractions; I just hoped that James would be able to contain himself when he knew I was having another one.

"Well, what do you think, any suggestions?" I asked.

"What about Charlotte?"

"Natasha"

"Anabel"

"Julia"

"Hope," April suggested quietly.

All of us looked at April, who suddenly looked very sheepish as her cheeks began to blush a deep pink.

"April, I think the name Hope is perfect," I told her.

I looked to our other kids, Christine and my husband, who were all abruptly quiet.

"What do you all think?"

The kids all nodded their heads in agreement.

"I think it's perfect too," James said with a smile. "That's settled then. Hope it is!"

I felt content knowing we had a name for our new baby and the name Hope felt right. We needed all the hope we could get our hands on, and many people were excited about our new baby, including the angels. We spent the next hour or so discussing the animals and the DNA storage units, as well as what the kids had been doing with their work and schooling.

When James and I finally got to bed, I was more than ready to sleep, and when James wrapped an arm around me, I could already feel my eyes getting heavier. He rested his hand softly on my bump, stroking my belly affectionately.

"See you soon, Hope," he whispered.

When I woke up, it was too a very painful contraction. I could feel my bump tightening and getting so hard that it felt like something was squeezing me. Automatically bringing up my knees I began to breathe through the pain, taking slow deep breaths, in and out. Keeping my eyes closed, I tried to relax the rest of my body. When it finally subsided, I slowly turned onto my back to see if James was awake.

"Are you doing okay, baby?" he said, answering my un-asked question.

"Yes, I'm okay," I told him with a smile.

My husband looked so handsome in the soft light, but I could see the concern in his eyes.

"Why are you so worried? We've done this all before," I said gently.

"You've not had to deliver a baby with wings before, Mel. I think I'm right to be more nervous about this baby. For you and for Hope. I'd feel a lot less nervous and worried if you were being watched over and checked by the angels. At least then, if something doesn't go right, they'll be there just in case," he pleaded.

Another contraction started, quickly building and taking my breath away before I had a chance to reply. As I breathed it away, I could feel James's anxiety building. When it finally finished, I turned to face my husband so I could see his face fully. With his brows furrowed and his eyes narrowing, his worry was clear to see.

"Ok, let's get up and call on Zanika and Harrik," I surrendered.

If I hadn't been so uncomfortable, I would have laughed as James tried to help me out of our bed. Hope was bearing down really low, and the pressure I felt in my groin area was awful. Just as he managed to pull me up, another wave of pain swept through me. I kept hold of James's hands, squeezing them as I breathed through it.

"Holy crap, Mel, I think you've broken my fingers!" James said, when I finally let go of his hands.

He stood there trying to shake his hands out, while trying to get his circulation back.

"I'm sorry, honey. I didn't realize I was squeezing them so hard," I told him honestly.

James led me over to the lounge area, but the last thing I wanted to do was to sit down. I waddled over to the large circular window and I placed my hands on either side of it, looking out at the stars that we were traveling past. As I felt another contraction coming, I braced myself, not even aware of where James was or what he was doing. When it had finally finished and my body relaxed, I was suddenly aware that James was behind me, and so were Zanika, Harrik and Christik.

"Damn you guys got here quickly," I told them with a smile on my face.

"How are you feeling?" Christik asked in a serious but friendly tone.

"I'm doing alright," I told her honestly. "They're coming quite quickly now, and they're definetely lasting longer.

Christik nodded and then she gave a look to Zanika and Harrik. Both of the angels smiled as they glided over to me, and as I stood there with my hands still on either side of the window, they used their healing power to check me over. When I looked down at Zanika's glowing hands, I could see her white glowing power flowing from her hands and into my body, passing through the silky dress I was wearing.

"You are close, Mel. Would you like us to flit you to the birthing room?" Zanika asked.

"Yes, I don't want everyone to hear me if I get the urge to start pushing in the corridor," I told her. "We need to wake the kids up before we go through, they'll want to meet their sister as soon as she's born,"

James was quick to act.

"I'll go," he said as he started to walk towards the kids' room.

I watched him open the barrier, and as I heard him trying to wake the kids, another wave of pain gripped me. By the time the pain and contraction had melted away, I opened my eyes to see all of our kids close to me in my peripheral vision. I straightened myself up and turned to face them, giving them a reassuring smile.

"It seems you're going to meet your new sister tonight," I told them. "We're going to go to the birthing room now, and your dad will come and get you when she's born, okay?"

Our kids were a mixture of emotions, excitement, trepidation, and concern. They were excited at the thought of having their sister, but they were also worried about me.

"You don't need to worry, nothing is going to go wrong with the angels by my side," I assured them.

Another contraction started, and it was a lot stronger than the last; both of my hands went to my hardening bump and I breathed through the contraction while trying to remain standing. Moments later, I opened my eyes and looked at my husband.

Before I could open my mouth to say anything, I felt a rush of warm fluid from between my thighs and I knew instantly that my waters had broken.

Luckily, James and I had explained to the kids when they were younger what happens when a woman has a baby, so when they looked down at the puddle that was now on the floor, none of them were freaked out. With a wave of Christik's glowing hand, the puddle vanished before our eyes, and I no longer felt the wetness down my legs and on my bare feet.

"Ok, we need to go now," James said, all business-like.

All of our kids walked over to give me a quick hug or kiss and as soon as they moved away Christik glided forward, placing her hands on James and me.

By the next second we were in the birthing room, with Zanika and Harrik gliding in with their sheer veils covering their faces and thin gloves covering their slender hands. James slowly walked me over to the nearest bed, helping me to slide my butt onto its surface. The pressure I felt between my thighs made me quickly turn onto my side before trying to lay down, and another wave of pain began to wrack through my swollen stomach. Harrik quickly placed his glowing hand on my arm, and the moment his healing power absorbed into my skin, the pain melted away. I could still feel the tightening of my bump and I could see it physically harden, making it look more egg-shaped as it tightened around my baby's body.

I was grateful for the angel's intervention and their version of pain relief. It was going to make my labor and delivery a hell of a lot easier. Within moments of the contraction easing off, yet another started, and this time I felt the urge to push. Instinctively I turned onto my back, bringing my knees towards me.

"She's coming," I told James, who was still holding my hand.

His eyes reflected his worry, and I knew he wasn't going to relax until our new baby was born and it was over.

"Push when you are ready, Mel," Zanika said, as she used her power to roll my thin dress, up and over my raised and bent knees.

I couldn't have stopped my body from naturally pushing, even if I had tried. I didn't know if it was because I'd already had four children or if it was because our new baby was different, but my body was doing all the work, and I was just going with it. When I felt the next contraction minus the pain, thanks to Harrik, I pushed as hard as I could, helping my baby to enter the world. A burning sensation between my thighs made it clear she was crowning.

"I can see her head, Mel, you are nearly there," Christik said encouragingly.

I took a moment to relax my body, but as soon as my head touched the soft pillow behind me, another contraction began. I automatically lifted my head and upper body, my hands gripping the sides of the bed, as my body's urge to push took over again. The burning sensation was awful, but I knew it would pass.

"She's coming, Mel, keep pushing!" Zanika urged.

I pushed with every ounce of strength I had.

"You've got this, Mel," James said as he placed his other hand on the back of my neck to support me.

"Ahhhhhh!" I screamed as I used the last of my energy to push.

I felt our daughter enter the world, shocked at the ease in which she came out. I was expecting a struggle, especially with her having wings. I looked down, and Zanika held our newborn daughter in her gloved hands, and she was surrounded in Zanika's glowing power.

"Oh my God, Mel, you did it," James said excitedly as he stared at our newborn. "And she's beautiful."

I smiled with joy and relief at the sight of our

new daughter. James was right, she was absolutely beautiful. Hope had wet, light blonde hair, long eyelashes and a wrinkled, scrunched up newborn face that I instantly fell in love with.

"She is beautiful," I agreed.

"Where's her wings?" James asked.

Zanika gently turned our baby over in her hands, and Hope cried for the first time, just like any other newborn.

"It is okay, baby," Zanika cooed to our daughter. "Her wings are soft," she said in surprise.

"Weren't your wings soft when you were born?" I asked Zanika.

"No, our wings are fully formed when we are born, but then our bodies are able to stretch to any size for a birth," Zanika explained. "Your baby's wings are obviously soft, because you are human, and your body is different from ours."

"I believe that her wings will become like ours, just as a butterfly has soft wings as it emerges from its pupa," Christik explained with a smile.

Christik glided forward and with a wave of her glowing hand, our baby girl was suddenly wrapped in a soft fluffy blanket, still crying. Zanika took our baby over to James, who was still stunned, and she placed our baby in his waiting arms. I could tell he was smitten with our daughter because it was written all over his happy face.

"Mel, we are going to deliver your placenta now," Zanika said as she glided back down the bottom half of the bed.

Harrik was still touching my arm, and to be honest I felt the gentle pull, but that was it. Within minutes, my delivery was over and Zanika was cleaning and healing the bottom half of my body with her power. I hadn't had a period since waking up, and the topic of periods hadn't come up with the girls or my daughters, and I realized that I didn't have anything for my residual bleeding. There was no need for me to worry. Zanika used her power again, and I was instantly wearing snug fitted underwear, with what felt like some kind of padding inside. '*Thank God for that*' I thought.

"Are you ready to hold our little bundle?" James asked with a beaming grin.

"Yes, I am," I told him with a huge grin of my own.

I gently took our baby in my arms and I watched her in amazement as she lifted her tiny hand, and began to suck on her little fist.

"I think Hope is hungry," Harrik said softly. "We also love the name you have chosen; it is very apt."

"Thank you, Harrik,"

“Christik, could you take me back to our suite so I can tell the kids and bring them back?” James asked the angel.

“Of course, James,” Christik answered.

James bent forward, placing a kiss on the top of my forehead and then on Hope’s, before walking over to Christik. The angel placed her hand on James’s arm and then they were gone. While he was with the kids, I took the opportunity to see if Hope would feed. Just like with our other children it took a little patience, but we managed it, and it was a relief when she took to breastfeeding like a duck to water.

“There are some things I'm going to need, Zanika,” I told the angel as she lowered my dress and covered my lower half with a fresh sheet.

“Do not worry, Mel, we have taken care of everything for you,” she said warmly.

Zanika glided towards the exit as Harrik held up his hand with his palm facing upward. It glowed for a second, and a thick folded cloth appeared. As Hope continued to feed, Harrik opened her blanket with his spare hand. I could see Hope’s body for the first time, and she looked perfect, ten toes and ten fingers. Whereas my other babies had clips on their umbilical cord, Hope didn’t. When I looked closer, it looked as if the end of her cord was already sealed and healed.

Harrik carefully and gently lifted Hope while she continued to feed, and he slipped the cloth under her bottom, unfolding it before lowering her back down. I watched as the angel lifted one side up to her belly and then the sides up over her hips, and just as my dress had turned into a swimsuit when it got wet, the cloth shrank and molded around Hope's little form.

"Won't she leak through the diaper?" I asked.

"No Mel, it will absorb everything and protect her skin," he answered with a smile as he wrapped her blanket around her once more.

Just as Zanika glided back in the birthing room, guiding what looked like a carved wooden crib, James arrived on Hulaz' arm with the kids, Nalik, Christine, Lindaz, Evest, and Christik. All of them had big smiles on their faces, and they melted before my eyes at the sight of our new arrival. Everyone held back, allowing April and Abigail to come up first, and I could see their instant love for their new sister.

"Mom, she's so tiny," Abigail cooed.

"Look at her tiny fingers," April said in awe.

Both of our girls stroked Hope's little face and hands as she suckled, completely oblivious. When they heard fake coughs from our other kids, they knew it was time to let the others through. Hope finished feeding and as I covered myself up, James came over and lifted Hope from my arms and placed her into Holly's.

"You're going to have one of these soon, honey," he told her with a grin.

Holly was beaming and Nalik suddenly began to glow so brightly that it was almost blinding. Luckily Hope had already fallen asleep after her feed. We could all tell how happy Nalik was at the thought of having a baby of their own. Slowly but surely, everyone got to see and hold our newest family member. While everyone was cooing over Hope, I relaxed and watched my family being happy and truly content for the first time in a very long time.

After a couple of hours, I was ready for my bed and some much-needed sleep. I could see that my family was tired too; happy, but tired.

"Can we go back to our rooms now please?" I asked Christik.

"Of course," she answered with a sympathetic smile, feeling my tiredness.

I slipped off the bed and let her flit me to our suite. Once back in our rooms and as the others flitted around me, I looked around in utter amazement. While I'd been busy giving birth, the angels had prepared our room for our new baby. There was a beautiful cream-colored crib close to our bed, a padded big chair for feeding, and near the entrance to the bathroom was a wooden changing station, with fresh angel diapers and everything else I'd need.

"We all have gifts for Hope, but we can do that tomorrow, when you've had some sleep," Holly said warmly. "We're going to go now, but let us know when you're ready for visitors, okay?"

"I will," I told our eldest daughter while giving her and Nalik a hug.

James was holding Hope in his arms again, and as I thanked the angels and the elders, he placed her gently into her new crib. By the time they had gone, and the kids had taken to their beds, I was desperate to freshen up and I knew I'd have to be quick, before Hope needed another feed. It was as if James read my mind.

"Go and get your shower, baby; I'll watch over Hope," he said, his face still beaming with happiness.

"You mean you'll coo over her." I laughed.

"Yes, exactly," he replied, quite proud of himself.

It was the best shower I'd ever had, and it felt like it was washing away all the tension from my tired body. I don't know how long I was in there, but when I came out of the bathroom feeling human again, James was sitting up on the bed with Hope laying on his thighs and she was wide awake.

"I think she wants to feed again," he said smiling.

I sat myself down in the padded chair, and James passed her to me as he slid himself off the bed, kissing me before making his way to the bathroom. By the time he came out Hope had finished, and I was burping her over my shoulder.

"How are you feeling, baby?" he asked as he sat on the bed next to us.

"I'm actually feeling really good," I told him honestly. "Better than expected. I'm tired, but I'm not sore or anything.

"Those angels are fricking good," James said, seriously impressed.

"Yeah, they are," I agreed as Hope let out a huge burp.

I could feel her relaxing in my arms as she started to fall asleep again.

"Is it just me, or do her wings feel like they're getting firmer?" he asked.

Both of my hands were on her back, and as I gently stroked up and down her back and her wings, they did indeed feel firmer.

"You're right, they do. It's going to be interesting to see what they're like tomorrow"

I carefully stood up and placed Hope back in

her crib while James got into bed. The moment I climbed in with him, the lights dimmed, and I felt my body relax against the mattress. I fell asleep as soon as I closed my eyes, too tired to even say goodnight to my husband.

CHAPTER 7

During the night, Hope only woke for one more feed. Luckily, she wasn't loud enough to wake James or the kids. I changed and fed her, then went back to sleep myself. When I woke the next morning, I laid in bed wondering if it was a dream or if I had actually had our daughter. A soft gurgle made it clear it was real. When I turned my head to the crib next to us, I could see Hope's little legs kicking in the air making me smile.

"Good morning gorgeous lady," James said as he woke and turned to face me. "I'll get her if you want to get sorted quickly."

"You're a gem," I told him as I got up and headed for the bathroom.

As I got ready, it felt strange no longer having my baby bump and with the angel's healing power everything had gone back to normal. I didn't care that I still had my stretch marks, I saw them as my badge of honor and James wasn't bothered by them either. The one thing that was still different was the size of my boobs; they were definitely bigger and until my bump had gone, I hadn't really noticed just how much bigger they had become. '*It's almost a shame they won't stay this size*', I thought to myself with a giggle.

I could hear the kids getting up as I was finishing my bathroom routine, and by the time I was done, everyone was awake and eating breakfast while making cooing noises at their new baby sister. It brought a smile to my face to see them enjoying our new family member. Hope was on James's lap facing everyone with her back against him and watching them with fascination. She had the same blue-green eyes as her dad and the same blonde curly hair as James had when he was a baby. As I looked at them, I wondered if her hair would darken to a darker blonde like her siblings.

"Good morning, family," I said as I walked in the lounge area with a smile on my face.

The moment our new daughter heard my voice her little legs began to wriggle free from her blanket, the material fell aside and suddenly her little wings began to open.

"What the hell," James cried out in surprise as he desperately tried to hold on to her.

Hope's little angel wings were completely dry, and the bone frames had hardened. James tried to hold her around her little waist under her wings as she splayed them out for all to see. Obviously, we knew she had her wings, but seeing them in their full display was something else. They were small but magnificent, covered in tiny white and silvery, fully formed feathers that glistened in the soft light. We were all amazed and completely speechless. She looked like a little cherub with her wings out and her little angel diaper on. As Hope couldn't hear my voice anymore, or anyone else's for that matter, our poor little baby started to cry, breaking me from my silent stare.

"It's ok baby girl," I said as I walked over to James and scooped her up in my arms.

James was sitting there in stunned silence with his mouth open and the blanket on his lap as I comforted our baby. Hope didn't really have any sort of control over her wings, and while I cuddled and settled her, they seemed to move all over the place.

"She's the coolest baby I've ever seen!" Anthony exclaimed with a face that mirrored the rest of my family.

"If we still had the internet and social media, I'd be sharing this everywhere," Harrison added. "She would definitely be a viral sensation."

"Make yourself useful and pour me a juice and some coffee please," I told the boys with a smile.

James walked over and stroked Hope's head as she started to settle and stop crying. Her little face nuzzled into my neck as he stroked. With my arms around her softly patting and stroking between her wings, they began to fold and close. Not both at the same time, but she got there in the end.

"I'd imagine she'll get better at controlling her wings with time," James said with a quiet voice.

"Yeah, I think so too, although I wasn't expecting that to happen for quite a while." I laughed.

"Bit of a surprise, wasn't it? I'm surprised I didn't drop her." James laughed.

"Your drinks are here, Mom," Harrison said, pointing to the table before grabbing Hope's blanket and draping it over her small shoulders.

"Thank you, darling," I said as he sat back down.

I sat with James and the kids while feeding Hope, and none of them seemed fazed by it. After everything they'd seen that was bad, it probably did them good to see something so natural as a mom feeding her baby. After all, there were no shops to buy formula anymore, so my girls would have to breastfeed too, when it was their turn. Once Hope was latched on, I enjoyed my juice and watched James and the kids discuss how exciting the previous day had been.

A knock at our archway entrance to our suite stopped the conversation in mid flow.

"Come in," James called out.

Christik and all the elders glided in gracefully, each with gifts in their hands and smiles on their angelic faces.

"How is our little Hope doing?" Christik asked as she glided to James, passing him the gift, all wrapped in a small thin piece of shimmering silver material.

"Thank you, Christik," James said, smiling.

"She's doing really well, and we've just had her first wing display which was a bit of a surprise," I told them.

"She appears very content, Mel, and we are all very happy. Especially for you and your family," Evest said kindly.

"The other survivors have not met her, but we can already feel everyone's happiness and hope, now that your daughter is here," Lindaz added.

Just as Lindaz said her last words, Hope opened her little mouth, releasing my breast, and I knew she was finished. Covering myself up, I turned back to Christik.

"Would you like to hold her?" I asked with a grin.

Christik looked absolutely thrilled and she held out her hands instantly. She was a natural and the moment she held her, she brought her up to her shoulder to burp her.

"This is for you," Lindaz said as she passed me her gift, wrapped in a soft pink material.

"Thank you," I told her warmly.

Looking down at my full hands, I began to unwrap Lindaz's gift and as I opened it, I was taken aback by what was inside. It was the most beautiful baby rattle I had ever seen. The rattle was made of two white oyster shells that were tipped with silver, so there were no sharp edges, and the handle was made of a stunning piece of dark wood with fine silver vines circling up to the shells. When I looked closely between the gap of the shells, I noticed it was filled with pearls. When I gave it a little shake it certainly made a rattle sound, and I knew that Hope was going to love it.

"Thank you so much, both of you," I said to

Lindaz and Evest.

James began to open Hope's other gift from Christik, and he smiled as soon as he saw it. Hope's present was a carved wooden animal set, with all the animals we had rescued before the Marilians had arrived, including the dugongs. Each little animal was carved from a different colored wood, and my heart swelled at their thoughtfulness.

"These are so awesome!" James declared as he passed them to the kids so they could see them too.

Christik and the elders stayed for about an hour, and they excused themselves when the next batch of visitors arrived. It seemed that our closest friends couldn't wait to see our new baby. The guys were just as soppy, cooing at Hope as much as our girlfriends. Derek positively melted when he thought Hope had smiled at him. Beccy gave him a stern look as if to say 'don't get any ideas', which made us all laugh.

Tracey arrived with Akhenaten and their thr-ee new daughters. They were like little magnets, instantly drawn to Hope. When each of their da-ughters had a cuddle with Hope, they were then content to play on the floor with Hope's little wooden animals, '*Well, we know what to get those little angels for their birthdays*' I thought. Everyone had brought gifts that they'd either made or found at the abandoned shops before the Marilians arrived. James and I were both touched by everyone's thoughtfulness, especially as they'd acquired or made the gifts before the battle.

The nice thing was that Holly was going to be able to use everything too. Our eldest daughter was watching Hope nearly the whole time she was with us, and so was Nalik. I could see and feel how excited they were to be parents themselves. '*Holy hell, I can still feel people's emotions*,' I suddenly thought to myself. I was shocked. After Hope was born, I expected not to be able to feel other people's emotions. I'd always had strong feelings about things, but this was different, and it now appeared to be permanent.

After our close friends left, our newest friends, the Jagu, arrived. Luckily there was a break in between, which I used to feed and change Hope. I was just trying to slip on an adapted baby robe that Hulaz had given us as they arrived.

"Let me help you with that," Jasmi said sweetly after they had all greeted us.

"Thank you," I told her gratefully as I struggled to get Hope's little wings in the back of the robe.

Hope didn't care, she was too busy trying to grab my long hair in her tiny plump fingers. Within a couple of minutes her robe was on, thanks to my Jagu helper.

"I can hold her while you dispose of her cloth," Jasmi offered.

I was grateful for the help, and Hope was extremely relaxed as Jasmi picked her up and held her.

"Congratulations to you all," Orchi said with his hand to his chest. "You are very blessed, James."

"Thank you, Orchi," James told him. "I'm feeling very blessed. Please sit down," James added.

The Jagu sat with James and the kids as Jasmi and I joined them around the table. Hope seemed extremely happy snuggling up to our new Jagu fr-iend. When I looked into Jasmi's eyes, there was the affection for Hope, but also a terrible sadness, and I could feel her loss.

"If your children are alive, we will help you find them," I told her.

"I know you will, Mel," she said quietly. "Our children are trained to be warriors from a very young age, they can look after themselves."

I smiled at her confidence. "Doesn't stop you worrying though does it," I stated.

Jasmi shook her head as she smiled at Hope.

"We have gifts for your new baby," Tuli said. "May we give them to her?"

"Yes, of course," James told him warmly.

Tuli got up and walked towards Jasmi and Hope. James and I looked at each other in confusion, as neither of us could see anything in his hands. Tuli knelt before our daughter and he placed his left hand on her little chest.

"You will grow with the heart of a warrior and protect your people, little one," Tuli said softly, and as he said the last words dark orange sparkles surrounded his hand for a split second.

When Tuli stood he faced James, bowing his head and placing his hand on his chest in respect. Orchi rose and was next to kneel before our daughter and placing his hand on her chest.

"You will always have love and respect for all life," he said as his own hand sparkled.

Next was Ros. "You will keep your ability to bond with other creatures, and it will grow stronger every day. You have a destiny to bring peace to the universe, little one," he told her as she stared at his feline face.

Dand was the last to approach Hope, and as he walked towards her, he took one of the decorations from his long thin braids. When he knelt in front of her, he reached up and attached an amber looking gem ring to her longest blonde ringlet before placing his own hand on her chest.

"We will always be there for you when you need us, Hope," Dand said with affection in his voice.

Both James and I were expecting the Jagu females to do the same, but it didn't happen, which surprised us. Neither of us felt we could ask about it. We just assumed it was part of their tradition and we were grateful for their verbal gifts and kindness.

"We spoke with Christik and the elders before we arrived," Dand said as he sat back down. "We aren't far from our world now. Before we get there, the angels want to return the Jeli to their home world. We should approach Cidari tomorrow, judging by our current speed.

"I wonder if we'll be able to go down to the planet as well," James said with an excited grin.

Dand's smile matched my husband's instantly.

"We are hoping to see their planet too. None of us have been to another world, although we have always looked to the stars and hoped we would have the chance.

"Well let's hope we get to visit this world together," James told him.

After the Jagu had left, we had quite a few more visitors who were excited to meet our new baby girl. The last to arrive were Harrik and Zanika, luckily with some much-needed food, especially as we hadn't had a chance to get down to the canteen.

"You are mind readers," I told them as they set down a heavily laden stone tray full of goodies.

"Actually, James reached through his communication device to tell us you were so hungry, that you could eat a moldy camel," Harrik stated with a smirk.

"Yuck, James. That's disgusting." I laughed. "But he is right; I'm starving, and I'm sure the kids are too."

The kids had decided to hang out in their room as the novelty of all the visitors had worn off, but the moment they heard the mention of food, they were straight out again. It was as if they had hearing superpowers when it came to food and their stomachs. Before long, Hope was sleeping peacefully in her crib and we were all tucking into the spread of food.

"Are you looking forward to visiting Cidari, the Jeli's planet tomorrow?" Harrik asked as he swept his blue shimmering hair behind his muscular shoulder and reached for some broccoli.

"I honestly can't wait," I replied, "and it's going to be interesting to see if creatures on another planet react to Hope the same way as earth's creatures."

"I'm excited to see how different another planet is," James told them. "It's one thing to see images from someone's imagination, but to actually see a different planet with our own eyes, that is going to be amazing."

All the kids had wide eyes as their imaginations ran wild, and the rest of our meal was full of their speculations. Harrik and Zanika had been to Cidari before, but they didn't give anything away to our kids. I think they enjoyed listening to the kids' ideas and predictions. When Harrik and Zanika were about to leave, Zanika looked into the crib at Hope before turning to face James and me.

"We have a gift for you that may be useful tomorrow," Zanika said with a smile.

The angel raised and held out her suddenly glowing hands, and in a blink of an eye she was holding what looked like an old-style baby papoose. She handed it to me with a smile and I took her offered gift, holding it up for James and the kids to see. I knew what it was, but it didn't look quite right.

"You are confused," she said.

"I know what it is, but it doesn't look like what I've seen before," I told her.

"That is because human babies do not normally have wings, Mel." She laughed.

As I looked at the cream-colored papoose, the

shape of it suddenly made complete sense. It was so soft in my hands, and it was made of a thick fleece type of material that I guessed the angels had made themselves.

"What the heck is it?" April asked curiously.

I held it higher for the kids to see.

"It's a baby carrier or papoose, as your grandma would call it. You wear it on the front or back of your body with the baby inside," I explained. "Only this one has two extra holes in it for Hope's little wings."

"Won't her wings get cold if they're not covered?" James asked.

"No, James," Harrik replied warmly, "her wing feathers act like insulation. Eventually she will also be able to do this."

To give us a demonstration, Harrik stepped away from us all, and we watched as he partly unfolded his large wings and slid them forward, covering his muscular form.

"When Hope has control of her wings, she will be able to keep herself warm and shielded when necessary," he told us.

As if on cue, I heard Hope beginning to murmur in her crib, so Zanika and Harrik bade us goodnight and left. The kids continued to talk and speculate about the Jeli planet while I changed and fed Hope, and they were still talking about new worlds as they all went off to bed. I got myself a shower and by the time I entered our main room, James was fast asleep on our bed with Hope sprawled on his chest. I could tell that she was as sound asleep as James, just by the sight of her relaxed wings that were draped down either side of his body. Not wanting our daughter getting into bad habits, I decided to put her back into her crib.

The one downside to having a baby with wings, was figuring out the best way to lift and hold her. As I looked down at her little body and her sprawled white fluffy wings, I was at a total loss. She looked so tiny and delicate that I didn't know how to start moving her. She looked so angelic and fragile. Leaning forward I softly touched her back in between where her wings connected and instantly her wings began to fold in reaction, making me jump. '*Well that's good to know*' I thought to myself.

Within seconds, Hope's little wings were folded neatly against her back, so without hesitation I scooped her up before she had a chance to relax them again. She was so tired that she didn't stir at all as I placed her in her crib.

CHAPTER 8

The following morning, we were so excited to be visiting Cidari, the Jeli's home, that when Christik and her elder parents arrived at the large meeting room, we were all there waiting for them. They smiled when they saw us through the big glass doors, sitting at the large wooden table. James and I had woken early with Hope, and as soon as we'd started to get ready, the kids had opened their barrier separating our rooms, already dressed and raring to go. Holly had arrived with Nalik not long after, just as eager.

After eating at the canteen, which had been

surprisingly busy, we'd made our way to the meeting room full of food and anticipation. James and I had even figured out how to get Hope into her papoose. Trying to fathom how to get her wings through the slits without hurting her had been quite a process. We figured out that while she was asleep her wings were just as floppy as the rest of her body, and we were able to lift her wings and slip them through without causing her any discomfort, thank goodness.

"It seems we are all ready to go," Christik said with a smirk, as she glided through the glass doors. "Come, we are meeting the Jagu warriors in the hangar," she added, waving her arm towards Lindaz, Evest, and the exit.

The Jagu warriors were indeed waiting for us when we arrived at the angel's hangar, and I could feel their anticipation as much as the anticipation from my own family. They stood in a line looking every bit like warriors, but I felt their anxiety as much as their need for adventure. The moment they saw us arrive, they all stood tall and straight before greeting us with bowed heads, placing their left hands on their chests in respect. We dipped our heads in return and then gave them smiles, the Jagu smiled in return.

None of us knew what to expect or how the day was going to pan out. We hadn't even felt the angel's main craft slowing down, let alone felt it stop outside of the planet's orbit. Before we left our rooms, we had tried to look out of our round suite window; unfortunately, from the angle of the craft there wasn't much we could see apart from millions of stars.

Without wasting time, Christik and the elders boarded one of the larger white crafts and the Jagu waited for us to follow behind them. As soon as we sat down in our seats, Christik took her place at the front of the craft, standing in the arch of the crafts control area. She placed her hands against the archway and immediately the large craft responded. Silver vines appeared from the sides of the ship, reaching for her shimmering skin and wrapping around her hands, wrists and arms like silver snakes.

As soon as the seats sucked us into place making us secure, I felt the Jagu's surprise and momentary alarm. I smiled at them in understanding. We'd all been taken by surprise the first time aboard the angels' crafts, and the Jagu were definitely out of their comfort zone. Orchi and his new clan soon relaxed as Christik began to glow with her power, and the craft started to move towards the main craft's exit.

"Do you think we could possibly see through the craft like we did at Cubanaz?" Abigail asked Christik with hope in her voice.

"Of course."

Christik's power glowed slightly brighter for a split second and the craft seemed to shimmer and change from the block white, to the same pearlescent appearance of the main crafts corridors, before turning see-through from the middle of the craft upwards. I was actually quite relieved that the bottom of the craft hadn't changed too. Floating in water was one thing, but floating in space was completely different.

The moment the craft was half transparent, we were looking in all directions, apart from the elders of course. Lindaz and Evest looked to the direction we were traveling, looking every bit the cool, calm, and collected elders they were. The rest of us, on the other hand, were looking like tourists on a tour bus. It was hard to keep our eyes fixed on one spot. There seemed to be a large planet or moon behind the planet Cidari that was half pale purple and half dark grey. I only assumed it was a moon because it appeared to have marks and craters like our own moon had.

The Cidari's surface changed from one color to another before our eyes. It was a constant swirling mass of colors, greens, blues, browns and reds, all swirling around as if fighting for dominance. I couldn't make out any land formations, bodies of liquid, mountains, or anything. So, I began to worry that the atmosphere may be moving solids and that's why nothing was visible.

As I sat on the craft with Hope fast asleep against my body, I tried to reason with myself. After all, the angels wouldn't put us in any more danger on purpose, I mentally slapped myself for thinking that at all. James, as always, seemed to pick up on my feelings and he reached over, taking my hand in his. The craft kept its course towards the planet, and as the tip of it began to make contact with the swirling colors, it was as if they blended together around the ship like paints on a painter's pallet. The sound of the contact was similar to sand being blown against metal, and the craft passed through without us feeling any resistance. In fact, that's what the atmosphere looked like, the multi-colored sand in the glass ornaments that people sold at beach locations.

I could feel my body beginning to relax as we made our way through, and within minutes the colored sand of the atmosphere began to thin to nothing. That's when I think all of us had eyes like saucers. As far as my eyes could see was a glistening ocean, almost lilac in color. I wasn't sure if the color was a reflection of the moon, or if it really was the color we were seeing. There were patches of dark red on the surface of the ocean that seemed to be flat, and it wasn't until we got closer that I realized they were islands, but not like islands I'd ever seen before.

The islands on the Cidari planet looked like they'd grown upwards and outwards from the ocean, like dark red flat mushrooms. Jagged rock crags seemed to cover the underside and the bases of them, with bright orange and yellow plants, like moss trickling down as if trying to reach the waters beneath. If I hadn't seen it with my own eyes, I couldn't have imagined it. I could hear the Jagu and my own family's gasps of awe and wonder as the angel's craft leveled and turned. We were flying, at what felt like only feet above the islands, and we were seeing some up close, all ranging in various sizes.

As the craft was turning, something huge burst from the lilac sea spraying the ocean water in all directions, before flopping its huge mass on one of the larger islands. It was the size of a large whale, but it looked more like a sea lion in body and head shape, with a row of paddle shaped flippers down each side of its huge dark blue body. We stared as the creature began to leisurely rub it's wide back against the island's surface, and it seemed to be enjoying itself immensely. However, the moment we flew close to it and it spotted us, it flipped over onto its belly and suddenly blew itself up like a puffer fish, with sharp spines sticking out of its form in all directions. Even its paddle fins became rigid before it began to roll off the island, splashing back into the sea without a trace.

We were all making noises of amazement as the elders sat quietly, enjoying our wonder and awe. Before we had a chance to talk about what we'd just seen, a large flock of something swooped down from the sky in flashes of green and orange, before diving and disappearing in the water too.

"What the heck were they?" Holly exclaimed, reflecting our own wonderment.

"They are what you would call a flying fish, although they do not look like the flying fish from your planet," Nalik told her.

"Our flying fish don't actually fly either," James added with a smile. "But those definitely did."

We kept a watchful eye out for anything else as the craft began to slow and descend, close to one of the smaller islands, but there was nothing more to really see. We felt the contact of the water against the bottom of the craft and we were soon watching the water level rise against the sides of the ship. That was when we really began to see life on Cidari. There was a whole different world beneath the lilac ocean, teeming with life everywhere that we could see, and it was all fluorescent.

In the distance, we could make out the large whale-sea lion creature or another just like it, and it glowed a stunning fluorescent green from each of its spikes and the tips of its many paddles. The island foundations were not what I'd expected as the craft steadily lowered. I assumed that the bases would be solid rock down to the ocean floor, but instead the bases of them split as they entered the water, branching out like strands of coral to the sea bed. Shoals of fluorescent creatures swam in and out of the stone strands, some stopping for a quick snack of something small that looked like tiny fireflies.

When the craft finally stopped on the sea bed with a light thud and the seats released us from the safety suction, we all stood straight away and began to actively look around as Christik and the ship disconnected. We didn't have a complete panoramic view as the back of the craft wasn't transparent, but it was still an amazing scene, and it was breathtaking. There were so many creatures of so many fluorescent colors, it was a feast for our eyes. Some of the sea creatures seemed similar to earth's, such as sea horses. Only the sea horses that we were seeing were bigger than us, and their bodies were smooth and were decorated with dark blue and silver flashes that reflected any light as they darted this way and that.

"Look at that one!" Christine exclaimed, as she pointed towards the sea bed.

At the base of one of the islands was a wondrous creature which had more of a mermaid form, in that the top part of it seemed more human in shape, but the bottom was like a Jellyfish. Instead of having a fish tail, it appeared to have a large pale green floating skirt, and from the bottom we could see lots of thin moving tendrils. At first glance, I thought it had some sort of crown, but as it began to swim towards our craft, it seemed to have a head full of bright red feathers. Well, that's what they looked like at least.

"I believe she is here to welcome back the Jeli we have brought home," Evest said as he rose from his seat to face our oncoming greeter.

Lindaz also rose, and Christik glided towards her parents.

The Jeli mermaid was very beautiful in her own weird and wonderful way, and as she swam closer I could see fluorescent colors, moving and running down her face and upper body, as if her actual blood was bioluminescent. Her eyes were larg-e pools of dark green, with flecks of red that matched her feathery hair, and when she opened her mouth to make a long call, it was hard to miss her delicate pouting lips. The sound she made was a series of clicking noises that had a slight whistle to them, and within seconds more mer-people began to show up, popping up from behind rock formations and large collections of colorful vegetation.

Before we knew it, we had a full welcoming party in front of the craft. They were a mix of males and female mer-people, and they all looked the same age. The males were smaller than the females with short red feathery hair, and the females all had the longer red feathers, with narrower faces and numerous breasts, giving me the impression that the females could bear more than one young at a time.

"The Quasi leaders seem to have all arrived," Christik said with a smile.

Christik moved to the middle of the craft so she was in full view of the Quasi leaders, and her body began to shimmer as she tapped into her power. Raising her hands, she started to make different motions in the air, and in the water on the other side of the craft wall, flashes of light appeared, moving in various shapes and intricate designs. It reminded me of when our kids were young, and they would make light shapes in the dark with sparklers. She was obviously communicating with them and as if to confirm my thoughts, I began to hear her in my mind.

'*Thank you for greeting us young ones*,' Christik told them warmly,' as the colors changed and moved.

One of the males swam forward and began to gesture just as Christik had done. His arms and hands elegantly moved this way and that, sometimes overlapping, almost as if he were doing a dance, and the colors appeared and moved in the water before him.

'*We are happy to see you, after such a very long time, Christik. Why are you here now*?' he asked.

'*We are here because the Marilian race destroyed the planet Earth, where some of your Jeli were dwelling. We also have many that we rescued, who were changed by the Marilians. The human woman with the infant behind me is Mel. She was able to change your Jeli back into their true form.*'

Suddenly all the Quasi turned to look at me, making me blush profusely.

'*Thank you, Mel,*' he drew in the water, which I heard through my com.

I smiled at the Quasi and dipped my head to them, not knowing any other way to say, you're welcome. Their gaze went back to Christik and the elders next to her.

'*We will take you to them,*' the Quasi male said, to which Christik and the elders dipped their heads in response.

The Quasi all turned and began to leisurely swim away in their group, while Christik glided back towards the arch of the control area on the craft. As soon as Christik started to activate the craft, we began to take our seats again. As I sat back down, Hope started to wake, and I knew she probably needed changing and feeding.

"That's good timing," James said with a grin.

"Please do not let our presence stop you from doing what you need to do, Mel," Dand said kindly.

I smiled in return and I could feel the Jagu's warmth and understanding. So, without any hesitation, I unstrapped Hope from her papoose with James's help and began to change her. We managed to get her changed easily, and the moment she began to wake up properly was the moment we started to become an animal magnet.

I could feel Hope's senses fanning out and the creatures around us responding. Not wanting her to get hungry, I latched her on as the Jagu and my family busily looked around at all the creatures that were suddenly very interested in the craft. Behind the Jagu, I could see what appeared to be a two headed miniature dragon with dark grey scales tinged with yellow bioluminescence, trying to rub against the side of the craft. Lots of different creatures were beginning to make their way towards us, and even the Quasi people stopped for a moment, floating in the water and looking at our craft.

As Christik set the craft in motion heading towards the Quasi people, they started to swim again.

In the distance, there seemed to be a higher concentration of light, not a bright light but a stronger more natural light, and we appeared to be heading towards it. The Quasi were very careful to lead us through the widest areas between the rock roots of the islands. As we traveled slowly but surely, we seemed to gather a growing audience which were trailing behind us. Hope was completely oblivious and was happily feeding, occasionally wriggling her legs and wings.

"We didn't see any life on the top side of the planet, are there creatures up there too?" James asked the elders.

"This planet is one of the few that has life only below its surface, James," Lindaz replied warmly. "Nothing is able to grow on the tops of the islands. Nearly every century, the planet's atmosphere lowers and destroys anything above. That is why the islands are flat.

"How long were the Jeli on Earth?" Christine asked.

Lindaz smiled at Christine as her peacock multi-colored eyes sparkled in the light.

"The Jeli were on your planet for millions of years. They are very different on their home world. They are healers, seers, and are able to forecast futures for the creatures here. The Jeli are revered," Lindaz explained.

"But all they did on Earth was sting people," Christine said, sounding utterly surprised.

When she spoke, I think we all agreed with her statement.

"The Jeli would only sting in defense, Christine. I believe that if they were able to use their healing and oracle powers on Earth, they would have. Unfortunately, they were captured by some and eaten. The Jeli soon learned that they could be prey," Evest added.

"Well thank goodness we're bringing them back where it's safe," James told them.

We seemed to approach the brighter light quite fast, and the islands appeared to be more spread out with their rock roots splaying out in wider arcs. The colorful moss plants looked bigger than before, and stuck to their flora were beautiful and colorful shells, all tinged with their own fluorescent colors.

Hope finished her feed and when I placed her against my shoulder to burp her, her eyes became wide. I knew that babies couldn't see very far when they were newly born, but Hope could obviously see all the bio luminous lights of all the creatures that were now around and following us. I could feel her excitement grow as her little body wriggled in my arms, and her little wings started to open and flop in different directions. Our kids giggled at their baby sister's obvious joy. Just as Hope gave the loudest burp I'd ever heard, bringing more giggles from our kids, the craft began to slow.

Ahead of us was what appeared to be a coral palace, decorated with the various colorful shells we'd already seen. I wasn't sure if someone had built it from scratch or if it had been created from a large coral mass, but it was absolutely stunning. The corals were various shades of reds and oranges, which were so vivid that the palace looked alive, and not just because it was covered in living shellfish. It vibrantly glowed in the water like a beautiful beacon, and we could see through the open arch windows and the door-less entrance that the palace was occupied.

We slowly followed the Quasi to the palace entrance, and all of us were silent as our eyes feasted on the amazing sight before us. As the Quasi people swam towards the entrance of the elegant palace, a form began to emerge. The creature coming out looked part human and part nature, in that he seemed to have a human form. However, he was covered in what seemed like deep red and green seaweed. The seaweed appeared to be growing out from his body, and the long tendrils lazily floated and moved around him, making him seem like he was in constant motion. Around the top of his head was what appeared to be a warrior's helmet, but it was made of the same kind of coral as the palace, and was decorated with the same bright shells. I could feel the power emanating from him and sense his self-confidence. I assumed he was their version of a royal. He was a very striking male and just like the Quasi people, he had flashing bioluminescent lines flashing down his face and the bare parts of his body.

The Royal male reached the top of the steps and he stopped, a broad smile showed shimmering pearl colored teeth, and his face lit up with friendliness. His dark eyes seemed to scan all of us until they connected with Christik's familiar face. His bright seaweed covered arms and bare hands began to move as he started to communicate.

CHAPTER 9

'Welcome back to our home, Christik. We are happy to lay our eyes on you once more,' I heard the royal say in my head with a very masculine drawl, as the bright shimmering shapes began to form in front of him in the water. *'I hear that you have brought our Jeli home, that makes us happy.'*

Christik began to move her own hands in reply. *"Thank you, King Ardis, we appreciate your warm welcome. We do indeed have your Jeli that were taken from here, as well as the young Jeli from Earth,'* she confirmed. *'We will open our hold for them now.'*

Christik glided towards the rear of the craft, disappearing as the back wall opened to her. Hope, who was still wriggling in my arms, began to gurgle at the Quasi King as their eyes connected. Her little wings started independently flopping around as her excitement grew.

"I think Hope likes it down here." James chuckled as he stroked her little cheek.

"Look!' Christine exclaimed. "The king is coming this way."

When I looked back to the palace entrance, King Ardis was beginning to descend the palace steps, but he wasn't swimming like the Quasi people who had brought us to the palace; he was walking. With every step King Ardis took, his body and movement sent out a powerful tremor through the water, like mini shock waves.

None of the creatures who surrounded us or who were near the palace seemed fazed by it as they gazed adoringly at their ruler. The king descended the last step and began to walk towards the craft, while Hope's legs started to bend and straighten, as if she wanted to jump up and down on my lap.

When King Ardis reached the craft, he placed his hand on the side of the hull that we could still see through, and Hope kicked out even more. I could feel her wanting to get closer to the king.

Standing up with her in my arms, I moved over to the side of the craft and Lindaz stood too, without me even having to ask her.

"It seems your daughter would like to greet the king," she said with a knowing smile.

"I think she'd like to greet all the creatures and people here." I giggled, feeling the truth in my words.

Carefully, I ran my fingers down between Hope's little wings, instantly making her fold them again before I turned her around in my arms, so she could see the Quasi king. Kneeling on the seat that Lindaz's had just moved from, I held up our baby girl in front of the impressive king. Hope wriggled in my hands, pushing her little bottom into my body, while leaning forward until her face made contact with the crafts hull and the king's hand.

There was an instant bright purple light the moment Hope and King Ardis connected, and a shock wave of power that made everyone and everything vibrate. I felt the wave of power rush through my whole body, and Hope squealed in delight. King Ardis smiled at Hope's obvious glee before retreating a small distance. His arms and hands moving again in communication.

'*You are all welcome to visit us, whenever you wish,*' he announced, giving us another friendly smile.

Not being able to communicate back, we all returned his smile, dipping our heads at his offer. Movement and dulled noises made us all turn our heads to the rear of the craft, and bubbles of air began to rise from the opening as Christik opened the hull. When the large intricate Jeli and the small earth Jeli began to float out into the open, we could feel the buzz of excitement in the water, crackling against the craft walls as if it were electric.

The Jeli obviously meant more to the creatures than we realized. We watched as the Jeli, large and small, made their way to the Quasi king, surrounding him and letting their long tentacles make gentle contact with his body. King Ardis closed his eyes and the Jeli seemed to come alive with various bioluminescent colors. It was as if the king was recharging them and likewise, the king appeared to become brighter too.

"What are they doing?" Orchi asked Evest curiously.

"The Jeli are sharing their memories with the king and foretelling the future, while renewing their bond," Evest stated as if it was just an everyday thing.

"Wow!" James uttered next to Orchi, with his eyes glued to what was happening.

Even Hope had settled and was watching the glowing greens, yellows, and other bright colors that were now emanating from the Jeli, lighting up the water around them. We waited patiently while the Jeli and the king communicated and re-bonded, and I could see the king's closed eyes flickering, as if he were watching a movie in his mind. Minutes later his eyes opened, and we were staring at eyes that were glowing like liquid gold, shining as brightly as the Jeli colors, and the king's face looked serene and at peace.

The Jeli released their contact with King Ardis, leisurely swimming away to what I assumed were their homes. I hadn't realized that Christik had already closed the crafts hold and was now standing next to us until the Quasi king looked directly at her and began to communicate once more.

'*Our Jeli have been through quite a journey*' King Ardis said in our minds, as his hands gracefully moved in the water, the light making intricate and beautiful shapes before us. 'T*hey only have flashes of memories from the time they were turned into Marilians, but I can tell you that the Marilians have destroyed many more races than we believed possible. You have a great task ahead of you, and our Jeli need to heal from their guilt. They know what the Marilians do.*'

Kings Ardis suddenly looked like he was carrying a huge burden, his body slumping with the weight of his words.

'*It is not their guilt to be burdened with or yours, King Ardis. Your Jeli have no responsibility for what occurred while they were changed. Please understand that the guilt lies with the one true Marilian, King Drakron, and his immediate counsel. They are responsible for all the deaths and destruction,*' Christik assured him.

As Christik finished her sentence I felt a change in the emotions of the angel and the elders, as if a new determination was developing.

'*We will not allow the Marilians to continue to destroy everything in this universe!*' she declared.

Evest and Lindaz glided to Christik's' side.

'*We will stop them before they can destroy us all,*' Evest stated, his body pulsing with white light as he spoke.

Lindaz was beginning to glow just as brightly.

'*Will you and your army fight for us*?'

The Quasi king's face went from defeated to defiant, as he mulled over his Jeli's guilt and shame.

'*We will! Call on us when you are ready for battle,*' he said, before dipping his head in farewell and respect.

As King Ardis turned his back and began to walk back to his palace, all the creatures around us began to turn and go back to their business. Even those who were extremely drawn to Hope all turned and left. I actually felt quite disappointed that our visit to Cidari was coming to an end, but like everyone else on the craft, I was feeling quite stunned by the angel's declaration, and I wanted to know more.

"I was hoping to explore this world a little before we had to leave," I told James disappointedly as I took my seat again with Hope in my arms.

"I was hoping for the same thing, baby," my husband said, giving me a sympathetic smile.

Everyone apart from the angels looked just as disappointed that we were leaving so soon.

"I am afraid we have no choice but to leave quickly, young ones," Evest said kindly. "The planet's big storm is coming, we can feel it."

"Will we be okay getting off the planet?" James asked, concerned for all on board.

"Our Own, our One, is more than capable of navigating the storm, so do not worry, James."

Everyone settled into their seats as Christik connected with the craft. James quickly helped me to get Hope back into her papoose, and I could feel her little body beginning to relax. No sooner had the silver vines wrapped around Christik's slender arms, we were moving slowly through the water and I realized that I couldn't see any of the creatures anymore. Everything had gone into hiding including the seashells, knowing or sensing the oncoming storm. It seemed strange to only see the rock roots covered in their colorful moss and nothing else.

As the craft picked up speed and started to ascend through the lilac water, I began to wonder where all the creatures had hidden. I assumed that they had shelters for when the storm came, especially as it was a regular occurrence. I didn't blame them for wanting to hide. As the craft headed upwards, I started to feel the resistance in the water. New currents were forming and were hitting the side of the craft, making it sway in a sideways direction. Christik didn't seem fazed by the currents at all and as I watched her, her body swayed with the craft as if they were one.

The closer to the surface we got, the more turbulent the ocean became, and I was suddenly extremely relieved that the craft had sucked our bodies to the seats. Hope was sound asleep next to my body, and as my body swayed with the motion of the craft, our baby didn’t stir one bit. I could see the kids getting nervous as we broke free from the ocean, huge crashing waves hitting the craft from all sides, and the kids reached out for each other clasping hands and linking arms.

The multi-colored sand atmosphere had descended, and all we could see was water and sand. Not even the flat islands were visible, and I could understand why nothing grew on the planet's surface. The noise of the sand hitting the craft was becoming deafening, and as Christik's began to glow with her power, Hope began to stir. The angel's power seemed to travel from her hands on the crafts archway, rippling through the hull in a wave, and by the time it had disappeared again, we were in silence.

As the craft soared higher through the storm it swayed with the bombardment as it did with the huge waves before. I knew that if we could hear the sand crashing against the craft still, we would be a lot more scared than we were. Everywhere we looked there was sand, and now it wasn't different colors like before; it was a dark, thunderous gray. Getting off the Jeli planet seemed to take more than twice as long as it did when we arrived. The pressure of the sand was hitting our craft in all directions, and there was no telling of our progress. Just as I was wondering if we were ever going to get out of the wild storm, we finally began to see the sand getting thinner and thinner, until finally we were free.

Heading towards the main craft, all of us looked back at Cidari, and it didn't look at all like it did before. Instead of the stunningly colorful, but turbulent looking swirls of sand, it now looked like one huge dark grey rock. No one would know that there was an amazing underwater world there unless you told them.

"We may not have been able to stay and explore, but at least we will get to see them again," James said, as if trying to soothe our disappointment.

I leaned against my husband's body, loving the fact that as always, he was thinking of everyone else. His words seemed to kick start the flow of conversation, and the kids began to talk to the Jagu about Cidari, wondering how they were going to help us fight the Marilians once more.

"Are we really going to take on the Marilians again?" I asked Evest and Lindaz.

"Yes, Mel, we no longer have a choice," Evest stated. "We have been thinking about it and discussing the Marilians since we left Earth. We feel that we do not have any other option."

Lindaz leaned forward, her eyes connecting with mine, and I could feel her internal conflict. They were created to be healers and protectors, not fighters and killers. This was going to go against everything that the angels were.

"If we do not stop the Marilians, then they will keep on killing and destroying. We cannot allow it and we regret not stopping them sooner," the elder said sorrowfully.

The journey back to the main craft was short. James, the elders, and I were entertained by the kids' conversation, who all seemed oblivious to the angel's emotional turmoil. Christik smoothly landed the craft in the cavernous hangar, and as soon as we began to disembark, the conversation from the kids soon turned to food and their empty stomachs. We all took that as our cue to head to the canteen, and when we arrived, it was teeming with people. As we walked in, I quickly spotted some of our close friends and I headed towards a grinning Tracey, Mimi, Andrew, Beccy, and her husband Derek.

"Are you guys having a party without us?" I asked with a grin of my own. "I'm glad you're all here, because I wanted to talk to you all."

All of their faces looked instantly intrigued. The kids had all headed straight for the food with James, and the Jagu took seats with me, joining our friends.

"We've just got back from dropping the Jeli back to their home world, and before we left the angels dropped the bomb shell that they're going to take on the Marilians, once and for all," I blurted out.

"But they're angels," Mimi exclaimed in total shock.

"Trust me, Mimi, they don't want to hurt anyone, even the Marilians. I can still feel the elders' pain and guilt from destroying the Marilian ships. That's why we need to convince them to leave the fighting to us, and any other race who want to join in the fight."

There were nods of agreement from everyone. None of us wanted the angels to try and be something they weren't, even if it was for the greater good. They were angels and the purest race in the whole universe, a race that every other race looked up too. We couldn't let them lose that, no matter what.

"We need to have a meeting with them and tell them. Plus, there's no point in us all going to our new planet, if we need to fight the monsters again," Tracey said with her now familiar look of determination.

"Agreed," Derek and Andrew both said together.

"So, let's get everyone on our new home planet and while we're heading that way, we can find out which races are with us," Tracey added.

"You can count on the Jagu to fight. All of our tribes will," Orchi stated with pride.

We all nodded in respect and gratitude to Orchi and his people. It was going to be interesting to find out exactly how many races would be willing to fight and how many of them there were going to be.

When the kids and James came back with their food, we all ate and discussed the possible races who might help us. James and I tried to describe the aliens that I'd healed, and we all tried to guess their possible physical defenses. Of course, it was all complete speculation. None of us had a clue what the other aliens were capable of, but as we talked, it made us feel that we were at least doing something.

With near perfect timing, Hope began to stir, and I knew she was hungry and needed changing again. As we said goodbye, I could sense our friends fighting spirit being renewed. Our kids decided to catch up with their friends, excited to tell them all about their experience on Cidari, so James and I headed towards our suite. By the time we got close to our rooms, Hope was wide awake and trying to grab my long hair.

Hope's diaper was disgusting when I changed her, stinking enough to make my eyes water, and forcing James to hold his nose in an overly dramatic way, making me giggle. It was nice having some quiet time with our new baby, and as I sat in new comfy feeding chair tending to Hope, James sat upright on our bed watching us adoringly.

"I still can't believe she's here," he said with

an affectionate smile.

"I think she came just at the right time, to be honest. She's definitely helping the kids to get over everything that's happened."

"It's a shame we're going to have to do it again," he said with a deep sadness to his voice and in his eyes.

"There's going to be more of us this time. Those evil monsters aren't going to stand a chance, James," I tried to assure him.

"But we don't know how many of them there are, babe, and the moment we attack, they're going to recall all their ships," he said earnestly.

I took a long deep breath, not wanting Hope to pick up on my concern, as well as her dad's.

"Well, we'll just have to take their ships out first before we hit their planet," I told him confidently, giving him a wink.

"I think when you're finished feeding Hope and she's back in her bed, you're mine, my badass wife," he said with a wink of his own.

'*Trust my husband to want to get frisky while the kids are out*' I thought. Hope actually fed longer than normal, and by the time she'd finished, was burped and back in her crib, James was snoring softly on our bed. There was no way that I could sleep. The Marilians were on my mind and I was wracking my brains, trying to think of a way of finding their ships before we attacked their planet. The Marilian ships could be anywhere in the universe, and we needed to get them before they had the advantage. I was still awake when all the kids came back, and it was at least an hour after they'd all gone to bed before I finally felt my eyes growing heavy.

CHAPTER 10

It was two days later when Christik and the elders invited us and some of our close friends to the large meeting room to discuss the Marilians. During those two days James and I had been trying to think of ways to locate the Marilian ships. Unfortunately, we came up with nothing. When we arrived at the meeting room with the kids, most of our friends were already there, and we took the empty seats amongst them. Derek, Beccy, Andrew, and Mimi arrived just after us and everyone seemed just as preoccupied as we were. There were half- hearted smiles and greetings between us all, but I got the impression that they all had been pondering our new situation too.

"Thank you all for coming today," Christik said warmly. as she rose from her seat. "We know you have all been thinking about the Marilians as much as we have, and we would appreciate your thoughts and ideas. We believe that between us all, we can think of the best way to deal with the Marilians, once and for all. We would like the Viziers to join us in our discussion."

The meeting room grew quiet as Akhenaten rose from his seat and raised his palms in the direction of the middle of the table. Just like we'd seen before, a silvery white sphere began to form before us, and once it was fully formed the square images of the Viziers appeared as the sphere spun around slowly.

"Thank you for joining us for this meeting, Viziers," Christik said respectfully before dipping her head in respect.

The Viziers all responded with dipped heads. There was no need for the Viziers to touch their throats to change their language this time. All of us in the meeting room were wearing communication devices now, which was going to make conversion a lot easier, and help the conversation flow.

"After visiting Cidari, the elders and I have decided that the Marilians need to be stopped permanently. However, there are key issues with our decision. The main issue is that we do not know which Marilians are true blooded Marilians from birth, or who have been changed. This means we have no true numbers of our enemy," Christik explained.

"We also do not know where they all are," one of the Viziers stated.

"Precisely," Christik agreed.

"So, we need to find the ships first and figure out how we can change those Marilians first before capturing the true blooded ones," Tracey added, "How the hell are we going to do that?"

"We already know that Mel's gift can be magnified with our power helping her, we just need to be able to locate the ships and get on board them without being detected," Evest told us all.

The sphere slowly spun before stopping again.

"We have the Longs, they can use their invisibility to board the ships," one of the viziers said confidently. "If Mel and our elders touch the Longs, they will be invisible too."

"That is an excellent idea, Elmnack. Now we just need to find a way of locating the ships," Lindaz stated with a tinge of frustration in her normally calm voice.

"The Longs have invisibility?" I asked, surprised that we didn't know already.

Christik looked at me with a smile on her face.

“The Longs are very unique creatures who have the ability to bend the light around themselves, making them invisible to almost any other creature. Unfortunately, not all Longs have the ability, which is why so many were lost when the Marilians attacked their planet,” she explained.

“Why didn’t they use their ability when the Marilian monsters attacked our planet?” Tracey demanded.

“Because they did not feel the need to, Tracey. It takes a lot of their concentration and energy, so they only use their ability when they absolutely have to” Christik told her gently.

“So, back to how we find the Marilian ships then,” Derek said, getting the conversation back on track. “Do you happen to know of a race who has the ability to locate them for us?”

“The Impa’s have the ability to locate nearly anything,” one of the Viziers said, her tone making it clear that she was happy with her suggestion.

“You are correct, Allik, they do,” Christik agreed. “We will have to visit them from our world, as we are nearly there and many weeks from their planet.”

"What about the Jagu? Aren't we supposed to be taking them home?" James asked.

"They wish to come with us, James," Christik told him. "They have the same fighting spirit as you do."

"There's one more thing we need to discuss while we're all together," I said nervously, not knowing how the angels and elders were going to react. "None of us want you angels to fight, or force yourselves to hurt or kill the Marilians. We all feel that you are the one pure race in the universe that other races look up too and admire, and we don't want you to have to live with any guilt."

After blurting out my words, I took a deep breath and waited for their response. I could feel everyone's relief that our feelings had been made clear to the angels. We knew they were capable of immense power, but none of us wanted them to do what wasn't in their nature.

"There should be plenty of us and other races who will fight, and we will definitely need your help deflecting fire and freezing any smaller ships," James added.

Evest and Lindaz rose from their seats, standing either side of their daughter.

"We understand," Evest said. "We do not want our angels tarnished either. We will be more effective defending and doing what comes naturally."

The relief in the room from my family and our friends was palpable. I was relieved that the angels and elders didn't need much convincing, but they were a logical race and they knew what their strengths were. Christik looked back towards the slowly turning sphere.

"Keep your course to our home. We will have another meeting once the elders and I have spoken with the Impa's," she told the Viziers.

As soon as she'd stopped speaking, the Viziers all dipped their heads in respect to everyone in the room before disappearing from the sphere one by one.

A couple of days after the meeting, there was an immense buzz on the angels' main craft. We were about to arrive on the angels' home planet, and I wasn't sure who was more excited: the angels or our fellow humans. It had been a very long time since the angels had been back to Anunaki, traveling from planet to planet saving other races, so I could understand why they were so excited. I was sure that the angels' loved ones were just as excited to see them all.

When we started to approach the Angels' planet, we were invited to the main control room by

Christik, and we were thrilled. We'd all been excited when we came into dock on our Disney cruise when the kids were little, but this was taking it up a notch. My family and I, along with our friends, all stood in front of the rows of angels and consoles with Christik, staring out of the control room's vast glass window.

The planet of Anunaki was like nothing I'd seen before, but it was also similar to what earth had looked like, in that it was covered in green areas and silvery blue areas, which I assumed were land and water. The main difference between earth and Anunaki was that the Angels' planet didn't have just one ring around it like some planets, it had many. They circled Anunaki at different angles, over-lapping each other from various distances. The rings looked magical, almost as though the planet was surrounded by glitter dust. The planet was so large that I knew we'd have no problem flying through between the rings.

The craft made its way through the rings surrounding the planet, and as we approached, I could see the rings were made of rocks, which appeared to be embedded with some kind of silver metal. '*No wonder the rings look glittery*' I thought as the light from the craft reflected off the stones. The distance between the rings was a lot further than I first thought, and our craft glided towards the planet's surface at a steady pace.

As we approached with the other large crafts and the planet became larger, I began to see shapes in the areas of land and what looked like circle patterns. I didn't know what they were for, but some of the shapes looked like creatures.

"Do those things look like weird animals to you?" James asked as he pointed to a large land mass in front of us.

It was as if he'd read my mind.

"That's exactly what I was asking myself," I told him honestly. "They remind me of the Nazca lines and their surrounding images that were discovered. Anthony showed them to me on google."

There were no visible fields of crops or dark colored roads, no large cities or towns that I could see, like we would have seen on Earth's surface. I began to wonder where exactly the angels lived. None of us spoke a word as we got closer to the planet, and I wondered if we were all thinking the same questions.

As we neared, not only did I see more animal shapes on the natural looking landscape, but there were henges dotted around too. '*Are those star passages like we had on Earth*?' I thought to myself, remembering the day when Christik and the angels had reactivated our Stonehenge. The planet's surface loomed closer with each moment and soon it appeared that the surface wasn't as flat or as natural as I first thought. Not knowing what to expect, my brain was trying to figure out what my eyes were seeing.

It wasn't until the craft appeared to be sinking into the ground that I realized there were buildings and layers of various stone structures, but they were all covered with plants. It seemed as though the buildings were built beneath the top layer of the planet. Everything was covered in different vines and flowering plants, with trees sprouting from wherever they had seeded.

The craft effortlessly lowered towards the lower levels, and angels began to appear in the rounded windows of the buildings that we could see in front of the craft. Just like onboard the main craft, the angels had different colored hair and their faces mirrored their happiness that their loved ones were home again. By the time our craft landed softly on the lush grassy ground, there was a huge crowd of waiting angels, and I could feel the excitement grow from the angels onboard our craft.

Christik turned to the angels at their consoles. "You may leave your posts and see your families," she said with a smile.

The green haired angels didn't need any further encouragement, quickly and gracefully turning off their consoles and gliding out of the massive control room. The room suddenly felt even bigger once it was empty of all the angels, and realization suddenly hit me. I was actually on the angels' planet, and I wasn't only excited, but nervous too.

"I have angels taking everyone to their temporary accommodation," Christik said as she turned to face us all. "I thought you may like to stay in my dwelling with me and my family."

Christik looked at us questioningly. I was touched and honored at her suggestion. I looked at James, our kids and our friends, who all looked at me as if to say, '*what are you waiting for*?' before turning back to her.

"We would all be honored to stay with you and your family, my friend," I told her with a huge grin and a dip of my head.

Christik led us out of the control room and as we followed her to the main hangar. There were many angels and people leaving their rooms, getting ready to leave the craft.

"What about our belongings?" I asked, thinking about the kids' things, especially Hope's belongings.

"They are all being transported to your new

rooms, Mel," she assured.

With my mind at ease, we followed Christik onto one of the smaller crafts, and once onboard we were greeted by Evest and Lindaz. After greeting the elders while Christik connected with the craft, we were soon making our way out of the hangar. Luckily for us, Christik automatically made the top half of the craft transparent allowing us a full view of her planet. Hope began to stir, and it was as if she could feel all of our excitement for a new adventure. No one batted an eye as I began to change and then feed her; they were all too busy, looking with wide eyes at the angel's world. As soon as she was feeding contently, I joined my family and friends in unconcealed awe at the sights we were seeing.

Christik glided the craft through natural stone buildings of all different shapes and sizes. It was as if the angels had been influenced by other lands and planets, and then recreated what they had seen. Each stone structure had its own style and was made of various kinds of stone in so many different colors, and all the buildings were decorated with plants and trees. It was a true unification between a race and a planet. There were no words to describe what we were all seeing, and all we could manage were looks of wonder between us, which spoke a thousand words.

Anunaki was teeming with wildlife. I could see flying insects and creatures making their way in between the buildings, flying back to their nests on the outer walls and crevices. The creatures were just as colorful as the plants and flowers they fed and landed on, colors and shapes that we'd never seen before on earth. Just when we'd thought we'd seen everything, a flash of deep red and gold streaked past the craft and began to fly in front of us, leading the way. To my utter joy, it was Qiu in all his dragon glory. Hope stopped feeding, picking up on my em-otions, and she began to wriggle in my arms.

"It looks like Qiu may have missed you, babe," James said with a grin.

"I missed him too actually, I still feel our co-nnection," I told my husband with a massive grin of my own.

As if Qiu had heard me, he turned his black horned, massive head towards us in mid-flight, and if dragons were able to smile, I swear he did. Qiu swooped and flew with graceful ease between and around the buildings, guiding us out of the angel's city. Abruptly the larger buildings stopped, and we were on the outskirts, heading towards what seemed like a smaller community, with single story stone buildings. The land around us was lush and green with areas of brightly colored trees.

"There's a dragon nest!" Abigail shrieked with excitement, as she pointed where she was looking. Sure enough, nestled in a long-grassed pasture was what looked like a crop circle, a flattened area of grass that was such an elaborate pattern, that it would have made a beautiful design for material or a picture. In the center of the crop circle was a beautiful deep purple Long, with short black spiral horns and long black spiked tail, which was curled around her young. A much larger, charcoal grey and dark green Long was watching his family from a short distance away, but he looked up to our craft as we neared. The large male didn't appear worried about our presence and he turned his large dragon head back to his resting family.

"The area those Long were nesting in looked like the crop circles we had appearing back on earth," Derek said to Lindaz and Evest, who were sitting next to him.

The elders smiled at Derek's observation.

"On earth you had the puffer fish who would make patterns in the sand, on the bottom of the sea bed to attract his mate. Here on our planet, the Longs do the same to attract the attention of their mate," Evest explained. "Every Long has their own designs to attract the mate they are meant to be with, and as you just saw, they are very successful at it. Although most Longs prefer to be in colder temperatures, as was the climate of their lost home world."

"If you like, we could take you to where most of the Longs live in our world," Lindaz offered.

Suddenly, everyone was saying yes please and thank you. The elders and Christik all chuckled.

We headed towards one of the larger settlements, which had a large triangular courtyard in the center. Qiu swooped down, landing gracefully in the middle before making his way to the side of the courtyard, while allowing us the room to land the craft. Within moments Christik was disconnecting from the craft and the elders were disembarking, leading the way to their home. As we all stepped off the craft and looked around the simple but elegant courtyard, sweet smelling flora scents drifted in the warm breeze, reminding me of late spring back home. The buildings were all made of stone like the angels' large city. There seemed to be more decorative markings on the structures, which were similar to the Hieroglyphs on the main crafts archways, although these markings weren't glowing like the crafts did.

Various vines wound around the pillars that were lined up at the building entrances, and strange multi winged birds flitted around the small red flowers that nestled amongst the vine leaves. All of us were turning and looking around, before realizing that Christik and her parents were gliding towards what looked like a larger entranceway.

"I think we're on the move!" Tracey said loudly, getting everyone's attention.

"I'll catch you up," I told our friends with a smile. "I want to say a proper hello to Qiu."

"I'll see you in a few minutes baby," James said, before kissing me on the cheek and giving Hope a kiss on her blonde covered head, as she slept in her papoose.

I watched my family and friends follow the elders into their home and noticed that Christik was staying behind.

"I will wait for you, Mel," she told me wa-rmly.

Giving her a grateful smile, I turned on my heel and walked over to my magnificent dragon fri-end. Qiu lowered his massive blood-red, scaled head and his gold nostrils flared as he huffed like a lion would. I placed my hand on his long snout, just above his nose, and instantly our contact began to shimmer a deep purple. I felt it from my hand and through my body. Straight away, Hope woke and started to wri-ggle her legs and arms in excitement, feeling the power and connection too.

'I've missed you, my friend.' I told Qiu with all my heart.

'I have missed you too, young one' he said. *'I felt you arriving and wanted to welcome you. I live in the ice peninsula, and I would like to take you there, so you may see my home and meet my clann,'* he added.

Butterflies appeared in my stomach at the thought of seeing where Qiu and most of the others lived, and Hope began to babble, as she wriggled more against my body. *'I would really like that Qiu, and I'd be really honored to meet your family*, I told him as I lowered my own head, my forehead gently touching his stunning face.

'Go, get settled, and I will come for you once you are ready,' he said in my mind.

Lowering my hand, I took a few steps, dipping my head to my dragon friend and showing my respect. After Qiu did the same, he shot his wings up in the air, lifting himself off the ground with ease, before flying away. I turned back to Christik with a huge grin on my face, while cradling Hope's wriggling bottom in my hands as she kicked her legs.

"It seems that Hope isn't as good at hiding her excitement as her mother is." She chuckled.

"It was really good to see him and yes, I am so excited about seeing his home and meeting his family," I replied, "Do Longs have large families?" I asked as we started to make our way inside.

"Yes, they live long lives, and some may have up to four young in their lifetimes. Not all Longs find a mate, so they help raise the young in their clann, by teaching them important skills," Christik explained.

"Like going invisible?"

"Yes, and learning to hunt for food."

CHAPTER 11

Christik glided through the large pillared entrance and into the cool building. The inside of the building was just as bright and natural looking as the holding craft had been, with everything made of either stone or wood. Inside the reception area, the light-colored stone beneath my feet was pale and smooth. Through the glassless window on the oppos-ite side, more vines were creeping their way through.

The angel turned left through an archway, and we walked through a large open lounge area. There were no sofas or chairs; instead large, round flat padded daybeds hung from the ceiling, from what appeared to be some kind of thick brown jungle vines. They reminded me of the old Tarzan show from when I was younger. The day beds looked big enough for at least four angels or six to seven humans, and I liked the way they seemed to encourage people or angels to sit or lay together.

After walking through the lounge area, we came to a hallway which had at least six arched, pale wooden doors. We walked to the third door and Christik knocked politely. Moments later April answered the door with the look of a very happy young lady.

"Mom, I have the cutest birds flying into my room," she stated gleefully.

"Well then, you will have to show me," I told her, relieved that the kids were taking this all so well.

April opened the door wide for us to enter and the room was a hive of activity. James was whizzing around the main room, putting all of our things away, and I could hear our other kids laughing and joking between themselves.

"Hi babe. Hi Christik. Has Qiu left?" he asked.

"Yes, but we'll see him in a couple of days," I told him.

Not wanting to stop my busy husband, I turned to Christik.

"So, what's the plan for the rest of the day? Is there anything you need us to do?"

"Just make yourselves at home and when you are ready, join us in the gathering room for a meal with me and my elders," she said before dipping her head and gracefully leaving our new room.

Our rooms were just as nice as the lounge area or gathering room as Christik had called it. There were soft beds plus, our own smaller day beds, as well as our own bathroom like the main craft. All the kids were thrilled that the wildlife was able to fly in through the windows and inspect the new guests. There was no fear from the creatures and why would there be, the angels lived in harmony with everything. Except the Marilians now, of course. Once everything was packed away and I had fed, bathed and changed Hope, I sat on the daybed with our new daughter. I waited for the rest of my family while listening to James, April, and Abigail talking about all the birds and creatures they could see from the room's large window.

Before long, we were making our way to the gathering room. I could hear lighthearted voices and laughter as we approached. Tracey and Akhenaten's adopted girls were already there with Mimi, and as soon as they spotted Abigail and April, they were soon running to our girls and jumping into their arms. We made our way in as Christik, Evest, and Lindaz entered through the other entrance. Their arms were laden with platters of food and drinks for everyone, placing them on side tables that weren't there before. James and I got on the nearest daybed and thanked Evest as he passed us by. Mimi giggled as she watched Tracey's girls and ours began to look for more creatures around the window frame.

"Where's Tracey and Akhenaten?" I asked Mimi. "Are they ok?"

Mimi started to wiggle her eyebrows comically.

"The girls are here and they're alone in their room, guess what they're doing?" Mimi said, emphasizing the word alone before bursting out with a big belly laugh.

"Trust Tracey to seize the moment," I giggled.

"Oh, trust me, Mel, I don't think that her angel was fighting her off!"

Once we'd all finished laughing, James reached forward, touching my hand.

"Would you like some food, baby?" he asked as he slid off the day bed.

"Yes please," I told him, realizing just how hungry I was.

What do you think of this world so far?" I asked Mimi and Andrew as I laid Hope on the soft daybed in front of me.

"It's amazing," Andrew said honestly. "It's like nature has taken over and everywhere I look, there's some kind of insect, bird, or animal. I love it!"

"Ditto," Mimi added just as Christik came over to join us.

The angel slid onto the daybed effortlessly and a lot more gracefully than I had, even with a drink in her hand.

"Our planet wasn't always like this," Christik explained. "We once made the same mistakes as mankind, and we did not respect our planet. When we were on the brink of extinction, we made the changes to heal our planet. We have dedicated ourselves to protecting our planet and other worlds ever since. We somehow knew it was our purpose."

"You don't mind the wildlife coming into your homes?" Mimi asked.

Christik held up her free hand, and it started to give off a slight white shimmer. Something yellow flew in from the open window, spinning through the room and between the hanging daybeds, before landing on Christik's open and glowing palm. It looked like a flying, yellow tulip with large petals rotating like a helicopter. There were short stems from the yellow petals, and they all were attached in a circle, on the top of a large caterpillar looking creature. As soon as its stubby little legs touched down on Christik's hand, its yellow petals, or should I say wings, began to slow their circular motion until they finally stopped. Its wings opened and closed like a real tulip flower, and then it closed its wings and kept them closed. It was then that I saw a head and two little beady eyes looking at me.

"We like living in harmony with our planet's creatures," Christik said.

She smiled at the creature on her palm, who was turning on her hand studying us. Its stubby little legs were tapping against her skin as it turned, making it sound as if it was lightly tap dancing.

"We wander all over our planet, sometimes encroaching on a creature's homes or living areas. So, we should be open to sharing our living areas with them too," she added.

"I wish we'd had the chance to live like that on our planet," Mimi's husband Andrew said with sadness in his voice.

"At least we'll get the chance to live differently on our new home," I said with a smile.

The rest of the evening was light-hearted, with the elders and Christik telling us stories of planets that they'd been to, and different races they'd met. By the time we got back to our rooms, we were all feeling very content and full of food, and our minds were full of the mental images of other alien races from the descriptions the angels gave us. As we climbed into bed, none of us had any trouble sleeping.

For the first time since she'd been born, Hope actually slept through the night, waking James and I as it started to lighten outside. When everyone was ready for the day, we made our way to the gathering room to have breakfast with everyone.

"What's the plan for today?" I asked Christik as we both selected food from the side tables, while James occupied our wide-awake baby girl.

"We are going to visit the Impa's, so we can ask them if they would be willing to help us locate the Marilian ships," she replied.

"We're all going?" I accidentally squeaked with unapologetic excitement.

Christik smiled knowingly.

"Yes," she said as her smile grew on her beautiful face. "The Impa's are also known as sky people. The indigenous people that were on your planet are descendants of the Impa's."

My mind was blown by this new information, as images of indigenous people popped into my mind, wearing their stunning feathers and beaded necklaces.

"How is that possible?" I asked, feeling very surprised.

"Just as some of Jeli were relocated to earth while we were healing their planet, so were the Impa's while we were healing their world. We cannot force a race to relocate back to their home world if they wish to stay where they are," Christik explained.

"Did the indigenous people know they were from another world?" I asked, still feeling flabbergasted.

"Yes," she said, as she finished loading her plate. "Most of the elders from the tribes called themselves star people, because their ancestors were not from earth. We have some of their descendants here with us now on our planet. They will be coming with us to meet their race and original home world, Tiyami."

"Heck, I thought I was excited. I bet they can't believe it," I said with a huge grin. "It's going to be awesome to meet them too."

Word soon spread around the gathering room about our upcoming visit to the Impa's home world. We were all excited, wondering what they would be like and if their world was similar to our own.

By late morning, we were all boarding the craft that was still parked outside Christik's home, and our nervous excitement was growing. Christik had explained that we were going to meet the descendants of the Impa's at the gate, and I thought of the Gate of the Gods in Peru immediately. We'd already witnessed the elders arriving and the Longs, but none of us had travelled through ourselves and my nervousness were growing.

The quick journey to the gate was fascinating, as we flew over more images on the natural plains of the angel's planet, and viewed more henges, some larger than others.

"Why are there henges and images on the ground here, Lindaz?" Derek asked politely, as we flew over what looked like another alien creature created in a long grassy hill.

"All of the images you see, can be seen from space if a craft or ship is close enough, Derek," Lindaz explained. "We want other races to know that we have met their race before, and they are welcome here."

"Well that makes sense to me," he stated to everyone within earshot. "What about the long lines on the ground?"

"Many of them are from crafts and ships," the elder said. "They are a more natural version of your airplane runways."

I could tell from Derek's expression that her answers had only created more questions for him, but he didn't want to miss out on anything else on the ground, so he kept them to himself.

A short time later, we seemed to be approaching a circular grassed area where the grass was visibly shorter. Inside the grass area and around the outer perimeter were dark stone arches, similar to the Gate of the Gods. As soon as we landed and Christik opened the rear door, we disembarked just as another craft was arriving. '*They must be the Impa's descendants*' I thought to myself. I was excited for the other human survivors, even though we hadn't met them yet. It wasn't often that people got to meet their long-lost relatives, especially in such weird circumstances. When their craft landed and the rear door opened, I was surprised by the nervous excitement that I felt coming from the people inside because it was so strong.

The indigenous people were of various ages, with a few elders and a large group of middle-aged males and females, plus some older children around the same ages as our own kids. They were a friendly group, and as soon as they disembarked, they walked over to meet us, introducing themselves and saying hello. There was only one who wasn't particularly friendly. He didn't feel like a loner to me, but I did feel a very negative vibe coming from him, which I couldn't understand. He was introduced by one of the elders as Running Bear and when we tried to say hello, his look showed how unimpressed he was.

"Don't mind Running Bear," the Indian elder named White Wolf said while rolling his eyes. "He has never believed the stories that were passed down through our generations, about our tribe coming from the stars, but he will soon," he added with a twinkle in his eyes.

Just as I was going to ask White Wolf about the younger man, I stopped myself. Christik was gliding towards the circle of arches and I really didn't want to miss anything. White Wolf turned to see what I was looking at, and before long all eyes were on the angel. James quickly walked over to join me, taking my hand in his.

"Shall we?" he asked with a wink.

Within minutes, we were all following Christik and the elders to the circle of arches, and they were a lot bigger up close. Two lighter stone pillars stood at the entrance and hieroglyphs were etched in the middle of them. As we walked between them, I could see that they were pitted and worn with age. I could feel the buzz of power within them, making my skin tingle. The darker stone arches inside the circle all had lighter stone centers with hieroglyphic markings too. Christik began to walk towards the center of the magical site. I could see there were large circular indents in the middle of them, which were already filled with gold.

All of us were intrigued, wondering what was going to happen next. For those of us who'd already experienced Christik's power, we had some sort of idea of what to expect, although none of us could really imagine what was going to be on the other side of the star passage. Christik glided to the front of our group, smiling at the mix of people before her.

"Please wait here for a moment," she said with a dip of her head, her peacock, multicolored eyes sparkling as she spoke.

The angel glided towards one of the arches to our right and she stopped, standing a few feet away from the megalithic arched door. I could feel her power building even before she started to raise her arms, and by the time her hands began to glow with power, I could feel the magic all around me.

"I can feel your hand tingling in mine," James whispered in my ear, making me smile.

"You wait till she activates the star passage." I giggled.

Hope was starting to feel it too, and I knew

she was starting to wake up in her papoose. I turned my gaze straight back to Christik and the stone arch she was standing in front of. The angel had turned her palms, so they were now facing the stone arch, and the gold inside the circular indent in the middle of the door was starting to glow. We watched, fascinated, as the gold turned into a molten liquid, traveling across the stone surface, reaching the hieroglyphs where each symbol was filled with the precious metal. The wind picked up around us, our hair being blown in one direction and then another, and the bottom of my dress began to whip around my legs. Hope began to wriggle in her papoose against my body, so I let go of James's hand, wrapping both of my arms around her, while shielding her from as much of the wind as possible.

As soon as all the hieroglyphs were filled, the gold inside the central indent began to swirl. The gold moved slowly at first and it was mesmerizing, watching it move in a circular motion, while getting faster and faster. Christik's power flowed, growing stronger as the golden whirlpool sped up dramatically inside the stone door. Those who hadn't experienced Christik's power first-hand began to huddle together through instinct, making them feel safer. The stone door started to softly glow as the golden whirlpool began to shimmer, and then there was a bright burst of golden light, as the stone door vanished leaving a gold shimmering barrier in its place.

When Christik started to rein in her power, the wind around us began to die down, until finally we could hear each other's heavy breathing, and murmurs of "wow" and "that was amazing". Many of us, including the Indian men had to sweep our messed-up hair out of our faces. As always Christik and the elders looked no different, with their long angel hair lying straight down their backs, with not a strand out of place.

When I looked around, many of our friends, old and new were telling each other how amazing it was. To be honest, even though I'd seen Christik's power in action before on many occasions, it never ceased to amaze me. Christik turned away from the shimmering gate of the star passage to face us, and as she smiled the light from the glowing barrier made her face look even more beautiful and magical.

"Are you all ready?" she asked.

There were many "Yeses" and nods from those who were still speechless from what they'd just witnessed, and I could feel how anxious many of them were.

"Please follow me, one at a time," Christik told us all softly.

Christik turned back to face the gate and we all stood and watched as she began to glide forward. The angel made contact with the barrier and its glow brightened as she seemed to melt through it, vanishing before our eyes. My heart began to pound in my chest as my nervousness grew. Hope started to gurgle and kick her legs against my very warm body. Tracey, our confident friend strode forward, looking back at Akhenaten once, who smiled at her lovingly, before she passed through the star passage with purpose. '*My God, that woman has no fear*' I thought, admiring my friends unwavering bravery. Akhenaten bent down to their three little girls, telling them that their mommy was waiting for them. We were all impressed as their girls went through with no hesitation, just like their mom.

After Akhenaten went through the star passage gate himself, James took my hand in his.

"You go first, baby, and I'll make sure all our kids come after you," he said with a wink.

My husband could tell by my body language that I was nervous, but he also knew that I wasn't scared. I trusted the angels with my life and the lives of my family. I knew they wouldn't let anything happen to any of us. Giving my family my best winning smile, I walked through all of our friends as confidently as I could, while stroking Hopes back through her baby papoose to soothe her. I stopped inches away from the shimmering barrier of the gate, pulled my shoulders back, and took in a slow deep breath. Then a thought suddenly popped into my head, '*Should I keep my eyes open or close them, hell, just do it woman*' I scolded myself.

Before I could give myself the chance of chickening out, I made myself walk forward with my eyes open. The barrier felt like tingling warm water as it touched my skin, and I felt a wave of power flow through my body. Flashes of glittering colors passed before my eyes as if I was traveling at speed, but I didn't feel like I was actually moving. The deep breath that I'd taken escaped my chest, and just as I was about to take another, a coolness washed over me, and I was stepping out into tall wildflowers. My eyes widened, darting left and right, as I desperately tried to take everything in.

"Wow."

CHAPTER 12

While my brain tried to take in everything before me, I started to walk forward and away from the gate I'd just come through. I didn't want to be in the way as the next person arrived. I could see Christik walking towards a stunning forest with Tracey, Akhenaten, and their girls close behind. As I waited for my family to come through, I looked around properly at my surroundings, and Tiyami was wild and beautiful.

Everywhere I looked there were trees, long grass, and wildflowers that swayed in the cool, sweet smelling air. The trees were thick with small green leaves, and their pale grey trunks seemed to have different long leaves sprouting from their sides.

Movement in my peripheral vision forced me to look away, just in time to see Abigail emerge from the star passage. As soon as she saw me a huge grin spread across her young face.

"That was the coolest thing I've ever done," she said breathlessly, with her grin getting wider.

I couldn't help but grin back at her beaming face.

"Come on, my darling, we'd better move back for the others," I told her, reaching an outstretched hand for her to take.

Within half an hour everyone was through the star passage, and were either telling someone about how they felt as they passed through, or they were busy looking around. Christik, Tracey, and her family were still waiting patiently by the nearest trees. So, once we knew that everyone had arrived, we began to make our way to Christik, with the elders in tow.

The cool breeze was pleasant on my skin, and the long grass and tall flowers seemed to sway out of our way as we walked through, almost as if the plants had a mind of their own. The ground was soft under foot, making it feel like we were walking on lush green carpet. Within minutes, we had reached the trees ourselves and I could feel everyone's emotions beginning to calm and settle, to eagerness rather than nervousness.

The trees were even prettier up close, and for a split second I swore I saw a tree trunk move behind Tracey. What I thought were long leaves coming from the sides of the tree trunks were actually long feathers that changed color as the light shone on them. '*What the hell*?' As my own emotions settled, I also picked up on new feelings of excitement and curiosity, but it didn't feel like it was coming from any of us.

"Are you ready to meet your ancestors?" Christik asked White Wolf and our new Indian friends.

The elder Indian man's face lit up at her words, and he nodded his head as eagerly as the others.

"Yes, and I think I can say that for nearly all of us," White Wolf said as he shot a look of disappointment at Running Bear, who rolled his eyes as if bored.

The elders and Akhenaten glided forward to stand either side of Christik, but with a good distance between them. Suddenly all four of the angels released their wings in magnificent splendor, while bowing their upper bodies respectively. My eyes were darting this way and that, trying to look for any signs of the Impa people, and I wasn't expecting what happened next. Hope sensed the Impa's before I did, and she began to turn her head from side to side, as her little legs began to kick against my hips.

Movement on the tree trunks caught my eye again, and this time I knew I wasn't just seeing things. The long dark feathers on the tree trunks began to bristle and move like they were alive, and as I watched completely fascinated, outlines of bodies in various positions started to appear along the length of the nearest trunks.

"Woah, what the fu…" Tracey began to say, before she quickly covered her mouth with her hand. She'd obviously got used to hiding her potty mouth, and didn't want her new adopted girls picking up on her bad habit. After some giggles from our group, including me and my family, we all turned our attention back to the trees that seemed to be coming alive. More definition of heads and limbs were appearing as we watched, and seconds later, slender light, grey people were peeling themselves from the trees. Some even had trickles of moss and tiny flowers still attached along their sides and backs, on their grey textured skin.

The Impa who had the most and longest feathers down his back, as well as the most moss and vivid colored flowers on his body, walked forward with the others following behind. I assumed that he was the eldest, and he was most definitely male, judging by the grey cloth around his waist that matched his skin color. The Impa walked towards the angels, and one by one he touched their foreheads with his own. I assumed it was his way of greeting them or his sign of respect.

As soon as Evest had been touched, he straightened himself, folding his large wings neatly behind his back in one graceful movement, with Christik, Akhenaten, and Lindaz following suit. Once the greeting was over the Impa walked back, so he stood in front of all four angels, his eyes quickly glanced over the native Indian people in our large group.

“It has been so long since our eyes have seen you friends,” the Impa said in a deep husky voice that matched his appearance.

“Yes, my friend,” Evest replied with a smile. “I see by your feathers that you are the new chieftain of your people, Swift Arrow. May your father rest in the stars,” he added.

All of the angels dipped their heads in respect to Swift Arrow and the memory of his father.

“My father and I smile at your return to our homelands,” he said, as he raised a hand to the sky. “What brings you and with so many?” the chieftain asked bluntly, although politely.

“The planet Earth has been destroyed by the

Marilians. We saved as many humans as we were able, and we will find them a new home. However, we have decided to try and take care of the Marilians, with help from our friends" the elder said, with a smile that made it clear what he was asking.

"We have seen what the Marilians can do. Come to our camp and we will talk more," Swift Arrow said, as he indicated towards the trees they had just come out from.

We talked quietly between ourselves as we walked through the forest, admiring the unusual things we were seeing, and pointing them out to each other. I could hear James excitedly pointing something out. When I turned to look, a fish-like creature with many legs scampered under a bush. One of our group called for us to look up, just in time for us to witness what appeared to be the smallest looking parrot-type bird I'd ever seen, but which was hovering above our heads like a hummingbird. Not for the first time, I wished with all my heart that I'd had a camera, so I could capture all the sights and creatures that we were seeing. I really hoped that one day Hope would get the chance to see and experience all the things that we were, when she was old enough to remember.

Soon the trees began to thin out and voices could be heard. Wherever we were heading, it was busy with people and children. Before long we spotted movement, and within mere minutes we all walked out into a large area surrounded by trees. Dotted around the meadow were the biggest and most impressive tipis I'd ever seen. Not that I'd seen any in real life, but they certainly looked a lot bigger than the pictures I remembered.

The Impa's tipis weren't made of animal skins and hides like the pictures I'd seen either, although they did seem to have a flap at the top, and at the openings to get inside. They still had large wooden poles coming out of the tops, and the outer walls of the tipis looked a lot like clay, hand smoothed over the framework. Colorful drawings were painted on the side of each one that I could see. Some had animal paintings, as if the creatures were in motion, while others had images of stars, plants, or trees. Each tipi seemed to have a theme, and I wondered if it had something to do with their owners' names.

As soon as the Impa people saw us approaching, they all stopped to look and stare. I got the impression that they weren't used to having visitors, especially visitors from a different world. All of the Impa's had various amounts and lengths of feathers, from the tops of their heads and down their backs. It appeared that it depended on their age. The older people had a lot of longer feathers, and definitely more moss and flowers covering their bodies. It was as if the nature on their planet was trying to cover their modesty as they got older.

The youngest Impa's were very cute, with short thin feathers on their backs and shorter black hair that was plaited by their ears. All the Impa's wore similar style clothing. The men wore cloth around their waists and the women wore long strips of cloth that covered their modesty. The Impa's all looked very different from the Indian people we were with, but after the birth of Hope, with her gifts and wings, I didn't doubt what Christik had said about them being the Indians' ancestors.

When the Impa people saw that we were with the chieftain, and some of their people already, their postures relaxed, and a few began to wave in wel-come. I couldn't help but glance at Running Bear, and he still looked completely unimpressed. The vibe I was getting from him made me think that he was hoping our visit was going to be a failure somehow.

When we reached the village, nearly all of the Impa's came to greet us. The older Impa's were clea-rly happy to see the angels, and I guessed that maybe the youngest of the tribe hadn't met them before. Swift Arrow held up both hands into the air and made some sort of loud noise that sounded like bird cry, making everyone quieten down.

"Welcome our travelers from the stars!" he declared in his deep voice. Instantly all the Impa's moved into action, all going in different directions. Swift Arrow lowered his arms and turned back to us, his eyes connecting with White Wolf.

"Come, we will talk while my people prepare for our gathering"

Swift Arrow started to walk, leading us through the tipis until we reached a clearing in the middle of their village. In the center was a big circle of long grass bundles, most of which had been trimmed and covered with colored cloth for sitting on. In the middle of the seating area there was a stone circle, filled with sticks and other dried vegetation ready for a new fire. I could see charred pieces of wood and blackened stones around the bottom, evidence of their previous fires. Swift Arrow stopped between the grass seats, next to a grass bundle that was higher than the rest. He turned, raising his arms out, as if inviting us in. Christik, the elders, and Akhenaten glided forward without hesitation, taking the seats on either side of the Impa chieftain, with Tracey and the rest of us following suit.

No sooner had our butts touched the grass bundles, Impa's came over with wooden cups and clay looking jugs of water. With every thank you, the

Impa men and woman smiled. I could feel their curiosity as much as it showed in their deep brown eyes. They were just as intrigued by us, as we were of them.

"We are happy that it was you coming through the star passage," the chieftain said, as his eyes scanned us all.

"You knew we were coming?" Tracey asked, her surprised voice reflecting my own surprise.

"We did, wife of Akhenaten," Swift Arrow told her. "We dreamt about you arriving. That is why we were waiting for you. We also knew that our people were coming home, and our friends needed us." he gave a knowing glance, to first White Wolf and then the angels.

"You knew we were coming too?" White Wolf asked, sounding just as surprised as Tracey.

"Yes, and we saw that you had lost your true selves," Swift Arrow stated, before turning to look at Evest and pointing to the waiting fire pit. "Would you?" he asked the elder, "My body is not as young as it was."

Evest smiled at the old Impa chieftain, before raising his hand to the waiting kindling. A burst of bright white power shot from the elder's hand, landing right at the bottom of the fire pit, making the bottom of it instantly light with new flames. I had no idea what kind of wood and vegetation the Impa's used, but the flames were beautiful, changing colors as the various twigs began to burn. I could have sat peacefully and watched the blue, green, red and purple flames for hours.

The Impa people started to join us within minutes, coming from all directions while carrying various foods on wooden trays. Some had large fish that were already gutted, tied with twine on thick, long wooden poles. White Wolf had fallen silent and we watched with fascination, as the fish poles were wedged between the stones around the fire, ready to be cooked, while the other food trays were placed on the ground around the stone circle. As soon as the Impa's had placed their foods, they all took seats on the grass bundles too. There were genuine smiles from the Impa's to the Indian people that were with us, and I wondered if they all knew they were related.

Once the last trickle of men, women and children were gathered around the fire, I looked around and smiled. The Impa children and babies were all sitting on or near their parents, and I could feel the love and closeness of the tribe. The Impa people were close and it brought back memories of when I was little, and the closeness of my own family. Unfortunately, our world had become a smaller place, with so many of my family moving away through marriage or work, and our family, like most had drifted apart. Swift Arrow stood from his seat and he made the bird call sound again grabbing everyone's attention. Very quickly the gathering of Impa's and humans fell silent and even the children became quiet.

"We thank you for sharing your food with our visitors from the Stars," Swift Arrow said, loud and clear for all to hear. "Please eat and enjoy."

The Impa's were very polite, picking up the nearest wooden platter of food or jug of water, and offering it to the nearest guests and other Impa's, while others went towards the fire to collect the cooked fish. Once we all had food in our hands and water to drink, conversation began to flow. I was listening to a young teenage boy asking Abigail about Earth, when I picked up on White Wolf asking Swift Arrow about his ancestry and I turned to listen.

"But I'm confused," White Wolf said politely, his eyebrows furrowing on his aged face. "If we are one and the same people, how can we look so different, and what did you mean that we had lost our true selves?"

"I told you all it was a load of crap," Running Bear chipped in, his voice ladened with disdain.

White Wolf and the other Indian people shot glares at the younger man, who had the decency to lower his eyes with embarrassment.

"I'm sorry for my son's rudeness," White Wolf said to everyone's surprise.

None of us had realized that the two men were related. I felt bad for the Indian elder for having a son who didn't believe in, or respect their ways and history. The chieftain gave White Wolf a sympathetic look of understanding.

"Your ancestors looked like us," White Arrow stated matter of factly, "we are all able to shed our feathers and our natures markings, we are even able to change the color of our skin. Those before us sought refuge on your world like many other races, and they found themselves in a place where it was ice and snow. Once the angels left with those who wanted to come home, the rest of our people shed themselves, to cover their bodies with furs from the creatures they hunted for food. Over time they forgot their true selves, only remembering that they were from the stars."

"So, our friends are permanently different to your tribe now?" James asked the chieftain.

"No," White Arrow said bluntly while shaking his head. "The Impa is still within them."

White Wolf gave his food to a young man who was sitting next to him, and then he stood up proudly with his shoulders back and his head held high.

"How can I become my true self?" he asked the Impa chieftain, with confidence in every word.

I was surprised that the Indian elder would want to rush so quickly into changing himself, but then, he'd obviously always been a true believer of the stories past down from his forefathers.

"You would need to drink the juice from the starberri. It is what we drink to enhance our dream sight," White Wolf explained.

"I'd like to do it please," White Wolf said, nodding his head respectfully at the chieftain.

Swift Arrow nodded his head to a female Impa who placed her food down and swiftly left the gathering. I found myself like many others, watching everything and placing food in my mouth, as if I were at the movies watching a dramatic film.

"This is going to be fricking awesome!" Tracey stated as she grinned at Akhenaten.

Almost as if on cue, Hope began to wake due to the excitement that was beginning to build. Discreetly I slipped the papoose off my body while James held my food, so I could change and feed her. Everyone was busy talking about what was going to happen next, and I tried to keep up with the conversations as I tended to our daughter.

"What is the starberri juice?" one of the Indian women asked as White Wolf sat down again.

Swift Arrow bent down to one of the platters of food, picking up a small vine which was ladened with deep, dark, red berries.

"These are starberri's, they are a sacred food for us. These sacred berries have everything our bodies need. When we have hard long winters, these are what get us through. When they are cooked with the sacred Itchu lake water, the juice helps to enhance our sight," the chieftain explained.

"What do you mean, your sight? Is that just while you are sleeping?" Derek asked curiously.

"They do not just enhance our dreams of what is coming next, our spirits can leave our bodies and search for what we seek,"

"Wow, that's amazing," Derek said, just as the Impa woman returned with a clay jug that was painted with images of stars and some kind of writing.

I didn't know if it was because I was a mom or because I was naturally protective, but suddenly I was nervous and a little worried. '*What if something goes wrong; what if the Indian people don't have enough Impa in them, for it to work and it makes them sick*' I thought. I turned to look at the angels who were sat with the chieftain, and none of them seemed concerned whatsoever. My eyes connected with Christik's and I instantly heard her voice in my mind.

'*You have nothing to fear for your new friends, Mel*', she assured.

I smiled at my friend and at the fact that she always knew how I was feeling, and knew what to say to put my mind at ease.

The Impa woman walked between the other tribe members and people until she reached the chieftain, bowing her head and holding the clay jug out to him with both hands. Swift Arrow nodded his head to her respectfully and she turned to go back to her seat. Instantly, without the chieftain having to say a word, the closest Impa's began to make room for their elder, sliding and moving the platters of food and jugs of water to the next person, and the next person, down along the circle, until finally the chieftain and the angels had a completely clear area.

"White Wolf, come forward and be released into your true self."

CHAPTER 13

The Indian elder stood from his grass bundle seat without any hesitation. I could feel his nervous excitement and anticipation as it grew. This was a man who believed one hundred percent in the legends of his people, and he was not only wanting to be true to himself and his beliefs, but he also wanted to prove his son wrong. Just as White Wolf took a step forward, his son grabbed his arm, and the elder turned to look at his doubtful son.

"You know this isn't going to work, don't you?" he asked with a shitty tone to his voice. "You're going to look like a fool in front of our people!"

I could sense the elder's heart breaking at the lack of faith and respect from his only son, and my heart sank for him. Instantly there was an awkward silence that washed over the gathering.

"You have so much to learn my son," White Wolf said sadly. "You need to have faith, even in the things you can't see and touch."

Running Bear's hand dropped back into his lap as he looked into his father's eyes. Although I couldn't see the elders face, I imagined that his eyes showed the disappointment he felt at his son's words and actions. He turned away from his son and straightened himself before walking steadily towards the Impa chieftain. As soon as White Wolf reached Swift Arrow, the chieftain raised the decorated jug up to the elder.

"Are you ready to become who you really are?" he asked.

White Wolf's eyes reflected the colorful flames of the fire, almost as if they were reflecting the elder's excitement and desire.

"Yes, I'm ready."

"One small sip is all you will need. Please remove your top clothing," Swift Arrow told him.

With not one single doubt in his mind White Wolf slipped his light-colored top off his body and let it drop to the grassy floor. Taking the offered jug and raising it to his full lips, he took his sip and handed back the jug to the Chieftain.

The gathering was silent. Even the young children and babies were quiet as we all waited to see what would happen next. Seconds passed and Running Bear scoffed, breaking the silence.

"You will show respect," Swift Arrow told him loudly, showing his authority.

The younger Indian, shocked at being called out by the Impa, lowered his head in embarrassment just as his father's head lifted to the heavens.

His father's shoulders and arms shot backwards as he gave a small 'ugh' sound, and we watched as a grey patch of color began to appear on the elder's chest. The grey color started to spread outwards, up to his collar bones, to his sides and down his torso, his skin texture began to change too. He gave another 'ugh' sound as black dots began to appear in a rough circle on his back, and spots of green started to show on his bare left shoulder, tricking down the left side of his chest. The spattering of dark brown chest hair fell from his body, and suddenly the elder bent over, placing his hands on his knees. His son, like the rest of us humans was speechless, and I could see his suddenly worried expression.

The black spots on the elders back grew outwards from his greying skin, going from spots to thin black spikes. They kept growing until his back started to look like a pin cushion. The greyness carried on spreading along his body, seeping down his arms and down his back, torso, and up his neck to his face, until finally his whole upper body was covered. The spots of green began to look like small blisters, and within moments, they appeared to burst into moss on his newly textured grey skin.

Seconds later, tiny little blue flowers bloomed on his moss patches, and the dark spiked cluster on his back started to fluff out into magnificent feathers just like the other Impa's. He reminded me of a butterfly emerging from its pupa. White Wolf panted with short, shallow breaths as his body changed, revealing his true self, and he was a sight to behold.

Everyone remained silent as White Wolf caught his breath. Minutes passed and then the elder straightened his body, raising his arms to study the new look and feel of his skin. Then he looked down at his chest and torso, running his hand softly over the moss and tiny blue flowers, his natures markings.

"That was freaking unbelievable," Tracey blurted out, not realizing at first that she'd said it out loud. She quickly turned to Akhenaten, who was rolling his peacock eyes at her in mock shock. Tracey quickly looked at her little girls who both sat on Akhenaten's knees.

"I'm sorry, my little poppets. Mommy didn't mean to say bad words," she told them, before turning back to White Wolf and the Impa chieftain.

"But that was blooming epic! How do you feel?" she asked, voicing what most of us were wondering ourselves.

White Wolf looked at Tracey with a beaming smile.

"I feel absolutely amazing. I feel like I did in my twenties."

Running Bear stood and gingerly approached his father. His eyes studied the new changes on his father's body, until finally he reached him and looked him in the eye.

"I'm so sorry that I didn't believe you, Dad," the younger man said with a voice full of emotion and regret.

He turned to Swift Arrow and bowed.

"Can I be next?" he asked, which surprised us all.

Through the course of the afternoon and evening, one by one the Indian people asked to be changed into their true selves, and each transformation was as amazing as the last. Just like the Impa's, their feathers and natures markings varied depending on their age, and they were all elated with their new forms.

"Will we now have the sight too?" White Wolf asked Swift Arrow after the last of his new tribe was transformed.

"Yes, and you will be able to seek what you desire too," the chieftain told him. "You all will."

"We seek the Marilian ships so they can be stopped forever," White Wolf said bluntly. "They murdered our people, killed our planet, and their reign of destruction has to end."

"You don't want us to fight with you?" Swift Arrow asked, as he looked at White Wolf and then glanced at the angels.

"We would be honored to have you by our side in battle Swift Arrow, but we would understand if you did not want to put your people in harm's way. We do need your help to locate their ships, as White Wolf has said. So, we can stop them before we attack their planet," Lindaz explained.

"You intend to kill them?" Swift Arrow as-ked.

"No. We intend to heal those who were ch-anged, and capture the king and the true blooded Marilians, so they can't kill or change any race aga-in," Evest said with conviction.

"Then we will help you," the chieftain told

the angels. “Come, you will be our guests tonight, and we will come with you when the sun rises.”

The Impa’s couldn’t have been more hospitable hosts. As we left the newly transformed Impa’s talking by the fire, listening to their history, we made our way to one of the large tipis that was going to be ours for the night. We were led by one of the Impa women, to a tipi with a strange looking bear creature painted on the side, and writing I’d never seen before. Our friends had been led to other tipis and when we entered ours it was surprisingly cozy.

A small fire was burning inside a small, stone hearth, giving off a surprising amount of heat. Around the hearth were two large beds on the floor for me and James, Anthony, and Christine. Plus, smaller beds for the kids. We thanked the Impa and she left with a smile, leaving us to settle down for the night. Out of curiosity I lifted the furs and blankets that were on the bed to see what we’d be laying on, and found flat stitched cushions that smelt similar to pine needles, but they were soft like feather downing. The kids all looked as tired as I felt, and Hope was finally fast asleep against my body.

The next morning, after a very deep sleep, I woke to Hope wanting to be fed and desperately needing a change. Recognizing the smell from her angel made diaper, I decided to take her outside, not wanting to stink out the whole tipi and make my family suffer.

I crept out of the tipi with Hope in my arms and her things in a bag over my shoulder, and was surprised to find White Wolf sitting with Swift Arrow at the gathering place. They were talking quietly between themselves, and I wondered if they'd been there all night or if they'd woken early like Hope. Not knowing where else to go I made my way over to the two elders, hoping that they wouldn't mind me joining them.

"Good morning," I said warmly as I reached them. "Would you mind if I sat with you?"

Both of the Impa men smiled with their eyes as they did with their lips, and they seemed genuinely pleased to see me and my baby girl.

"Please, join us," Swift Arrow said, patting the empty grass seat next to him.

"Have you been up all night talking?" I asked them with a smile.

"No, it seems that we are both early risers," White Wolf grinned. "Maybe it's an age thing."

"I thought I'd be the only one up," I told them. "I'll apologize now for anything nasty you smell, I'm afraid this little one needs changing,"

Both men smiled as if to say, we've been there and done that.

"You do what you need to, Mel," said White Wolf with a wink.

As I changed, fed and burped Hope, I listened to them talk about the stories White Wolf was told as he grew up, and what really happened according to Swift Arrow and his knowledge. It reminded me of when I was a child playing Chinese whispers; how a story starts off being told one way, and then every time it's retold one or two details are changed, until finally the real story and the last retelling of the story, are completely different.

"How did you sleep in your new form?" I asked White Wolf when their conversation paused.

The elder looked thoughtful for a moment.

"It was strange to be honest," he said with a small smile. "I slept deeply I think, but I had the most vivid dreams I think I've ever had in my long life. They were so real that I could smell things and even feel things, as if I was really there."

"What did you dream about?"

"I was dreaming about the Marilians, Mel, and I really think we can stop them," he said confidently. "Last night I dreamt that I was in a dark, orange stone room, and the Marilian king was talking with around ten others. I think they were all true blooded Marilians, and if they are the only ones who are true Marilians and we can change the others, I really think we can stop them."

My heart was pounding in my chest at his word. I really hoped he was right, but what would we do with them if we managed to succeed? I had to trust that the angels had an idea about how to imprison them, or put them somewhere where they could be contained permanently.

"We'll have to make sure that we change as many Marilians as we can, so we have the numbers we need to attack their planet," I told him, "and I think you should tell Christik and the elders about your dream too."

We talked for a while longer and gradually everyone else began to wake and came out of their tipis. I took Hope back to our tipi just as a young Impa teen was leaving. We smiled at each other as he left, and I went inside to find my family getting up. There was a clay wash bowl and small cloths next to it on the floor by the glowing embers of our fire pit.

"Are we all supposed to use the same bowl of water to wash with?" April asked with a stunned look on her face.

"Don't worry, honey," I told her, smiling at the face she was making. "Just wet your cloth to wash your face, we'll get showers as soon as we get back to Christik's dwelling okay?"

Before long, we were semi washed and were making our way to the gathering area with everyone else. Just like the night before, the Impa people were showing us their hospitality. They were bringing out wooden trays of flat bread, sliced meats, and fruits. I was expecting my family and friends' faces to light up at the sliced meat the Impa’s were offering, but that wasn't the case. Personally, I was enjoying our new vegetarian lifestyle, and it wasn't just because so many of earth’s animals had died either. I actually felt better in myself, and I was beginning to think that was the case for most of us.

After tucking into a hearty breakfast, the Impa’s who were coming with us said their farewells to their families. It was touching to see them holding hands and touching foreheads. They were a close-knit group of people, and it felt good to know that we were the same now too. Some of the younger, newly transformed Impa’s stayed with the tribe, but most were coming with us, including the newly changed Running Bear. It was as if he was a different person, no longer the moody, glum man he was. If I hadn’t had recognized him, I wouldn’t have believed it was the same man, who was now chatty with everyone.

Christik led us back to the star passage which was still glowing and active. This time there was no hesitation from any of us as we walked through, and when we came through the other side to the angel's planet, there were four crafts waiting this time. In less than an hour, we were back at the angels dwe-lling, and while Christik showed her new guests to their rooms, we all took the opportunity to get our showers and change. Holly and Nalik wanted to hear all about the visit, and while I fed Hope, I told them everything.

"It's going to be a massive advantage if you, the elders, and the Impa's can pull it off," Holly said as she held and burped her baby sister.

"I know we can do it," I told her, feeling more confident than ever. "By the way darling, I'll need you to look after Hope while I'm gone, if that's ok."

"Sure, but what about feeding her? It's not as if the angels have formula," Holly said with a smirk.

"I am sure we can help you with that, Mel," Nalik assured, as Hope let out a big burp, taking us all by surprise.

While Holly played with Hope, James and I decided to take a walk around the dwelling and have a little time to ourselves. It had been quite the whirl-wind of events and I felt like I needed a breather, even if it was only for a while. James held my hand as we walked through the dwelling and into the cou-rtyard. As soon as we were out in the warm breeze, we could smell the scent of the flowering plants and trees. James led the way, walking around the stone buildings and heading towards the grass area behind. When we found a nice spot to relax in, we laid down on the grass holding each other and enjoying the moment.

The moment James began to run his fingers across my body, along my collarbone, I knew what he had on his mind. My body started to tingle as he pulled me closer. His lips met mine, his soft tongue probed as he started to kiss me deeply, and my body reacted to him. My hand moved to the back of his neck, my fingers moving through his thick dark hair, as I kissed him back with gentle pressure.

I could never seem to get enough of my husband's caresses and kisses. When we finally ended our long, passionate kiss, we were smoldering heaps on the grass. We took a few moments, just looking up at the clear blue sky, relishing the peace and quiet. It wasn't until we sat up to leave that I noticed the top wet patches covering my full breasts.

"Oh hell," I exclaimed, as I realized that I'd leaked breast milk during our tryst. "This isn't a good look to have in front of everyone. How am I going to hide this?"

James smirked and gave me a smoldering look.

"You're not really helping right now, husband of mine," I told him with a fake scolding tone.

Before I could say another word, James stripped off his loose top, folding it before giving it to me.

"There you go, baby, just hide your wet patches until you can get another shower and change," he said with a grin.

We headed back to the angels dwelling with me covering my chest with James's top, hoping that we could avoid being seen. Especially as James was walking around half naked in all his masculine glory, with a large satisfied grin on his face. However, luck wasn't on our side. The moment we tried to sneak into the main entrance, Tracey, Akhenaten, and their girls were walking out. The moment Tracey saw us, her face broke into a grin that said, 'I know what you've been up too'.

"Had a little accident, did ya?" she asked with a smirk.

My cheeks instantly began to glow with embarrassment. Luckily, their girls were too young to understand what their mom meant or what we'd been up too. Even Akhenaten started to smirk at James's huge grin as Tracey wiggled her eyebrows at us.

"Would you like some assistance before you

meet anyone else?" he asked with humor in his deep musical voice.

"Yes please, Akhenaten," I said gratefully, thanking my lucky stars that it wasn't anyone else we'd bumped into.

Without another word, Akhenaten approached me, raising his hand and tapping into his power. His hands began to glow, and as I looked down to my chest, I could see and feel the tingle of his power as my dress and James's shirt dried. Once the angel's power faded and he lowered his hands, I gingerly lifted away the shirt, relieved that there wasn't any trace of my leakage. With a smile, I gave James his top back, getting a wink from him in response.

"Thank you, Akhenaten, you're my hero." I grinned, showing my relief and gratitude. "Where are you off too?" I asked my still grinning girlfriend.

"We're taking the girls for a little walk. Christik is getting us a babysitter, so we can all meet and discuss our battle plan at their HQ," she stated.

It seemed a little weird to think of the angels having headquarters, but I guessed that they would have a main place to discuss important issues.

"Ok, we'll see you in a bit. Thank you again for the help!" I said as they turned to leave.

CHAPTER 14

By the time we got back to our room, my cheeks were no longer glowing a flushed pink. Holly was cradling Hope in her arms and our baby girl's eyes were starting to close. My heart was full of love as I witnessed the bonding between my daughters as Nalik looked on in awe. Holly's angel was definitely going to be a doting dad without a doubt. Anthony and Christine were standing at the open window tal-king quietly, and I could hear our other kids in the next room laughing and teasing each other.

"Christik has asked us to meet in the court-yard as soon as we're ready," Holly said, as soon as she noticed us walking in.

It wasn't long before we were all ready and, in the courtyard, waiting. Tracey and Akhenaten were waiting with us, and all the younger kids, including ours, were hanging out together in the gathering room. It seemed that our little tribe were quite relieved to be chilling out instead of talking battle plans, and I couldn't blame them. Small crafts soon arrived, and as they started to land in the large courtyard, Christik and the elders glided out to join us.

Soon we were boarded on the small crafts with our new Impa friends, and Christik was piloting the craft. Christik had kindly made the craft partly transparent, and we were all looking in different directions, admiring Anunaki's landscape. It appeared we were going in a different direction than before. Although we were still seeing similar markings on the ground of creatures and tracks, as well as wide rivers, strange forests and unusual rock formations.

As we flew over certain areas, we would see some of the planet's wildlife, and not just the odd dragon. At one point we flew over a herd of creatures who looked like huge hairy pigs, immediately making me think of herds of buffalo. They were trekking slowly across the grassland at a leisurely pace, that was until one of the dragons decided it was going to take one for lunch. Those of us that were looking in their direction gasped as the bright green dragon swooping from the sky, effortlessly raising its large wings back behind itself, as its taloned feet stretched and reached for the nearest creature.

The poor animal didn't stand a chance as the talons enclosed its body with a deathly grip. Everyone else turned to see what we were gasping and wowing at, just in time to see the dragon beginning to flap its massive wings, in its attempt to lift the creature off the ground. We could see the animal's legs trying to run in the air as the dragon ascended. The other creatures' instincts took over, sending them into a stampede across the ground, dirt and grass flying from their hooves as they fled.

There was no saving the creature in the dragon's clutches. The dragon tightened its hold, and the animal grew limp as it died. We flew on as the dragon and its prize flew off into the distance. Before we could even acknowledge what had just happened, we began to fly over clusters of buildings, which were getting larger in size the further on we flew.

I was amazed by the various designs of all the buildings, and it was fascinating to see the different angels going about their business as we got closer. The streets between the buildings had been reclaimed by Anunaki's flora too. Buildings and plant life were blended together in harmony. I tried to twist in my seat to take everything in. Which was tricky as my butt was still sucked to the seat, and I had Hope strapped to the front of my body in her papoose. Giving up, I focused on what was in front of the craft and my eyes widened at the huge buildings that were approaching.

The buildings were the angels' version of LA skyscrapers, only these were intricate structures with natural decorations. Small flocks of strange birds flew from the flowered vines and plants as we approached, swooping down the sides of our craft. While large nesting creatures just stayed in place and watched without fear. The largest of the structures stood out, not just because of its sheer size, but because there were decorative open walkways leading to it from the other large buildings. I could see not only angels walking along the walkways, but also some humans with them too. It was reassuring to see that our fellow survivors were settling in so well.

Christik and the other angels flying the crafts headed downwards, flying with precision under the oncoming walkways from the buildings on either side. Within seconds, we were landing at the base of what I assumed was the angels' headquarters. We disembarked the small craft, and followed Christik and the elders towards the main entrance of the massive white stoned building. The entrance was a large decorative archway with deeply engraved hieroglyphs, but instead of the frame being dark like on the angel's main craft, this one was made of a red stone-similar to the marble that was on earth. Tall pillars stood proudly either side of the entrance in wide rows, all made of the same red stone, small strands of ivy were climbing up their lengths. We looked up and around at the magnificent structures, in awe of their size and beauty.

Christik led us through the archway and into the main entrance. Inside were more archways heading in different directions, leading to long white corridors. It was intricately carved into beautiful designs and I wished I had the time to walk around and admire it. We followed Christik and the elders to an amazing spiral, stone staircase which was smack bang in the middle of the building foray, spiraling up from the ground floor to the top where it then branched out.

"Please tell me we aren't climbing stairs all the way to the top floor?" I asked, assuming that I probably wasn't the only one having the same thought.

Christik gave me a smirk, picking up on my dread while I waited for her answer.

"No, Mel, do not worry, we are only going up one level. We would flit you if we had to go to many levels," she said as her smirk became a smile.

The relief I felt was immense. I was very sporty as a child and into my twenties, but once I had the kids, I barely had time to take a shower, let alone do sports or go to the gym. James gave me a knowing look as if he could read my mind, and I rolled my eyes at the man who knew me so well.

By the time we reached the top of the next level, I was feeling relaxed and eager to discuss our plans for sorting out the Marilians. Christik and the elders led us down a long corridor, stopping at a room with heavy wooden doors. It was a large room and four red headed angels were waiting for us. The room was sparse, with only a massive stone circular table in the middle and wooden chairs set all around it. I could feel the warm breeze coming in, through three open windows that looked out on the nearest buildings. The red headed angels were all talking quietly as we entered, but the moment they saw us, they turned to us, dipping their heads in respect. Without even thinking about it, we all did the same.

"It is good to see you again, Vizier's," Christik told them with a warm smile. "We have much to discuss. I would like you to meet Swift Arrow, White

Wolf, his son Running Bear, and a few of the Impa tribal members," she added, indicating to our new friends.

Again, the Vizier's nodded in respect.

"Of course, you have already met our human friends from earth," she stated.

It suddenly dawned on me that the vizier's in the room were the same angels who had attended the meeting with us, via the communication globe. It was nice to finally meet them in person. With more smiles and nods all round, we began to take our seats around the large, dark wooden table. None of us had done anything like this before, and I felt the nervousness emanating from my friends and husband.

Just as the last member of our battle team had sat down, the wooden doors opened again, and the other elders glided gracefully to join us. Evest and Lindaz remained standing, nodding to their comrades as they took the remaining seats.

"I am afraid we do not have time for pleasantries. Time is of the essence, and the Marilians are killing and destroying as we speak," Evest said bluntly.

"Do we know where their ships are yet," asked the Vizier known to us as Mickiz.

"We do not. However, Swift Arrow and his tribe are here to help us locate them," Evest assured him.

Evest turned to the other elders in the room.

“How many races are willing to fight with us?” he asked with a ring of hope to his masculine but musical tone.

“All of them!” Eliz said with a confident smile. “Every race we have asked has said yes.”

“That’s incredible news,” I said, mirroring everyone’s surprise in the room. “How many races are we talking about?”

Christik turned and smiled broadly at me, cl-early thrilled with the good news.

“A lot more than I think we need,” she said as she turned to the rest of the table. “We need all races to select their best warriors for the battle and to be ready, for when we need them.”

“How will we get them all to where they need to go?” James asked.

“We will have to build star passages on each of the planets, so the warriors can pass through when it is time,” Lindaz answered.

“But won't that take too much time?” Andrew asked.

“Using our power, we can build them very quickly,” Akhenaten said thoughtfully. “The issue we have is getting the stones to create them.

“Don’t the races all have rocks and stones on

their planets?" asked Andrew.

"The stones have to come from the race you want to interact with," Akhenaten replied.

"Why, are they magical stones?" I asked as my curiosity began to grow stronger.

"Planets absorb the energy from the creatures that dwell on them. Stone and the land absorb the most. They do not hold magic as such, but we can use the energy with our own power to create what you call magic," Lindaz explained.

"So, how the hell are we going to get stones from the Marilian planet without them knowing we're on the planet, and," Tracey took a deep breath, "how the hell are we going to get there quickly enough before more die?"

"Marilia isn't the first planet that the Marilians have dwelled on," Christik said. "While we were healing their current world, the king mentioned that their race should have learned their lesson by now. That they had made the same mistake millennia ago, on the planet of their creation. If we can locate their old planet, there might still be just enough residual energy left for us to use."

Christik's voice grew more confident with every word that she spoke.

"Swift Arrow, do you think you can locate the Marilians previous planet?" she asked.

"We can locate anything we seek," he replied confidently.

Swift Arrow reached to the side of his body, pulling out a small clay bottle from somewhere in or around his loincloth. '*Where the hell was he keeping that*'? I thought to myself. When I happened to look at Tracey and Mimi, they seemed to have the same surprised look. Swift Arrow lifted the small bottle in front of himself and he pulled a stopper from the top. After taking a sip of the starberri juice, he replaced the stopper and the bottle vanished again somewhere on his person. The Impa elder placed his hands on the dark, wooden table with his palms flat, and he closed his eyes, and we waited.

Not a sound could be heard in the large, white stone room, and all eyes were on the Impa chieftain. Swift Arrow's eyes began to flutter rapidly, the long dark feathers on his muscular back started to bristle and move as if a strong breeze was passing through them. His fingers began to vibrate against the table, individually tapping the surface as if an electric cu-rrent was passing through his body. Only a few minutes passed, but it felt longer, and none of us could stop ourselves from watching him.

When Swift Arrow's eyes abruptly opened and his fingers tapped the table at the same time, it made us all jump apart from the angels. His pupils were so large that his eyes appeared to be completely black. We watched as his body began to calm. His feathers started to settle, and his eyes changed back to the previous deep brown, and then Swift Arrow turned to Evest.

“I know where the planet is,” he stated, “but I do not know how to show you the way,”

“I can help you show us,” Evest replied with a kind smile, and he glided to Swift Arrows side. “May I? he asked the Impa chieftain as he offered his open palm.

Swift Arrow nodded and without any hesitation Evest placed his open palm on top of Swift Arrow’s head while raising his other hand to face the center of the wooden table. We’d been around the angels long enough now to know that we were going to be shown what Swift Arrow had seen. As Evest’s hands started to glow an image of the angel's planet appeared, just above the table's center. We could tell it was the Anunaki by the colors of their world and the many rings surrounding it. Suddenly, the view of the image changed and instead of seemingly looking down on the planet, we were looking at the surrounding rings from the opposite angle, and facing millions of stars.

Without warning the image zoomed forward, and it was like being on the starship *Enterprise* traveling at light speed. Stars were no longer bright spots in the darkness of space, but were bright flashes of lines as Swift Arrow's sight traveled.

Just when I started to feel some motion sickness, the image slowed down and a dark brooding planet came into sight. It reminded me of Earth's moon, with large craters and surface scars, only this world appeared charred. It was larger than earth, but where Earth looked alive, this planet looked like death in different shades of grey and black.

"Thank you. Swift Arrow," Evest said gratefully. "We now know how to get there."

"When are we leaving?" Tracey asked with her get up and go, positive attitude.

Evest glided back to his seat and towards Tracey.

"I am afraid you will all have to remain here while we retrieve the rocks for the star passage, Tracey," he replied regretfully. "The Marilians previous planet is far away. We will have to travel extremely fast. Your bodies are not designed to travel at such speeds, and our crafts are not designed to counteract the harmful effects to you."

"Well Captain Kirk, that's not freaking good!" Tracey declared.

Tracey's reference wasn't lost on us humans, with many of us giggling at her humor, but Evest looked at her with confusion written all over his face.

"I think she is trying to tell you that she is disappointed, my own, my one," Akhenaten remarked.

Evest looked sympathetic.

"It is best that we go alone. We will not be long," he assured. "When we have retrieved the stones for the gates, and have built one on each planet, we will then need the locations for the Marilian ships. We will meet up again on our return."

That night back in the angels dwelling, I was tossing and turning so much that when Hope woke up for a feed, it was actually a relief to get out of the bed. After feeding, burping, and changing her, she was just as awake as I was. Not wanting to wake the rest of my family, I decided to take my baby girl for a little walk around the courtyard. What I wasn't expecting was to find Tracey out there already.

I found my friend sitting on a stone bench at the side of the entrance, and I felt her sadness as soon as I got close to her. I approached her quietly with Hope in my arms, hoping that I wouldn't make her jump.

"Tracey, are you ok, honey?" I asked, feeling very concerned.

She looked up with a tear running down her

already wet cheeks, and her face was full of guilt and anguish.

"No, no I'm not ok," she sobbed, as another tear trickled down her flushed skin. "When is the pain going to stop?"

"You're talking about John?" I asked, feeling her heartbreak.

"Yes," she admitted. "I keep trying to put on a brave face and pretend like everything's okay, but every time I feel any happiness, the guilt makes my heart crash and burn."

Tears streamed down her flushed face as she admitted how she was feeling. Sitting down next to her, I wrapped my arm around her shoulder, while trying to keep hold of Hope. I could feel all the emotions that were coursing through her body, and I wanted to make it all go away for her.

"Have you talked to Akhenaten about how you're feeling?"

She looked up with defeat written all over her wet face, and she used a hand to try and wipe away some of her shed tears.

"I have and he uses his power to help me, but as soon as I think I'm getting a handle on things, it all comes crashing back," she explained through her sobs.

"Tracey, we don't know what could've happened during our battle with the Marilians. John could've just as easily been killed during the fight, or he could've died from his heart condition as we were leaving. You're not responsible for any of this, and you have to let your guilt go," I told her, meaning every word.

She laid her head against my shoulder, letting her tears flow, while knowing that I wouldn't judge.

"You do know that you gave John the best years of his life, don't you?" I asked her.

"Damn right I did," she said, and I knew she was trying to smile.

"I think he's happy wherever he is, that you are surviving and flourishing," I added, giving her shoulders a squeeze.

"Tracey, my own, my one?" a strong masculine voice said from the entrance.

I knew it was Akhenaten immediately, and I released my friend from the hug. I stood and lifted her tear-soaked face.

"We'll talk more tomorrow. I'll make sure we get some girls time, ok?"

Tracey nodded and I walked away with Hope falling asleep on my shoulder. Akhenaten looked at me with concern on his beautiful angel face.

"Taking her pain away isn't helping her, Akhenaten," I told him gently. "She has to face it, and then you both have to deal with it."

The pain in his peacock colored eyes showed that he was hurting for her, and I knew he only wanted to make her happy.

"Thank you, Mel," he said gratefully, before gliding away to be with her.

Sneaking back into my room, so as to not wake James and the kids, I placed Hope in her crib and slid into my bed. I fell asleep hoping that tomorr-ow would feel a little brighter for Tracey, Akhenaten, and their girls.

CHAPTER 15

The next day was just as beautiful as the day before, with sunlight streaming in our rooms' open window. I woke to the sounds of two birds fluttering around our room, and began to feel like Snow White in the dwarves' home. It was lovely, but strange, to have creatures coming into our living area whenever they felt like it.

After we'd all got ready for the day and were having breakfast in the gathering room, Christik glided in with a smile on her face, and what looked like a bunch of silver bangles in her hand.

"Your Long is waiting for you, Mel," she stated, as her smile grew. "You will need these, it is going to be cold where you are going."

We slid ourselves off the hanging daybeds and walked towards the smiling angel.

She was obviously enjoying our curiosity and our excitement that Qiu had arrived.

"What are they going to do to stop us getting cold?" I asked, pointing at the bangles.

"Put yours on and you will see,"

Christik handed me one of the silver metal bangles and I placed it on my wrist. I could feel the coldness of the metal, and also a little buzz of its magic or power. As soon as it was on my wrist, the bangle started to shrink in size, until the whole thing was snug against my skin. It began to glow as if it was getting hot, and what I can only describe as a force field started to seep from the bangle, coating my skin in a protective layer.

Everyone stared as the protective barrier worked its way up my arm, then my shoulder and chest. Once it met the center of my chest, it spread, tingling as it traveled down my other arm, torso and up my neck. Within moments I was completely covered from my hands to my feet. Apart from my skin still tingling, I felt fine and completely normal.

"I have a small one for Hope too," Christik said, as she reached for our baby and slipped a tiny bangle onto Hope's little wrist. We watched as the same thing happened to our baby, and because she was sleeping warm and snuggly in her papoose, she didn't know any different.

"What does this do?" I asked Christik.

The angel took a few steps back and she raised her palms to face me, her hands beginning to glow.

"This," she stated calmly.

An arctic wind burst forth from her hands, instantly making everyone around me jump and dart away. Once they were at a safe and warmer distance, they stood gaping as the freezing wind flowed over and around me, as if I were a car in a wind tunnel chamber. I couldn't feel even the slightest chill, but I could see icicles forming on the nearest daybed cushion. Christik reigned in her power and the freezing wind instantly stopped. I could hear every-one shivering with teeth chattering, because the temperature in the gathering room had dropped so much.

"Who would like one?" Christik asked with a smirk.

There was a sudden rush of bodies passing by me and making a beeline for the angel. When James and our kids reached her, Christik handed each one a silver bangle, which they instantly put on their wrists. Within minutes everyone was protected from any temperate changes and we were ready to go.

The excitement I could feel emanating from my husband and kids was very strong. They had all witnessed me riding Qiu, and I knew they were all dying to try it themselves. They were just as impr-essed with Qiu and the other Longs as I was.

When we walked out into the courtyard, Qiu was indeed ready and waiting for us, but he wasn't alone. I was instantly impressed by the magnificent sight of five huge dragons, all of them uniquely different. I recognized Qiu immediately and I could feel our bond connecting straight away. Out of all five of the dragons, Qiu was the only red dragon and the only one to have horns. I walked towards him and as soon as I was standing in front of him, he imm-ediately lowered his head to gently touch mine.

'*I have been looking forward to this day*,' I heard Qiu say.

I lifted my head again to look at my friends' dark eyes, "So have I, my friend," I replied with a big smile. "I can't wait to see you home and meet your family and clann."

I was sure that my dragon friend was smiling at me again, but even though it was hard to tell, I could feel him smiling. Qiu lowered the front of his body, the sharp pointed scales running down his spine disappearing from sight, as he lifted his front leg to allow me to climb up. The kids watched as I placed a foot onto Qiu's leg, while gripping his blood-red scales. I pulled myself up, with James behind me pushing my butt. It wasn't as easy climbing up with a growing baby in a papoose strapped to my front, as it had been during the battle. Once I was settled on top of Qiu's back, the other four dragons lowered themselves for the kids and Christik.

Anthony and Christine climbed onto a dark green dragon, as did Harrison and Christik. Holly and Nalik mounted a deep brown dragon, while Abigail and April climbed the back of a jet black one. Once everyone was settled on top of their dragons, I felt Qiu's power thrumming through his body connecting with me. I'm sure if my feet had been touching the ground, I would have felt all the dragon's power as they prepared to fly.

"Hold on tightly!" Christik called out, as the dragons arched their backs and bent their large muscular legs.

Qiu shot up to the clear light blue sky first, his power and speed was breathtaking, literally. I was grateful that Hope was facing my body with her head resting against my breasts, so she could breathe normally. I held on to Qiu's scales with one hand, Hope with my other, and James wrapped his arms around us both protectively.

As soon as we were high enough, Qiu leveled out and we began to glide over the landscape. My instinct was to turn and check on the kids to make sure they were behind us, but I didn't want to chance slipping off. Instead, I touched the com at my throat and reached out to Christik.

'*Are the kids alright, Christik*?' Before she had a chance to answer, loud, excited shrieks of 'woooo whooo' and 'yeah!' Rang through the sky.

'*I believe that answers your question for me*,' Christik said humorously.

I completely lost track of time as we flew over very different terrains, going from lush fields, forests, deep canyons, and then over mountains that were so big that it made earth's mountains seem like small hills. After a while, everything below us became more sparse and whiter. None of us could feel the temperature dropping, but we could visibly see the dusting of snow on the ground, covering everything that was growing down there.

Before too long, everything was covered in a thick blanket of snow, and we were flying over a stunning winter wonderland. We flew over huge frozen lakes that looked like mirrors, reflecting the sun's rays, making me wish that I had sunglasses. The temperature was clearly dropping to arctic temperatures, judging by the thick trees we saw which were covered in ice, making them look like tree popsicles.

As the snow became thicker, ice formations began to appear. Huge clusters of ice jutted out from the snow, and it wasn't until we flew over them, that I realized they were built in patterns and there were dragons inside. They were dragon nests, just like we'd seen in the long grass on the way to the angels dwelling, and we glimpsed flashes of color as Qiu glided over them gracefully. The further we went, the closer together the nests were. I was starting to expect a frozen dragon city or something, but suddenly, the ground below us seemed to fall away.

Qiu swooped and began to swerve in midair. As he did so, a huge frozen canyon came into view, with what appeared to be large frozen nests built onto both sides. My stomach flipped as Qui began to circle while slowing down. When I looked around, I could see the other dragons doing the same with our kids and Christik on their backs.

As we slowed and neared the dragon canyon, I could see some of the dragons perched on the edges of their nests, some with food in their mouths for their young. Other nests had dragon heads sticking out of them checking who was arriving, but none of them appeared alarmed or concerned by our arrival.

On the last sweeping circle, Qiu slowed so

much that I was a little afraid we would drop like a stone. He arched his back, making James and I rise as he descended down the side of the canyon. The rock wall and nests passed our vision as if we were in a glass elevator passing floors, until he finally grabbed a nest with his long and powerful talons. Qiu's legs and body absorbed the impact, and for a moment I felt James and I both vibrate. I desperately looked around to find Christik and our kids. One by one I saw them land on nests, secure on top of their Longs, their faces lit up and full of complete awe.

'*Lower your heads*,' Qiu said in my mind.

I did as I was asked and dipped my head, with James following suit behind me. Hope wriggled in her papoose, disturbed by my movement. The nest was made from chucks of ice, which had obviously been carefully placed at the entrance, to what appeared to be a cave. I could see the joins of the ice blocks, which I assumed had been heated and left to refreeze and connect.

The nest was empty and the entrance to the cave was massive. I couldn't tell if the cave was made or natural, as there was no smoothness to the entrance, but also no tool marks either. Qiu effortlessly slinked over the edge of the nest, landing on the rock base, which was covered in tree branches, before walking into the entrance.

Inside it was pitch black, and although I knew I had nothing to fear, my heart still began to pound in my chest. Qiu took a few steps and then he shot some of his fire breath out into the darkness in a big sweeping arc. At first, I thought he may have been lighting torches, but instead the walls of the cave began to light up with a golden glow.

Our dragon friend walked forward in large strides, and as we walked past the glowing walls, I noticed that the glow was coming from small stones embedded in the rock that Qiu must have activated. The cave was a lot bigger than I expected, and my heart rate settled as we walked forward with Qiu occasionally breathing his fire to illuminate our way.

After a few minutes we could see a stronger light in front of us and sounds of movement. The cave appeared to be getting bigger, and after a few moments we emerged into the biggest cavern I'd ever seen. The cavern was as wide as it was tall, with tunnel exits everywhere at various heights, which I assumed led to other nests. There were Longs everywhere, in all different colors and sizes, some with horns, others with wings, and they were magnificent.

While some of the Longs were sitting alone, we could tell that some small groups were family. They brushed against each other like lions in a pride, with their young protected in the center of their group. I smiled as some of the young dragons vanished and reappeared, becoming nervous from our unexpected presence. As Qiu walked into the cavern, our kids and Christik entered from other entrances and our kids' eyes lit up in surprise and wonder. When the other Longs saw Qiu's presence, they began to dip their heads to him, in either respect or submission.

Qiu walked towards a large, sleek black dragon who was standing next to a young red one. Both had large silver horns that almost touched at their tips, and deadly silver scales sticking up and running down their backs to their long tails.

The young dragon was clearly happy to see Qiu, and it began to patter its front legs on the stone ground in excitement. As soon as we were close to the female and her young, Qiu rubbed his large head against the female's neck and she brushed her head against him. The young dragon pattered forward and started to rub its smaller, red scaled body against Qiu's front leg. Qiu responded by rubbing his muzzle against the side of the young one's slim body.

After greeting what I assumed were his family, Qiu lowered his body and lifted his leg. Taking the cue, James released his hold around my body, swinging his leg over and sliding himself off Qiu's back. I wasn't as graceful as my husband unfortunately and struggled to get down with his help, while trying not to squish our baby. As soon as we were back to standing on solid ground, we walked gingerly towards the front of Qiu and his waiting family.

'*Mel, James, this is my clann, and my family. My mate, Anari and my young one, Razen,*' Qiu said, his deep gravelly voice filling my mind.

James and I both dipped our heads to Qiu's family and his clann in respect, as Christik and our kids walked over.

'*It's our pleasure to meet you,*' I told them genuinely.

I pointed to our arriving family who were all beaming next to our angel friend.

'*This is our family, Holly, Nalik, Anthony, Christine, Harrison, Abbey and April, and of course you already know Christik.*'

Christik smiled as she heard me include her in my family and I felt her affection and happiness. They all dipped their heads, and Abigail gave a giggle as the young Razen began to rub against her thigh affectionately. She in turn, began to stroke the young dragon between his horns, and Razen started to do a dragon version of purring, which came out as a cute long growl.

It wasn't long before many other young dragons wandered over to greet our young family, and soon the noise and commotion woke our baby daughter.

'*Come with me Mel, so you can feed your young one,*' Qiu stated.

We left the kids enjoying their dragon experience, following Qiu up a slope that wound its way around the cavern, leading to a natural rock platform with large flattened boulders. I sat down and began to remove Hope from her papoose to feed her, while watching my kids fussing over the young dragons.

'*How old is Razen*' I asked Qiu.

The dragon's eyes moved to look at his young one.

'*He is one hundred and four of your earth years, which is very young for a long,*' he replied with pride in his tone. '*He will lead the clann when I part this world.*'

After feeding Hope and the kids had joined us, Qiu declared that he wanted to show us their land. He explained that although some of their clann wanted to live close to the angels, most of them preferred to live together away from others. Qiu also told us that they'd caused quite a lot of damage to the angels' structures when they'd first arrived, and looking at his massive body and very long tail, I could only imagine.

We followed Qiu as he led us towards one of

the entrances, breathing his fire to light our way. The kids followed behind with their new baby dragon friends trailing next to them, and their parents taking the rear. We walked for at least ten minutes down the glowing corridor, and by the time we came to the end, Hope was fast asleep again.

At the cave entrance there was no nest, but an arctic wind blowing past and huge snowflakes falling from a cloudy sky. We walked out into a vast snow-covered flat land, which was dotted with more dragon nests made of ice. Some were a lot more elaborate than others and a few were breathtaking.

'*Some females are harder to impress,*' Qiu said, with humor in his voice, picking up on my thoughts.

'*So I see,*' I told him with a giggle.

“You think yourself lucky I didn't expect you to build me an ice sculpture!” I told James with a wink.

“I would’ve done it, if that’s what it had taken, hot stuff,” my husband replied with a wink of his own.

As we walked around and between the dragon ice nests, the falling snow began to thicken. Huge white snowflakes landed on our bodies, melting in seconds. Without warning, the wind picked up and the snow fakes seemed to swirl violently in all directions down to the snow-covered ground. Instinctively we looked up to the sky, just in time to witness a large green and black dragon, who was wanting to land with a huge block of ice in its mouth. Instinctively we all backed up, giving the dragon the room, it needed. Its enormous wings flapped wildly as it tried to navigate itself between the nearest nests, until finally it touched down with a thud.

The moment the dragon landed; it dropped the huge ice chunk on the ground with another thud. None of us moved as we watched the Long study his nest, deciding on where to put it. Without warning, he took a deep breath and released his fire on the half-built nest before him. We could see the surface of the ice melting and within seconds he grabbed the ice chunk in his mouth, dropped it into place. It was so cold that in mere seconds the ice was frozen again and the block he'd just added was secure. Like a dragon on a mission, he didn't waste any more time, opening his massive wings and lifting off again.

'*Well that was a nice surprise!*' I said, thinking how lucky we were to have witnessed the nest building.

'*Do all Longs build nests?*' James asked as our kids began to freely walk around and explore.

'*Yes*' Qiu answered. '*We use whatever mat-*

erials are available.'

Qiu took us on a tour of the dragon's land, while introducing us to his family members and leading clann members. As soon as Hope decided she was wanting to be fed again, Christik suggested it was time to make our way back. We walked back to the entrance of the cavern. When I looked back to check on the kids, I noticed that we had accrued a few more baby dragons who were trying to play and interact with the kids. Our kids were seriously in their element, even Holly and Anthony. Just as I turned back in the direction we were walking in, another huge gust of wind surged down on us, sending the snowflakes down and then up in our faces. For a moment I couldn't see anything apart from white snowflakes.

It was another enormous dragon, but this one wasn't carrying ice, it was carrying a large animal carcass. The dragon was blood-red in color just like Qiu, with the same gold tendrils on his body. It landed in front of us and the entrance, blocking our way and it roared loudly. It felt as if my bones were actually vibrating.

'*Why have you brought these humans to our home, brother*?'

Instinctively, Qiu and Christik quickly moved forward, becoming shields from the seriously angry dragon. I felt my whole body starting to tingle. When I looked down at myself, I was glowing blue as my new power kicked in to protect us.

'*They are my guests Wang, and you will treat them as such*,' Qiu told him.

'*After what they did to us*?' Wang roared. '*Are you going to be their pet*?'

Qiu moved so fast he was a blur of red and gold, shooting forward and grabbing his brother by the throat with his huge taloned claw. Wang swiped with his own claw, hitting Qiu squarely on the side of his head.

"Back away!" Christik shouted, as she quickly raised her palms, creating a gold shimmering barrier between us and the fighting dragons.

Christik didn't have to ask us twice. We all turned and ran from the fight, grabbing Abigail and April on our way. Nalik instantly flitted Holly a safe distance away, his natural instinct to protect his new wife and mother of his unborn baby. Within seconds, we were safely away from the fight, shielded by one of the ice nests. We watched as the two dragon brothers began fighting with no holds barred, lashing at each other and biting down with their lethal sharp teeth, while Christik tried to protect the nests and young.

The fight was nasty, and we watched in horror as Qiu sliced through Wang's jaw, leaving a black bloody flap of skin and red scales. Wang twisted away, hitting Qiu with the full force of his razor-sharp scaled tail and our dragon friend went flying through the cold air. Christik tried to shield the nest that Qiu was about to hit, but unfortunately Qiu's body got in the way. He demolished the ice nest with an almighty crash, and the ground shook like an earthquake. A loud roar of pain came from underneath the broken ice and my heart sank. As Qiu quickly picked himself up while trying not to cause any further destruction, a very pregnant and enraged blue dragon emerged.

'*You*!' She roared.

She got to her taloned feet and shook herself off, shards of ice flying off her in all directions. Her orange eyes were blazing with fury as her nostrils flared.

'*You destroyed my nest*!'

CHAPTER 16

In a blur of blue, the female dragon launched herself at Wang before Qiu or Christik could try and stop her, taking Wang by surprise. Her strong jaws opened as she reached him and she clenched them down onto his neck, her teeth sinking into him, as if his thick scales weren't there. The force of her body's impact knocked Wang to the frozen-snow covered ground, and there he laid with her sharp teeth embedded in his throat. I didn't know whether it was guilt that stopped him from trying to fight back, or the fact that she was a pregnant female, and he didn't want to harm her and the young one she was carrying. Either way, there he laid, submissive and not moving.

We were all panting with hearts pounding hard in our chests from the adrenaline rush, not quite believing what had just happened. The shrill sound of Hope beginning to cry broke us all out of our stunned trances. As I stood up from my crouching position to try and comfort my hungry and rudely awakened baby, Qiu began to stride towards the female long and her prize.

'*Fucang, I am just as much to blame for what has happened to your nest. I am sorry*!' Qiu told her, grabbing her attention.

Her eyes darted towards the clann leader, and I could tell that she was snapping out of her blind rage. Fucang's jowls billowed with her heavy breaths, but she didn't release. Wang was struggling to breath beneath her, and we could all hear his wheeze and slight gurgle as blood ran down his throat.

'*Please release him, Fucang.*'

Hope became louder with her hungry cries and as much as I was trying to comfort her, she wasn't calming down. Fucang finally released Wang and he sputtered trying to take in a deep breath. His black blood oozed from his suddenly open wound. Fucang turned away without a second glance and she strode over to Qiu and Christik. She looked at Qiu with her eyes still blazing and her large brows furr-owed.

'*You will both collect what is needed so my mate can rebuild our nest*,' she declared.

She then strode towards us, her large pregnant belly swinging as she moved, and she stopped in front of the nest we were shielding behind.

'*Take care of your young one, there will be no more fighting this day*,' she said confidently.

Fucang dipped her head, then in one huge swift movement she took off and flew into the snowy grey sky. Christik glided over to us, placing her hand on Hopes little face and as her power gently flowed into our daughter. Hope began to quieten, falling back asleep.

"I will get you back to the cavern so you can feed her as quickly as I can," she said with a small smile.

"Thank you."

Qiu was already standing over his brother by the time Christik had glided back to them. A pool of black blood was now forming underneath Wang's weakening red scaled body. Christik glided within inches of the wounded dragon, and she raised her palms to the seeping, bloody holes in his flesh. As soon as her hands began to glow and her power flowed, the blood ceased, and the deep wound-the size of large knife lacerations started to close and heal. Taking the opportunity while his brother stayed still and quiet enough to listen, Qiu moved forward.

'*Brother, these humans are no threat to us. These are not the same humans, and the past is the past,*' Qiu told him calmly.

'*They are all the same, Qiu; they take what they want and that includes us,*' Wang said angrily as his voice began stronger.

'*These humans are different, Wang. Earth has been destroyed; the humans that remain have been punished enough for their mistakes,*' Christik told Wang as her healing power continued to flow.

'*I will never be a human pet, ever again,*' Wang roared, just as Christik finished healing him and started backing away.

Qiu allowed his angry brother to skulk away and then take flight. We walked towards Christik and our dragon friend, still feeling a little shaken from what had just happened. It was different when something scary happened and you weren't prepared for it, especially when you thought you were in a safe place and your guard was down.

'*I am sorry you had to witness that,*' Qiu apologized. '*My brother is still angry even after all this time.*'

'*What happened to him?*' I asked.

'*During our stay on your planet, my brother was captured in China and he was given to the emperor as a gift. We were very young and not yet powerful enough to defend ourselves,*' Qiu explainned. 'T*he emperor was a cruel man, and he did terrible things to Wang before I was able to rescue him.'*

'*I'm so sorry that your brother went through hell on our planet Qiu,*' I told him, while witnessing the sadness and guilt in my friends' eyes. '*I don't think any of us remaining humans would or could do such a thing.*'

'*I know that, Mel, but trying to convince my brother is another matter completely,*' he replied.

Another gust of wind stopped our conversation. We looked up to see it was Wang again, and this time he was carrying a huge chunk of ice. He didn't even look over, but instead headed straight for the ice nest that he'd helped destroy, dropping the chunk of ice next to the icy ruins.

'*I will help my brother,*' Qiu stated. '*Christik will lead you home. I will see you again soon, young one.*'

Qiu dipped his head to meet my own and without another word he strode away and took flight, as did his brother. Christik waved her hand at the entrance to the cavern indicating for us to move, and as we entered, she used her power to activate the light stones. I couldn't stop thinking about Wang and what he'd been through. Whatever the emperor had done to him, it had left very deep emotional scars that were still very open and deep. Just like Tracey, he was going to have to eventually face his wounds and deal with them. Then I began to wonder if maybe my family and I would be able to help him. Why else would I have such a bond with Qiu, maybe it was all meant to be?

While I fed and changed Hope, Christik gathered the Longs who had brought us. By the time they had gathered to take us back to the angels' dwelling, Hope was clean, fed, and gurgling in her papoose, while kicking her legs against my body and trying to grab my long hair again. Just as I was wondering who I was going to fly with, as Qiu was obviously busy, his mate Anari gracefully slinked over, dipping her head in respect.

'*I would be honored to take you back, Mel,*' she said as her beautiful eyes gleamed in the light stones glow.

After saying farewell to the Longs who had made us so welcome, we mounted our new dragon friends. Heading in different directions as before, the dragons led us down the rock tunnels, back to their ice nests built onto the sides of the canyon. Anari was just as comfortable to ride on as her mate. She eff-ortlessly took off from the edge of her nest, swerving away from the other side of the canyon and ascen-ding into the snowy sky, with her young one, Razen flying behind us.

The journey back was just as smooth, and I was impressed that Razen managed to keep up the whole way. Although, when we landed in the angels courtyard, he was panting heavily with his head do-wn, his curved horns touching the ground. April and Abigail walked straight over to him after thanking the dragons for the ride. They began stroking the young dragons dark red scales, until he was back to pattering his feet again in happiness.

Holly and Nalik kindly offered to take Hope back to our room, so she could sleep in her crib, while James and I talked to the dragons while they were resting. Like most people, I didn't know dra-gons were real until Christik and the elders had summoned them. What had really surprised me since meeting them was the fact that there were so many different kinds. It wasn't just the fact that they were different colors, it was the various horns, tendrils, wings, body shapes, and the way they moved.

'*How come you're all so different?*' I asked

Anari as she watched our girls making a fuss of Razen.

'*Before the Marilians came to our world, it was beautiful, and we were many. There were clann's all over our world and certain species were adept at surviving in different environments*,' she explained. '*We were spread all over our world and although we did interact, we lived with our own clann's. Back on our home world, my clann lived in an underground cavern with its own lagoon, where we could fish and swim. Now, there are so few of us, we cannot risk our race dying out by living separately.*'

'*We completely understand what you mean*,' I told her.

'*We all want to stick together since we lost our planet too*,' James added.

Once the dragons were rested enough, they flew back to their icy home. I knew that the kids were going to miss their new and not so little dragon friends. Razen and the other young ones were tiny compared to their parents, but they were still a lot bigger than our own kids. As soon as they were gone, we headed to our rooms, exhausted from the day's excitement.

We had offered Christik the bangles that had kept us so warm on the dragon's icy peninsula, but she told us to keep them on for the time being. As I began to fall asleep, fiddling with the bangle on my wrist, my mind started to go over my mental images of Wang's face, full of anger and pain. I hoped that we could change his mind about humans in general, and make him realize that we weren't all monsters like the emperor he once knew.

The next day was calm and peaceful. Christik showed us more of the area around her dwelling, and we even got to pick some wild fruits and vegetables, which were the weirdest things I'd ever seen. One of the fruits was from the dragons' planet, and the angels had managed to grow it there. Aptly they had called it the Long berry fruit. The outside of the fruit felt like soft black leather and it was as big as a grapefruit. Christik showed us how to peel it like a banana, from the top and downwards. Inside it was packed with jelly balls the size of marbles. I put one of the jelly balls in my mouth and popped it with my teeth. In the next second my mouth was full of the sweetest juice I'd ever tasted. By the time we had finished, we all had baskets full of food ready for the gathering room.

When we walked back to the dwelling's courtyard, there were visitors waiting for us, standing with Lindaz and Evest. It was Razen and two more of the young dragons. I looked around and I couldn't see any of their parents anywhere.

"Hi," I said to the elders as we dipped our heads. "Did they fly here on their own?"

Both of the elders smiled with humor. "It appears that Razen remembered the way, and he misses April and Abigail. Also, the little females seem to miss Harrison." Evest smirked.

"Well, I hope they don't get into trouble with their parents. We've already witnessed two angry dragons so far." I laughed. "Do their parents know that they're here?"

"Yes, they know," Lindaz said with a smirk matching her husbands. "Ahh, here they are now," she added, looking up to the clear blue sky.

Sure enough, when James and I looked up we could clearly see one huge red dragon, a black one, and a green dragon. It wasn't until they flew closer that I realized Qiu had come with Anari to collect Razon, and only one other dragon had come with them.

"Couldn't you get hold of the other parent?" I asked Lindaz, feeling worried for the parents, as only a parent would be.

"Do not worry, Mel, these young females are twins, like Harrison and Abigail. It does not happen very often, but it is known to occur from time to time," Lindaz explained.

The three dragons all landed together with a thud in the courtyard, and when I turned to see where their young ones were, I failed to contain a giggle. All three of the baby dragons were actually trying to hide behind our kids. Unfortunately for them, they were so big that it wasn't working. It reminded me of my kids when they were small and playing hide and seek. They all went through a little stage of thinking that if they couldn't see us, then we wouldn't be able to see them. It was very funny back then, and watching the baby dragons doing the same thing made it even more hilarious. I started to laugh aloud, and it wasn't long before James and the elders were laughing too.

As I looked from the hidden baby dragons to their parents, who were trying to look stern, I tried to control my laughter. Qiu roared and all three of the young ones peered from around our kids, before trotting out completely to face the music. We could tell that the little dragons were sorry and were regretting their decision, just by the way they were hanging their heads.

"Qiu, I know that you are upset with the young ones, but just bear in mind that this is their first encounter with humans, and also other twins," Lindaz said gently.

Qiu dipped his head and I saw his body beginning to relax as his mood lightened.

"Would you like to join us for our evening meal?" Evest asked them while their young were brushing against their legs apologetically.

The Longs decided they would join us and the Impa's, so instead of eating in the gathering room, we all had a picnic in the courtyard, Impa style. The elders and Christik acquired grass seats for us to sit on around a fresh fire pit, and we ate a feast of new fruits and vegetables, while the dragons told us more about what their world had been like.

Even the Impa's were asking questions about the Longs long lost planet. The Longs obviously still missed their home world, and for once I was relieved that humans did not live as long as the dragons or elders.

Our new generations wouldn't know any different once we were on our new world, and my generation would have those memories of Earth. It was a relief, but it was also sad that our young ones wouldn't get to experience what we had. The one true blessing was that we had survived and so had our animals and plants. We still had our history and were able to tell the next generations how amazing Earth was, but also tell them the mistakes we had made as a race.

When the dragons had rested enough, they left to make their way home and the rest of us stayed by the fire pit enjoying each other's company. Tracey and Akhenaten had their girls on their knees, wrapp-ed in their arms, and the girls were beginning to fall asleep.

When Tracey's eyes connected with mine, there was hope in them that wasn't there before. I could feel that she was starting to feel better, and I was so relieved that she and Akhenaten were finally on the same page. Within an hour the kids were all in bed and it was just us adults that were left.

"You will be pleased to know that the gates for the star passages have been completed." Evest said.

"Wow, that was fricking quick!" Tracey blu-rted, saying what we all thought.

"The Marilians' old world was uninhabited, which made it very easy. Then, between us and each race, we were able to build them very quickly," the elder explained.

"Is that how you built the henges and ancient cities on earth?" James asked.

"Yes, although we did take our time, showing your ancestors the best ways to build them, to make sure they lasted," Evest replied.

"I always wondered how those stone Easter

Island dudes got to where they were, now I know," Tracey said with a smile.

"I watched a documentary about Easter Island and wondered the same thing," I told her.

She raised her eyebrows at me, as if to say, I know right.

"So, what's next?" I asked the elders. "The search for the Marilian ships?

"I can't wait to take those monsters down!" Tracey blurted before anyone else could answer.

Akhenaten took Tracey's hand in his and gave her an understanding smile. As always, Tracey only said what the rest of us were thinking.

"That is the next step," Lindaz stated. "If you are still willing to help us," she added, as she turned her gaze to Swift Arrow.

"Of course," he told her. "We all want this to end."

"Then it is settled," Evest declared. "Tomorrow morning, we will all meet, and with the Impa's help we will locate the Marilian ships. We will then organize the teams to take the ships."

"What if we use their own ships against them?" James interjected. "We're going to take control of them anyway, so we might as well use them to our advantage. It would also make things a lot easier transporting all the changed ones."

"Excellent idea, James, on both counts. We will take the ship that is furthest away from Marilia and work our way to their home world. As Mel is the only human who can change the Marilians, she will have to protect you all in her power capsules, so you are not harmed at our crafts' high speed," Evest said. "She can release you once we get close to the last ship.

Butterflies were forming in my stomach as we talked. It was nerve wracking enough, planning and preparing for our battle on earth, but this was going to be a lot trickier and there were so many things that could go wrong. I suddenly felt a massive weight on my shoulders. '*What if I can't change the Marilians under such stressful conditions? What if they catch me before I get the chance to change them*?' The weight of my part in the plan and the thought that everything depended on me, made my shoulders sag, and I placed my head in my hands. I immediately felt James's hand beginning to stroke my back.

"Mel," Christik called.

I looked up to see everyone looking at me with understanding. Even our friends who couldn't actually feel my emotions.

"Please do not worry, you do not carry this burden on your own," Christik said calmly. "The elders will be with you, do not forget."

I had temporarily forgotten that the elders were going to be doing it with me, and I would have Qiu by my side too. I gratefully started to feel a little better, but those damn butterflies in the pit of my stomach wouldn't quit.

"I haven't seen Orchi and the rest of the Jagu since we got here, are they doing okay?" I asked.

"They are back on their world, Mel." Christik said warmly. "It seems that there were more survivors than we thought. Orchi and the others are helping their people and gathering warriors."

I felt everyone's relief because the Jagu still had a planet to go home too, and that so many had survived.

We talked a while longer before going to bed, and as I laid next to my husband, my mind reeled with Marilian faces, their huge ships and flashbacks to our battle on earth. This new fight wasn't just about humanity this time, it was about all worlds in the universe and all life.

"You can't sleep either?" James whispered, not wanting to wake our oblivious sleeping baby.

"No, I can't," I whispered back, while turning in bed to face him. "what if we fail?"

"Baby, there's always going to be the chance of failure, but what choice do we have. If we don't try, the Marilians could come back to whatever new planet we're on and try to destroy us again. I don't want that fear hanging over our kids' heads, especially as they know first-hand what it's like. We have to try for our kids and everyone else, and we have more back up this time, don't forget."

I knew James was right and as I looked into his big blue-green eyes, I could see his determination. Moving closer, I kissed my husband on his soft full lips, while thinking again how lucky I was to have him. He wrapped me in his arms and for a while I felt safe, while wishing he was going to be at my side throughout our whole mission.

CHAPTER 17

Having not slept at all well, I was still feeling very tired when I woke the next morning. Especially as Hope had woken twice for feeding and managed to stink out the whole room after filling her diaper. Once again, I was grateful that the angels dwelling had open windows. So luckily it didn't linger, and I was able to go back to sleep for a while.

The kids were up and dressed in no time, and I think they were secretly hoping that Razen and his two little female dragon friends were going to pay them another visit. James and I had to explain to them that the young dragons were going to have to stay safe at home like they were. We also had to tell them that today was the day that we were going to try and take down the Marilians for good.

Our breakfast meal in the gathering room wasn't relaxed as it usually was by any means. Even our boys, Anthony and Harrison, barely ate a bite. We knew that they wanted to come with us and be part of the mission, and as much as we understood that, we wanted to keep them safe. Our kids were the last of humanity, and there was no way that we were going to put them at risk. Not when we had other races to help us this time.

When Harrik and Zanika arrived to stay with the kids, I was very relieved. It was going to make things easier for them when they had familiar faces and friends with them. Plus, I knew that our angel friends would keep our kids updated as to what was happening.

After getting changed into our battle gear, which the angels had saved luckily, we were geared up and ready to go. It felt reassuring wearing battle clothes and even though it was just clothing, it put us all in the right frame of mind. After hugging the kids and giving Holly the milk, I'd put by for Hope, we were ready to leave on the waiting craft in the court-yard.

The butterflies in my stomach had turned to rocks and I just couldn't shake the feeling. Christik sat next to me on the craft and when she sensed how nervous and tired I was, she placed her hand on mine and I could instantly feel her power flowing into me. The rocks in my stomach melted away, making me feel recharged within seconds.

"Thank you," I told her gratefully, giving her a smile.

She dipped her head, knowing what a difference it had made, before releasing my hand again. The ride to the angel's headquarters was smooth and quiet until James broke the long silence. The angels didn't do small talk, so it was a relief to have a distraction.

"Are we going to be able to watch Swift Arrow and his tribe locate the Marilian ships?"

"If the chieftain is happy to have an audience," Evest responded.

"We do not mind you watching," Swift Arrow said with a smile. "Some more of my tribe are coming to help us seek the Marilian ships, as we do not know how many there are," he explained. "They will be meeting us at the headquarters."

"Have you ever had to seek anything like this before?" I asked, still feeling curious about the Impa's and their way of life.

"There have been times when we have had to search for something important during my lifetime. Our planet can be harsh at times and sometimes we need to seek a new place to dwell, to keep our tribe safe. Mostly we use our starberri's to hunt and monitor the weather," the chieftain explained.

For the rest of the journey, Swift Arrow told us about some of the things that had happened on his world and with his tribe. They were ancient people, and I got the impression that he had enough tribal stories to keep us listening for years. It was nice to know that his tribe's past was kept alive through the tradition of storytelling, and that they were always learning from their past.

When we arrived at the headquarters, another craft was already there, and red headed angels were flitting the Impa people to wherever we were going to hold our meeting and seeking session. By the time we had disembarked, the other Impa tribal members were gone and the guard angels were back to take us.

When Christik flitted me to the meeting, I found myself in a round, cavernous stone room with a beautiful glass ceiling. It was multi-colored and blended as if someone had painted it with a wide bristle brush. Huge sand colored pillars surrounded the opulent room with vines twisting around them that had crept inside from the many large open windows along the top of the circular wall. There was no furniture in the room, but from the indents and scrapes on the light stone floor, I could tell that the room had been well used, and was maybe emptied for our use.

The only things remaining or were placed in the meeting room were at least thirty big fat cushions made of the same cloth as our normal clothing, and the rest of our close friends. It was great to see so many friendly faces and it also helped with my nerves, knowing that we were all in it together yet again. There were hugs and hellos all round, but we knew that we didn't have time to catch up properly. Once everyone was in attendance, including the other elders, Evest walked through the circle of large cushions to stand in the center.

"When you are ready," he said to Swift Arrow.

With a nod of his head, Swift Arrow walked forward to take a seat on one of the silvery cushions, with White Wolf, Running Bear and the other Impa tribal members following their lead. Before long, all of the tribe was seated and ready to begin, reaching to the sides of their clothing to retrieve their small clay bottles of starberri juice.

The rest of us stood around the circle of Impa's watching in fascination. I could feel that I wasn't the only one who had nervous butterflies again. The Impa tribe, on the other hand, all seemed very relaxed. I envied the way they seemingly controlled all their emotions, and they reminded me of meditating monks.

Lifting their small clay bottles to their mouths, they all removed the corks and took a sip of the powerful juice before laying the bottles on the stone floor before them, and we waited. As soon as the juice began to work its magic, I could feel the buzz of energy in the room. With the nervous excitement coming from us humans as well as the Impa's, the energy was quite overwhelming. I felt a gentle hand on my upper arm and looked to find it was Christik giving me a little support.

All eyes were on the Impa's and when their bodies started to quiver, the elders began to move. Evest glided behind Swift Arrow, Lindaz moved behind White Wolf, and the other elders glided to some of the other tribal members. Even Akhenaten joined in as the energy level in the room rose.

The Impa tribe sat with their legs crossed with their hands flat on their knees and their fingers started to tap on their bare skin. The long dark feathers on their backs bristled and moved as the starberri juice worked its magic.

Surprising us all, one of the tribe who was close to Akhenaten threw her head back and her eyes began to flicker rapidly. Straight away, Akhenaten was behind her and he placed one open palm on her forehead, holding his other up to the center of the circle.

As her body quiver grew stronger, Akhenaten's hand started to glow, and in the middle of the circle an image began to form. It was showing us space and the image zoomed through the stars and planets, changing direction, then zooming again. We watched in silence as the Impa female showed us the way to what we sought.

After a few minutes, the image slowed, and we appeared to be approaching a lush green planet. Seeing so much green was a good sign. It meant that the Marilians hadn't been there long enough to destroy the world. The image banked around to the right side of the planet, and there was the Marilian ship, menacing in its stationary position next to the planet. Then the image melted away.

'*That's one*,' I thought to myself, while feeling a bit more hopeful that we might actually succeed. White Wolf was next to find another Marilian ship. Lindaz, who was already next to the Indian chieftain, was there immediately to show us the way. Again, we watched the image before us, zooming through stars and around planets.

As we watched the images, I really began to grasp just how big the universe was, and that living on earth had been like living in a small bubble, unaware of the true vastness around us. Yes, most of us had at some point seen photos or film footage of space and planets, but we were now seeing way past what had ever been seen by a human before.

When the image before us finally halted, we were looking at another Marilian ship hovering over a mixed brown colored planet with streaks of blue, and a single thick ring slowly moving around its center. I couldn't tell how much damage the Marilians had already done. It was hard to tell whether the planet normally looked so brown, or if that's what the Marilian monsters had done to it, but I knew that the blue streaks were a positive sign.

The Impa's magic was working and with each ship found, my confidence grew a little more. However, not all of the Impa's were able to find ships, which was fantastic news. Fewer ships meant less work for us and more chance of success. All in all, the Impa's tribe found eight Marilian ships between them and I felt a massive relief that there weren't more. Once the last Impa came out of their trance like state, they all took a few minutes to recover.

"How sure can we be that all the ships were located? our friend Luiza asked the elders.

Swift Arrow turned and looked at her with confidence, pulling his shoulders back and straightening in his back. "We always find what we seek," he told her with a matching confident grin.

Luiza returned his smile and when she looked to Evest he was nodding his head in agreement. The room was full of chatter, and our friends nervously talked about what they had just seen. It was becoming very real, and the nervousness was building even more in the room.

"Let us go over the plans!" Evest declared, getting everyone's attention.

Within seconds, all eyes were on the elder in anticipation.

"We will sort you all into your groups and you will be taken to your assigned crafts. You will fly to intercept your Marilian target, and you will wait for us to join you once we have completed our task," Evest explained. "We are going to take the first Marilian ship, then we will travel to the next and nearest target to do the same.

"What about their smaller ships down on the planets they're destroying?" Andrew asked, his eyes narrowing with concern.

"We will take the controls rooms first and once we have full control, we will get the Marilians to summon their ships back. Mel will have to use her power to neutralize the crews. Their smaller ships will dock on their main crafts, so we can disable those Marilians as soon as they land," the elder told us.

There was a long pause while everyone went over the plan in their minds.

"What's next?" I asked, wanting to get going before my anxious nerves got the better of me.

"Next we will help you to encapsulate everyone here, so we can safely transport them without causing harm," Evest said as the Impa's began to stand, moving their padded cushions to the side of the room.

The elder turned to our friends, who were standing in nervous small groups around the room. I looked at their nervous, anxious faces, hoping that they wouldn't be feeling that way all the time they were in their fluid capsules.

"Could you all come forward, please, and form a circle around Mel?" Evest asked.

I wasn't sure what was happening, because I thought we were going to encapsulate our friends in small groups. However, I trusted the angels and I knew I should go with it. As everyone began to surround me in a large circle, Lindaz, Evest, Christik, and the other elders stood around me in a smaller circle too.

There were more elders this time, which meant more power, and I suddenly realized how we were going to encapsulate everyone all in one go. Once everyone in the room, including the Impa's were surrounding me, Christik and the elders all placed one hand on my body, until I had hands on my chest, back and both of my shoulders. '*Good thing I don't get claustrophobic*' I thought to myself as I began to feel the tingle of their power through their palms.

"Are you ready?" Christik asked, gently squeezing my shoulder reassuringly.

"Yes," I told her with a nervous smile.

I closed my eyes, aware that every one of my friends were probably watching me closely. Not everyone had seen what I could do with this new power since my dormant angel genes were activated. I began to feel like the nerdy kid I was at school, standing in front of all the cooler kids, about to read out the essay which they'd wished they'd written. I tried to relax and tap into the power within me, but as I took long breaths and tried to locate it within my being, nothing was happening.

It had been easy before, because my emotions had been driving me. When James was attacked, I was in panic and fear mode, and when I changed the

Marilians, I could feel the hatred coming from them in waves. This time, all I could feel was friendship, love, anticipation, and nervous energy. My frustration started to build, as did my embarrassment, because everyone was waiting.

"Remember how you felt when James was attacked, Mel," Christik whispered quietly in my ear.

Keeping my eyes closed tightly, I nodded and began to relive the events in my mind, the sight of Kay's burning, blood-red eyes and the feel of her hatred towards us. The sight of her flinging James over the bannister and the thud of his body on the floor. It was enough to stir my horror and anger again, and I could feel the strong emotions surging through my body.

All of a sudden, my whole body felt as if it was bursting with power, the angel's hands feeling hot on my skin as my power met theirs. I opened my eyes and we were glowing with a bright blue shimmer. Christik and the elders held their other arms out towards our friends, their eyes wide with surprise.

Our combined power flowed through the angels and me, until suddenly there was an explosion of dark blue light. As it left my body, my legs gave way beneath me, Christik catching me with her strong but gentle hands.

While I tried to stand on very shaky, wobbly

legs, I looked around at our friends. They were all frozen in the blue fluid capsules, every single one of them. Some had their eyes open wide in surprise, while others had taken to closing theirs. They were all motionless with not even the slightest eyelash flicker. James looked as if he was just having a deep sleep, his body was relaxed, and it told me how much he trusted me and my new gift.

I steadied myself and gained the strength back in my legs, with Christik's help. While catching my breath, I watched as the red headed angels flitted each of our friends to their designated craft, ready to fly to their battle position. '*I can do this, I can do this*' I kept telling myself as my friends vanished with the angels.

I'd never had to do something so important, where everything relied on me, and I was really feeling the pressure. As always, Christik and the elders picked up on my feelings. Christik and her father, Evest turned to stand before me, Christik taking my hands in hers, letting a little of her power soothe my worries.

"Please do not worry Mel. Even if we only liberated one ship today, it will be a great achievement," she told me softly.

She was absolutely right. If we did only manage to take one ship, that would still be hundreds of

Marilians stopped and changed into back their true selves. Plus, we would be able to return them to their original homes. I knew I had to be more positive, we were doing this for everyone.

"You're right, everything we achieve will be a bonus," I replied, feeling the truth in the words as I spoke to them. "Let's go."

Without saying another word, Christik gently gripped my forearm and we vanished. By my next breath, we were standing beside Christik's large craft in the middle of acres of flat land, surrounded by other huge crafts, and Qiu was sitting next to ours waiting patiently. I walked up to my dragon friend and lowered my head in respect. Like always, our respect was mutual, and he proceeded to do the same, lowering his head until it touched mine. I could feel Qiu's anxious energy. He was ready for anything and his determination was strong and infectious through our connecting bond.

'*We can do this, Qiu,*' I told him, feeling more confident now that I had him at my side. An abrupt rumble from the ground and a massive who-osh sound broke us from our moment. I had no idea where the sound came from, but logic told me it was one of the crafts. I looked around just in time to feel and see another of the angel's crafts taking off. It lifted off the ground until it was clear of the surrounding crafts, before tilting into the direction it needed to go. Then whoosh, it shot forward at such speed that all I saw was a flash of bright light and then clear sky again. When I turned back to Qiu and Christik, the angel waved her arm at the open craft doors. Qiu began to shrink in size as we walked towards the large craft, and I boarded the waiting vessel.

As Christik led me to the main control room, I assumed that Qiu would be traveling and waiting in one of the larger holding rooms on board. The control room was bustling with angels and flashing control lights as they all prepared for take-off.

Christik calmly glided to the center of the control room and I followed, not really knowing what I should do with myself. The front glass window of the craft was clear, and I watched as other crafts rose, tilted, and then shot off into space, leaving no evidence of their departure.

"We are nearly ready to leave, Mel. You need to think of our last battle and tap into your power, so it protects you," Christik said, as she faced me.

After what had just happened at the headquarters, I knew she was right. My gift was definitely tied to my emotions and it was going to be the only way to activate it. Closing my eyes, I tapped into my memories of our battle with the Marilians. Their burning blood-red eyes, big shaggy haired bodies and their razor-sharp talons slashing through the air. Fighting them alongside my family and friends, watching Anthony getting sliced across his chest and his blood running from his wound. Immediately I felt the buzzing sensation as my power, my gift began to grow within me. After mere seconds, I could feel it inside and out, making my skin tingle and the hairs standing up on the back of my neck. Opening my eyes, I looked down at myself and I could see the blue shimmer pulsing from my body.

"I'm ready," I told her, while hoping that my power was going to be enough to protect me, James, and all our friends.

Christik raised her arms out to her sides and the craft began to ascend in the air. I watched through the clear glass window as their land sprawled out before us, with trees and grassland as far as I could see. The view from the window changed as Christik bent her arms upwards and the craft began to tilt. The strange thing was that the control room didn't tilt, as if it was independent from the rest of the craft. Christik dropped her arms down pointing towards the front, and before I could take another breath, we were shooting forwards at such speed that everything before my eyes was a total blur. The pressure on my body was immense, and it felt as though I was being squeezed all over. I was helpless.

CHAPTER 18

I didn't know how much time had passed. It could have been seconds, minutes, or even longer. When the pressure finally began to subside, I fell hard to my hands and knees, desperately trying to draw air into my oxygen starved lungs. My knees began to throb from the impact as I gasped for breath, while beads of sweat broke out on my tingling skin. Gentle hands softly gripped my shoulders and I felt the soothing and healing power that I knew was coming from Christik.

"Are you ok, Mel?" she asked as she helped me rise to my feet.

I wavered for a moment, swaying where I stood between the rows of consoles, with Christik behind me holding me up. I nodded to her, not quite ready to try to speak. My eyes started to finally focus and as I stared out of the front glass window, I could see the large, lush green planet that the female Impa had shown us. There, right next to the planet, was the menacing Marilian ship and we were very close to both. Panic began to rise in my chest.

“We’re too close, they're going to know we're here!” I shrieked, while trying to turn to face Christik.

She let her hands drop to my arms as I turned to face her.

“We are hidden, Mel; they cannot detect us, that ship or their small ships on the planet,” she assured.

Taking more deep, long breaths, I tried to control my racing heart as Christik’s power helped me to calm down.

“I hope everyone else doesn’t feel what I felt as we were traveling here,” I told her. “I’ve never been deep sea diving, but I imagine that’s what it feels like.”

“I don’t think the others will feel as much as you did,” she said with hope in her voice. “Are you ready?”

“More than I’ll ever be,” I told her, trying to sound a lot more confident than I actually felt.

Christik released my shoulders from her grip and she turned, leading me through the aisle between the consoles. The angels on either side nodded their heads in respect, and it wasn’t just out of habit, it was because they knew what we were about to do. ‘*We can do this, we can do this*,’ I began telling myself again, as I thought of James, our children, and all the other human survivors, while walking down the long corridor to meet Qui and the elders. ‘*This isn’t a revenge battle, it’s a universal intervention*’ I thought.

By the time we reached the holding room, I was feeling more confident and determined that we were going to make a difference. I’d had the epiphany that I was only one person, and if the worst came to the worst, my life wouldn’t matter if it meant saving so many others.

All the elders who I was familiar with were waiting with Qiu. Evest, Lindaz, Mikaz, and the others all dipped their heads as soon as they saw us, as did Qiu. We nodded back in respect and I made a beeline for my dragon friend, who looked weird in his shrunken state.

He wasn’t misshapen in any way, but it felt

strange seeing him so much smaller. Qiu lowered his head and we briefly touched foreheads as Christik began to lead the way to the center of the holding room.

As soon as we were in the middle of the cavernous white room and stopped, the elders surrounded Qiu and they all placed their hands on his deep red scaled body.

"You need to place your hand on him too, Mel," Christik said. "Otherwise you won't be invisible to any Marilians that may be near when we arrive."

I may have been feeling more confident, but my hands were trembling with nerves as I placed them on Qiu's thick neck. His hard-red scales felt cool against my fingertips and I felt us connect, his power and mine. Our connection gave me just the confidence boost that I needed to shed the last of my nerves and worry about what was to come.

Christik placed her own hands next to mine, and I felt a strong tingle in my fingertips. It was coming from Qiu and as it grew stronger, I felt it spread over my skin like the silver bangles power had. Only this time it felt like cool water flowing over my skin. Before long the feeling passed and I assumed that we were now deflecting and bending the light around us, making us seem invisible to the naked eye. Hopefully, even if the Marilians were alerted that someone or something had got onto their ship, we would have enough time to take control.

“Ready?” Christik asked.

I nodded to her and took a deep breath. The elders and Christik started to glow all over their bodies and I felt their power pulsing through Qiu’s scales and into me. Then everything went dark. For a few seconds it was as if I no longer existed: there was nothing, no light, no sound and no feeling.

Then all of a sudden, as if a switch was flipped, we were back. We were on the Marilian ship and smack bang in the middle of their control room. Thankfully it was a completely different layout to the angel’s craft, and even though Qui had appeared on top of some of their equipment, there was minimal damage.

The Marilians were roaring at each other, confused as to why their ship had been suddenly damaged with no visible explanation. My eyes darted from side to side, taking in their positions and numbers. My heart was racing in my chest as I took in the sight of their needle-sharp teeth and deadly razor talons, while my body shivered from flitting.

‘*Now, Mel*’ Christik shouted in my mind.

I set my inner power free as soon as I felt the

elders' power connect with me. For a moment I was blinded by a bright, purple shimmering light as the burst of power filled the control room.

I felt vulnerable as I tried desperately to blink away the light that was still in my vision, even as the bright purple burst faded away. Even though I knew we were surrounded by Marilians, I couldn't hear anything apart from my own breathing. Trying to control my rapid breaths as my body started to regain some normality, I focused my vision on Qiu's red scales under my hands, willing them to come into focus quickly.

As soon as my eyes began to focus on Qiu's blood-red scales, I turned to look around the Marilian control room. It was eerily silent. All the Marilians who were in the control room were frozen inside my blue fluid capsules. They hadn't stood a chance of escaping our combined power blast. Some were frozen, lent against their control panels, while others looked like they were about to walk. I could still see their confusion and annoyance in their fiery red eyes. It sent chills running down my spine.

"Act quickly!" Evest declared, removing his hands from Qiu and gliding up to the closest frozen Marilian.

Christik and the other elders followed suit, heading for the nearest Marilians, and I watched as they appeared to scan them with their glowing hands. Qiu moved swiftly to the exit doors of the control room, making sure that we could do what we needed, while being protected.

"It is safe to heal this one," Evest said as he turned to me.

I quickly walked over to Evest and the Marilian, my legs still slightly shaking, but my shivering had stopped thank goodness.

"Is it a true Marilian?" I asked, as I looked at its nasty looking snarled mouth.

"It is a Jagu warrior. He will be an asset for our task."

Evest placed a hand on my shoulder while he held his other glowing hand in front of the encapsulated Marilian. I stared at the Marilians needle sharp teeth and imagined it trying to bite me. It was enough to get my power active again, and as soon as I felt it flowing through me, I let it flow into the Marilian.

The Marilian changed before our eyes and like before we watched as its long shaggy hair disappeared, absorbing into its body, being replaced by the short silky Jagu fur. Its eyes turned from the blazing, evil red to a deep amber and its talon shrunk to cat-like claws, which were just as deadly.

Within minutes we were looking at a male Jagu warrior. Without wasting time, I used my power with Evest's help to release the Jagu male from the fluid capsule.

The blue fluid reacted as it had before. Tiny little ripples began to form along the fluid's surface, gradually becoming more turbulent as the miniature waves travelled along the length of the Jagu's body. The capsule was soon one big violent body of fluid and I sensed straight away when it was time to absorb it back into my body. As soon as I felt the change, I kept my arms steady, reaching for the fluid with my mind. It reacted immediately and I felt a slight chill as the cool fluid touched my open hands, absorbing into my palms.

As soon as the Jagu male was free, he lunged forward, swiping through the air with the only weapons he had: his claws. Before Evest had a chance to stop him, he slashed his claws across my arm, making me cry out in pain. I ducked to the left to avoid the oncoming Jagu, just as Evest managed to grab him, subduing him with his power.

"Be calm!" Evest said, his voice booming in the control room.

The Jagu's pupils enlarged as his eyes focused, homing in on the elder. Evest then said something in the Jagu's language. In the next moment he was placing an angel communication device around the warrior's neck and giving him traditional clothes that he magically produced. I was too busy watching them interact to notice that my blood was dripping on the floor, but I was aware of the pain in my arm. Christik glided over the moment she felt my pain and by the time the Jagu warrior was calm and dressed, I was fully healed and ready for the next one.

While Evest quickly explained to the Jagu what was happening and why we were there, I helped Eliz heal and change another Marilian. By the time we were down to the last few, I was feeling a lot more confident. There were a couple of Marilians that we couldn't change, because like the Jeli, they wouldn't have survived without their natural environment.

We had two true blooded Marilian's that were left, and they were going to be a challenge. I took a long, sharp army knife from a sheath strapped on the side of my thigh and held it up ready to use it, giving another blade from my waist to the Jagu warrior.

Some of the aliens I healed looked like they didn't need any extra weaponry; they already looked like they could kill or hurt the Marilian's with what they had. I could have studied all of them for hours, admiring their spikes, claws and defensive attributes. I just had to hope that they would all step up and help. Christik told them individually what we were doing, while I was changing the next Marilian. We just had to trust them to help us with our mission.

"Are you ready to release the first true blooded Marilian?" Evest asked as calmly as ever.

I envied the fact that the angels were always so cool, calm and collected. Nothing seemed to faze them, even with so much at stake.

"Yes, I'm ready," I replied, as I walked between the other aliens and up to the frozen Marilian.

My eyes scanned the frozen in time Marilian and as hard as I looked, I couldn't see any differences between the true blood and the changed ones. Everything was the same, from the fiery-red eyes, the thick shaggy hair covering its muscular body and its height.

It was a blessing that the angels could tell the difference. The Jagu warrior walked to my side joining me, with the borrowed blade in his hand ready to defend us both. I quickly looked at him and he gave the slightest of nods, indicating that he was ready too.

This time it was easy. I took a deep breath and only had to look at the Marilian for a second or two, before I felt my inner power flowing through me. It felt effortless and natural. As soon as we saw a flicker of movement, the Jagu and I were on high alert. The Marilian's eyes instantly began to dart left and right, trying to gauge what was happening. He let out a snarl of anger as he clocked me, the other aliens, the angels, and Qiu, who was glaring from the closed exit.

The Jagu warrior was fast, instantly raising his razor-sharp blade to the Marilians throat as I continued to absorb the fluid, while our alien allies changed into defensive positions.

The Marilian and the Jagu warrior may not have been able to verbally communicate, but the Jagu's bladed message was clear as it pressed against the long, brown hair and skin of the Marilians throat, 'submit or die'.

I could tell that the Marilian was counting how many of us there were, calculating its chances against us. He knew how powerful the angels were and by the confusion on his vicious looking face, he was clearly unsure of how and why they were taking over its ship. Taking advantage of the Marilian's confusion, Christik glided to my side as the last little bit of blue fluid flowed into my hands.

"There is no win for you in this scenario, Marilian!' she told him, her eyes shining with her inner power. "This human and Jagu warrior will think nothing of ending your life after what your race has done to them and their worlds."

I didn't know whether the Marilian could sense the truth in Christik's words or if he could see it in her peacock eyes, but his body relaxed in defeat as he looked again at our numbers. Our alien comrades and Qiu glared at the Marilian with pure hatred and loathing. I lowered my hands and backed up to give the Jagu Warrior and Christik some room.

"We will guard this one while you take the rest of the ship", one of the aliens said, who looked like a cross between a human and pangolin.

He stood next to another of his kind, and I wasn't sure whether they already knew each other or not, but they appeared capable of handling our Marilian prisoner.

"What about the other Marilian?" I asked, glancing at the other frozen monster.

"We do not know whether we will need her yet, we will see once we are in their hangar," Lindaz said.

All the elders and Christik glided towards Qiu at the exit of the control room, placing their hands on his red scaled body.

"We are going to project your power energy outwards to the rest of the ship. Hopefully we will get all of them," Evest stated calmly, while the rest of the aliens moved up to take our flank, either side of the control room doors.

I nodded to the elder and placed my hands on Qiu's body and my pulse began to race as I waited for the unexpected. With one hand touching Qiu, Evest used his other to open the doors with his magic. The thick grey, almost black metal doors shimmered for a second, then they opened with a loud scraping noise as they slid away. Two Marilians were on the other side of the doors, sitting at control panels that were built into a long metal corridor. They both turned to look who was exiting and their eyes blazed with confusion.

They couldn't see us or Qiu, but they couldn't see through us either and their fighting instincts kicked in immediately. They were out of their seats and coming at us within seconds. Even before the angels had time to react, two thin darts flew past me, missing my head by inches, before piercing the Marilians in their necks.

I turned quickly, trying to gage where the darts had come from. One of the aliens standing next to Qiu's long tail was smiling. The darts had come from the creature's hands and when I looked at them, I could see two of his talons were missing on his left one. The alien was very bird-like with small, light green feathers covering its body, only this creature had four legs all with the deadly looking talons. It was smiling at me with triumph on its small beaked face. By the time I looked back to the two Marilians, they were falling hard to the floor, landing with a hard thud.

Evest and Nical used their power to move the Marilians out of the way, allowing us to surge forward into the dank looking corridor. I may not have been able to feel the temperature of the ship and corridor, due to the bangles on my wrists, but I could certainly smell it. The scent of a rotting compost heap filled my nostrils and I almost gagged, while thanking my lucky stars that I wasn't pregnant anymore. Otherwise I definitely would have puked in front of everyone.

Once Qiu and the rest of us were out into the corridor, I felt the angels' power flowing through Qiu again and this time the angels didn’t have to tell me. They were using more power this time, more than I had felt before. I could feel it merging with mine and building within the core of my body, until finally I thought I might explode.

Just when I thought I couldn’t take anymore, the power tide switched. Suddenly it was all flowing from me to the angels, their outstretched hands channeling the power out in all directions. The purple light from the energy pulsed through the ship as if someone was turning on lights, and I hoped that it was working. We stayed in position, waiting for the energy to reach the end of the ship. I could feel our new allies' anticipation and itch to get moving.

After a few more minutes, Christik and the elders released their contact with Qiu and began to lead the way. Our allies began to flank down our side ready to fight if needed. I could sense that some of them desperately wanted to fight any Marilians we came across. Their hatred and pain of loss was as fresh as the day they were captured and changed. I was surprised that so many had kept their memories. None of them knew if their loved ones were dead or alive, and I knew exactly how that felt.

We slowly and steadily made our way through the ship passing encapsulated Marilians on our way, frozen in the act of either doing their job or just going about their business. We even walked in on two Marilians getting it on, frozen in place by my blue fluid. It wasn't our finest moment, and it was something that I wished I could un-see. Between us we checked every door we came to, making sure that we had got them all.

The ship was enormous, and it took longer than I'd hoped to get to the hangar, which was right at the back of the Marilian ship. Their hangar was massive, with only three smaller ships docked. There were spaces for at least ten in the hangar, which I assumed were down on the planet doing what they did best, destroying. We walked past five frozen Marilians and our allies spread themselves out either side of the hangars entrance. I followed Qiu and the angels towards the opposite end, where the Marilian ships would be entering.

We had nearly reached the doors when a Marilian leapt from the front of a remaining ship. It flew through the air, roaring with rage with its talon ready to slash. I grabbed my knife from my thigh, but I wasn't quick enough. The Marilian plowed into all of us, finally crashing to a halt against Qiu’s large body and while the angels rolled and gracefully leapt to their feet instantly, I wasn't fast enough. Before I knew it, the Marilians arm was tightly around my neck. My knife dropped from my hand.

Scrambling to find my feet, I tried to escape his hold. I could smell his stench as his muscular, hairy arm tightened against my throat. I couldn’t breath and I could hear the sound of my heart pounding loudly in my ears. I tried to grip his arm with my hands, trying desperately to pull it away.

I honestly thought I was going to pass out. Everything became blurry, shapes became blobs of color as my brain was being starved of oxygen. I could feel myself going limp.

“Mel, hold on,” Christik shrieked.

CHAPTER 19

I'd never heard Christik sound so worried before, and I felt a tingle of power at the same time that I heard the Marilian roar in pain. I was dropped to the ground in a heap as the Marilian released his hold from my throat and my fight or flight instincts took hold.

With my eyesight still blurry and my flight instinct winning, I scrambled across the metal floor, trying to get away, heading for what I hoped to be safety. I kept going until something soft got in my way, and I felt something resting on my shoulders. Calming words filled my panicked mind: '*you are safe*'. I stopped moving and my body involuntarily shuddered as I tried to catch my breath, while blinking to regain my vision.

When I could finally see again, and my breathing was settling down, I slowly tried to get on my feet. Standing on shaky legs, I turned to face the Jagu who had helped me.

"Thank you," I told him as I dipped my head before heading back to Qiu, Christik, and the elders.

They were near the dying Marilian as its blood pooled around its large frame from a large round wound in its chest. Even at near death, the Marilian was desperately trying to slash and bite at anything that was anywhere near it. Part of me felt bad that it was dying. It could have been a trapped alien like the others around us. However, it was hard to feel bad for something that would still kill you with its dying breath.

Christik and the elders were trying to freeze it with their power. I assumed so they could heal it, or so that I could encapsulate it, but it was moving too much and too fast. Its panic was evident, fueling its desire to do whatever it could. Seconds later it suddenly stopped, its blood-soaked body going limp and still as blood trickled from its mouth.

For a moment I didn't understand what had happened. Our alien allies didn't seem close enough to have been able to hit the Marilian with their natural weapons. A drip of the Marilian's blood landed onto my shoulder and when I looked up to see where it had come from, I saw the Marilian's fresh black bl-ood slowly trickling down one of Qiu's deadly horns.

"I had no choice, young one, it was either you or the Marilian," Qiu said with no regret in his tone.

I wasn't sure how to feel, apart from grateful. Grateful to Qiu for saving my life and that our mis-sion was still on track. Evest waved a hand and instantly the dead Marilian and its blood was gone without a trance. Then he turned to Qiu and with another wave of his hand, the blood on the tip of Qiu's black horn vanished.

"It was a true Marilian, Mel," Christik told me reassuringly as she glided to my side. "We need to move, the Spadee in the control room have made the Marilian recall the ships from the planet's surface. They will be here soon. Take cover everyone", she called out loudly for everyone to hear.

Straight away, the aliens all began to hide from view, concealing themselves behind the rema-ining ships that were left, some hiding behind the large mounds of trash that were dotted around. Some of the aliens even had camouflage abilities, blending into the black metal walls of the hangar seamlessly as their bodies changed.

"Mel, you are with us," Lindaz said. as she began to glide towards the side of the hangar doors. "As soon as the ships dock, we will hit them with our combined power."

Qiu and the other elders followed and once we were at the side of the doors, we all placed our hands on Qiu's body again. I felt the sensation of Qiu's power, and we began to wait. We had no idea how long the ships were going to take. Seconds turned to minutes and roughly half an hour later, just as I was starting to feel fidgety, the first of the smaller Marilians ships began to arrive back.

Noisy machinery moving made me jump, breaking the silence of the hangar. A barrier had been activated across the hangar door, protecting the hangar and any Marilians from the effects of space. Once the doors were completely shielded the huge, heavy metal doors began to open with a loud clunk. The loud scraping noise they made as they slid to the sides of the entrance was worse than someone scraping their nails down a chalkboard. The sound went right through me, and I clenched my teeth, cringing until the sound stopped.

I knew the Marilian ship was coming, but I didn't hear it until the tip of the ship passed through the glowing barrier. It sounded like metal vibrating against metal, and it showed how little the Marilians cared for their fleet. My pulse began to pick up its pace as I watched the ship emerge from the cold space beyond. The floor of the hangar was vibrating with the force of the ship's engines. It felt like forever waiting for the small ship to come all the way in and get into position to dock. I knew it was only minutes, but my nerves were making it feel longer than it was.

The moment the ship touched the floor of the hangar and its engines stopped I heard Christik in my head.

'*Now*'.

Immediately I felt the rush of power coming from the angels, passing through Qiu and meeting mine in my body's core. As soon as I saw the angels lift their palms towards the ship, I released our joint power. It wasn't as much as when we did the whole of the main ship, but the blast was enough to hit the small ship in a wave of power, flowing right through the entire machine and hitting every single Marilian on board.

We didn't have time to pat ourselves on the back for a job well done before another ship started to board. Again, we blasted the ship as soon as it moved into its docking position and its engines were stopped. By the time we had blasted four ships, I was thanking my lucky stars that the angels were helping me. There was no way in hell that I would have been able to do so many ships on my own. I was so relieved when we'd finished and there were no more ships to blast. At least we could have a small breather before we had to do anything else.

After all the action, the hangar seemed strangely quiet and eerie. That was until the hangar doors began to screech again as they started sliding across to close. When they were shut and the barrier disappeared, it confirmed that we had all the ships from the planet's surface. I was sure that the aliens down on the planet were probably wondering whether they should start celebrating that the Marilians had gone.

"We'd better send some angels down to make sure that we have all the Marilians," I told Christik, as our new alien friends and allies began to come out from their hiding places.

Christik nodded and as the aliens started to join us, she began to glide towards the nearest docked ship. I followed her and noticed that the elders were splitting up and heading for different ships, with some of the aliens going with them. Christik glided up to a side door on the nearest Marilian ship.

As soon as she held up a glowing hand to the thick, dark grey metal door, it opened with a piercing screech. The stench that wafted out of the small ship was even worse than what I'd already experienced, and I wondered if my nostrils would ever recover.

The Marilians obviously didn't care about maintaining their ships in any way, big or small.

Following Christik as she glided into the Marilian ship, I was trying to ignore the smell that was assaulting my nose. The inside was cold and dank, so no wonder it was stinking to high heaven. There was only one Marilian inside the opened corridor and it was frozen in one of my fluid capsules. Its eyes were scowling in confusion and its mouth looked like it was in mid snarl. It was clearly pissed about leaving the planet so soon. Christik glided passed the encapsulated monster, heading for the rear of the ship and as I followed the hairs started to stand up on the back of my neck.

After what had happened before with the other Marilian surprising us, I wasn't one hundred percent confident that we had trapped all of them on board. I was nervous, but also on high alert and ready for anything.

My hand went to the small but lethal knife, tucked into the waistband of my combat pants under my breasts and I slid it from its sheath. It was perfect for fighting in smaller confines.

Reaching the end of the corridor, I took a deep breath as Christik opened the door. It was where the Marilian troops were kept. Seeing so many in such close quarters made my blood run cold, even though they all seemed to be encapsulated.

You could tell that the blast of power had frozen them before they knew anything about it. I see that some were in conversation as they sat next to each other, while others looked like they were arguing, they're body language looking aggressive and fierce. There were even two of the Marilians encapsulated in mid-fight towards the back, while other Marilians were frozen while cheering them on. I could imagine them roaring "kill" to their fighting comrades, not actually caring who killed who.

Content that the Marilian monsters were out of action, Christik gave me a nod before heading out of their holding room. We made our way through the ship, passing other trapped Marilians, heading to the front where the controls and pilots were. I was keeping everything crossed as Christik reached the door and began to open it. I didn't have to worry.

The smile on Christik's face as soon as the door opened told me that we had trapped them all. Needing visual reassurance, I slipped past Christik and walked into their control room. As with their main ship, every one of them were frozen at their work stations. I smiled too, and my confidence in our mission was reaching new heights.

"Onto the next one then!" I told Christik brightly as my smile turned into a grin.

"Yes, onto the next," she replied. "We are going to leave angels down on the planet to help the survivors and complete damage control until this is over."

She turned and led us back the way we came. As we disembarked, I hoped that the elders had had the same luck as we did, and that all the other ships occupants were decommissioned.

As we emerged out into the hangar, it was like breathing fresh air. Which was saying something, considering the main ship stank too, just not as badly as the smaller one. We headed towards the main hangar doors, our numbers growing again as the others emerged from checking the other ships. The elders nodded to Christik to indicate that there were no escapees. There wasn't time to waste, to discuss everything that had happened, I was already thinking about the next ship. Qiu was waiting for us at the hangar doors, and we all made our way back to the control room. I felt good walking beside my dragon friend, it felt like where I belonged.

The two Spadee were still in the control room with the Marilian prisoner and the remaining encapsulated female when we arrived. The unrestrained Marilian looked a little worse for wear than before, and I wondered if he'd tried to take on the Spadee in an attempt to escape. Judging by the minor injuries to his face and body, and the fact that the Spadee didn't seem to have any injuries at all, the Marilian obviously got more than he bargained for. He looked utterly defeated, slumped between the two Pangolin looking aliens.

The smaller of the Spadee began to make clicking noises, and I looked to Christik in confusion. "He thought he could take us," Christik translated. When I looked back to the Spadee, the smirk on its face showed how funny he or she thought it was.

"I do not think he will try again," Evest told them with a smirk of his own. His eyes sparkling with humor. "Please brace yourselves, we are leaving for the next Marilian ship."

Everyone in the room either sat down or took a position so they were secure.

"Don't I need to encapsulate them again for the journey?" I asked Christik, following her to a large control panel near where Qui had landed hours earlier.

"You do not need to do that this time Mel, the Marilian ship is built for their softer bodies. None of you will be harmed, although you may experience some minor effects," she assured.

I nodded to her, showing I understood, and then I took position at a floor to ceiling pole near where Qiu was sitting. The elders glided to the other control panels and it didn't matter that the panels were lit with the Marilian markings, as the angels weren't going to use their fingers. As soon as they raised their hands and they began to glow with their power, I gripped the pole and braced myself for the unexpected.

When the angels' power started to flow through the control panels, the ship burst into life, with clunks, screeching, and bangs as the old and unkempt ship tried to do the angels' bidding. In front of us two large metal screens started to part, a zig zag forming between the separate sides as they opened.

It was a god-awful noise as they slid to the sides of the ship, but at least we could see out. I spotted the angels' main craft in the distance, as well as another angel craft that I assumed were full of the angels, who were going to help the planet's inhabitants.

"Brace!" Christik declared, as the angel's power glowed brighter.

I wrapped my legs around the bottom of the pole and gripped it with my hands as much as possible. Everyone else was doing the same, all gripping whatever they could. It was while I was watching them that I realized that there were small metal grips attached to all the control panels, so the Marilians obviously had to brace themselves during travel too.

I watched in fascination as one of the aliens slipped an arm like a sucker less tentacle, through and around a hand grip with ease. The two Spadee secured the two Marilians on deck. The encapsulated Marilian was wedged between two consoles with the smaller Spadee blocking any movement. The other Spadee was holding the other in a death-like grip, while using its spare arm and leg to grip the pole on the other side of me and Qiu.

Suddenly the ship rumbled loudly, and our angle started to change, moving away from the other angels' craft. Then as soon as we were in the right direction, which only the angels knew, the ship burst forward at full speed. Like before on the angel's main craft, we shot forward through space with stars becoming shooting long lights instead of static bright dots. I had no idea if we were traveling as fast as before.

I started shaking and feeling extremely hot, and I had to close my eyes from the scene before me. My whole body was vibrating, and it got so bad that at one point it felt like my bones were shaking from head to foot. I took slow breaths and began to try to think of anything but what was happening, while desperately trying to keep hold of the pole.

Minutes passed and I tried to hold on, but my

hands began to get slippery. Just when I thought I was going to be flung backwards against the ship, something gently pushed up against my back, holding me in place. Whatever or whoever it was, was vibrating as much as I was. I didn't even try to open my eyes to see who or what it was, I was just grateful for the assistance.

Finally, the ship began to slow, and as if I had been on a fairground ride, my stomach felt as if it was trying to move out of my body. I fought the force that was suddenly trying to lurch me forward, well aware that if I did, I would probably bash myself against the pole.

When the ship finally came to a full stop, the relief I felt was immense. I was still trembling from the strong vibrations from the journey and it reminded me of my trembling hands after sanding down the deck of our old house. I knew it would wear off quickly and I hoped the shaking of my legs and the sudden urge to vomit would pass just as fast. Opening my eyes, I tried to distract myself by looking around the control room. Everyone else apart from the angels looked quite queasy too.

We could see the Marilian ship in the distance, and from the look of the planet it was next to, they had already caused a lot of damage. It was starting to look quite dead, brown and burnt on one large patch that we could see, and I was dreading to think what they had done to the inhabitants and the creatures down there. I was abruptly furious, wanting to kick some Marilian ass. I knew the angels felt my emotions immediately, but I wasn't the only one who was feeling furious. I looked at our allies in the control room, following the angel's gaze and there were looks of rage everywhere.

The aliens, like me, were releasing their hold on the hand grips and anything else they'd had to hand. All standing and moving around to shake the trembling that was still in our bodies. I felt the pressure behind me relax and when I turned around, I wasn't surprised to see Qiu lowering his front leg. I walked over to him on my shaky legs, placing my hands on his neck.

"Thank you, my friend,"

"Next time hold on to me, I will keep you safe, young one," he said, and I knew he would.

"We have no time to waste," Evest said to us all. "We can only take who we need, the rest of you will have to stay here for now and await our Viziers and angels."

There was no dispute from our allies, but even I could feel their disappointment, it was so strong. Christik and the elders moved swiftly to gather where we had originally landed when first boarding the Marilian ship, while the other aliens parted to allow Qiu and I to join them.

The Spadee were doing a great job of keeping our Marilian prisoner subdued. It was quite strange to see one of them looking so defeated and sorry for itself. We placed our hands on Qiu and instantly felt the tingle of his power as we became invisible, the angel's power blending with it. '*Here we go again*' I thought to myself, but this time I wasn't nervous or worried. This time I was feeling pissed off that we didn't get there sooner.

CHAPTER 20

Luckily for us, everything went smoothly with the Marilian ship takeovers and by the time we prepared ourselves for the last Marilian ship, we were maybe a little over-confident. We had managed to appear unseen next to the planet and fairly close to our enemy's ship. Unfortunately for us, while we had been over taking the other seven ships, these Marilians had been very busy.

The planet was unrecognizable compared to what it had looked like when the Impa's were seeking it. It was now a dead husk of a world, and my heart felt broken as I thought of all the life that had been lost. I hoped that there may be some survivors down on its surface who we could rescue. I had to remind myself that the smaller ships that were now heading for their main craft probably held Marilians who had recently been changed too.

We knew we had to act fast. We were still on the first ship that we had taken over, leaving the other defeated ships to catch up with us once the next one was thwarted. Our new alien allies had been fantastic. All of them had helped with our mission, and their confidence and determination had matched our own.

Skeleton crews of angels were flying the other Marilian ships, and while we were preparing to take the other ships, they were getting ready to take the Marilian's home planet. The smaller Marilian ships which were streaming towards their main ship were leaving death and destruction behind. There were dark grey hues spreading across the planet's surface. I began to pray that the Marilians hadn't had a chance to use their world destroying weapon yet.

"Can you sense if they have destroyed the planet's core yet?" I asked, while hoping for good news.

Christik shook her head. "We cannot tell without being on the planet and touching its surface. We have to hope we are not too late."

"So, what do we do now?" I asked Christik and the elders. "Do we wait for the smaller ships to dock before getting on their main ship, or go now?"

The elders and Christik looked at each other for a moment as if they were deliberating.

"We will go now. If we act quickly, we can lock them in their hangar once the last ship is on-board. Hopefully they will be encapsulated with the rest of the ship," Evest said calmly.

Time was going to be of the essence, and we had to keep faith that it would work. I moved quickly to place my hands on Qiu with Christik and the elders, ignoring the sensations through my body. Within seconds, we were on the deck of the Marilian ship. All the Marilians ships had been the same, with identical layouts.

After taking over so many already, we were precise on where we needed to appear. Unfortunately for us, we couldn't predict where the occupants would be, and this time as soon as we appeared, I came face to face with one of the monsters.

As I stood in front of the Marilian with his hot stinking breath washing over my face, I resisted the urge to turn and vomit. It was as if something had died in his disgusting mouth and had got stuck between its razor-sharp teeth.

'*Let's do this now*' I told the angels and Qiu

through our coms.

The Marilians putrid breath in my face made it easy for me to access my power. Christik and the elders held out their glowing hands out towards our enemies and in seconds the Marilians we encapsulated, frozen in place.

A quick look around the control confirmed they were all out of action and we instantly moved to the large doors to exit. Considering Qiu was still very large, he seemed to move just as quickly as the rest of us. Eliz stayed where he was, making me turn when I realized that he wasn't moving with us.

"I will stay and close the hangar door when the last of their ships is onboard," he said, responding to my questioning look.

He looked down at the consoles, placing a glowing hand on one of the black, grimy panels before looking back up.

"They have not released their final weapon yet, we have time to retrieve survivors once we have control of the ship. I will alert our angels to come as soon we are finished here,' ' Eliz said with a calm and relieved tone.

Without missing a beat, I turned back and continued to move with Qiu and the angels. Evest opened the door, and as with the last few ships we'd recently taken over, the two Marilians on the other side of the doors were encapsulated with the rest of the control room crew.

“Should we blast the ship now or wait for the smaller ships to finish boarding?” I asked Evest as we passed the two frozen Marilians.

“We will try and get to the center of the ship before we blast them. Eliz can let us know when the last ship is onboard and the hangar doors are locked,” he said confidently.

I wasn’t feeling as confident. We had a long walk to the center of the ship, and there was no way of knowing how many Marilians we would encounter on the way. I knew we were still invisible because I could still feel the tingle of Qiu’s and the angels' power on my skin.

We headed for the hangar and it felt like every step I took, my heart beat a little faster in my chest. We moved as one and all the while my senses were on high alert. Abruptly Qiu stopped and his nostrils flared. ‘*I think someone is coming up ahead*’.

Slowly and steadily we moved, passing heavy metal doors on our way. I was so busy looking forward that I wasn't expecting the two Marilian’s, who Qiu sensed or smelled, to suddenly appear. One from an opening door on my side and the other ahead of us. Neither of them saw us, but they could smell me. I was close to the Marilian in the doorway, and he was instantly on high alert. I was dirty and sweaty, and he snarled loudly as his eyes darted left and right, trying to spot what he could smell.

As soon as the angels spotted the Marilian ahead of them, Lindaz raised her arm towards it. My instincts kicked in and without thinking I kicked out, hitting the other Marilian back through the door he'd come from, sending it skidding along the cold metal floor, before releasing my power in his direction. Lindaz's target didn't stand a chance either. As soon as she felt me, she released our joint power too, hitting her target and freezing him in place. Adrenalin was pumping through me and I wanted to get our job done. A quick glance through the doorway confirmed there were no others coming, and with a nod to the angels and Qiu, we pushed on through the ship. I wondered if they were resting after all their destructive activities, and that was why we weren't encountering any others in route to the hangar. Either way it was a blessing.

'*The last ship is docking, I am going to lock the doors.*' I heard Eliz say through our coms.

'*We need to get a little further*' I told him.

Christik looked at me over her slender bare shoulder.

"We have to do it as soon as they are trapped. Mel, give us all you have!"

I didn't have time to think about what Christik was asking, I just knew I had to try. My heart was now beating so fast in my chest that it felt as if it was trying to escape the confines of my ribs.

'*Now*,' Eliz declared urgently through our co-ms.

My pulse kicked up as notch as I instantly tapped back into my new power, unleashing every-thing I had in me. My head and back arched as the angel's power joined mine and it all burst from my body. The adrenaline in my system fueling it as much as the angels, then suddenly blackness took me.

I fluttered my eyes, trying to focus on the sounds around me. For a moment I didn't know wh-ere I was. My body felt weak and lethargic, but I could feel tingling on my arms, torso, and legs. Tur-ning my head to the side, I focused on a form near my left arm and as my brain and eyes began to clear, I realized it was Evest.

"What happened?" I asked as the memory of the blast came back to me. "Did we do it?"

"You really did give everything you had, yo-ung one," Evest said with a smile. "I never realized that you humans were so strong."

"But did it work?" I asked again while trying to sit up.

Evest placed his hand on my chest, gently stopping me.

“Let us help you, Mel, you are spent. We think it worked, but we will check in a moment when you have some strength.”

I knew there was no point in arguing with the elder. Just trying to sit up let me know how weak I was, so there was no way I’d be able to stand. I stayed where I was and let the angels share their power, while wishing I had an endless supply like they did. After ten minutes or so, I felt strong enough to get back on my feet and find out if we’d succeeded.

By the time we got to the hangar, I was fee-ling very confident. Every single Marilian that we’d passed or seen had been encapsulated. When Evest opened the hangar doors for us to check I finally relaxed. There were Marilians frozen every-where. Some had been encapsulated while trying to open the doors, while others were obviously banging on the doors in anger and frustration. Many were in the middle of disembarking their ships and some had even got into fights as they were getting off.

“We will let the Viziers know that it is done,” Evest said as he turned to me. “You need some rest and some food before we heal them and continue our mission.”

The elder glided towards me and surprised

me by taking my hands in his as the other elders and Christik all turned to look.

"You have done an amazing thing, Mel, and you have saved so many lives. We are honored to know you," he said.

I felt the truth in his words at the same time I felt the tears spring from my eyes and trickle down my face.

When the angels' main craft arrived and Christik had taken me aboard, I was so ready for a shower and a sleep. I also badly wanted a cuddle with my husband, but as he was still frozen with the rest of my friends, I knew I'd have to wait. It was very tempting to unfreeze them and have them travel with me on one of the Marilian ships, but having seen how disgusting they were and knowing how badly I stank, I decided that James and our friends were better off where they were.

I took my time in the shower, letting the refreshing water rinse away all the Marilian stench and grim. Even when I knew that the dirt and smell was gone from my body, I stayed under the water and let it soothe my muscles and skin. By the time I finished and made my way to the bed in our suite, I was dead on my feet, flopping on the bed ungracefully and letting sleep take me.

When I woke, I wasn't aware of how much time had passed and as I turned over and sat myself up, I saw that the angels had been in and left a food platter, some juice and coffee on the small table in the dining area of our room. My stomach growled at the sight and my mouth watered. The expression of being hungry enough to eat a scabby horse sprung to mind, and then I realized how disgusting that phrase was.

Without wasting another second, I headed for the table and the platter. The coffee was no longer hot, but it was warm and extremely welcome. By the time I'd finished, I was feeling satisfied, energized and raring to go.

After cleaning my teeth, braiding my hair ag-ain, and getting dressed in the clean combat gear the angels had kindly left, I made my way back to their control room, where I knew I'd find Christik and the elders. I was greeted with smiles from the elders as I walked into their control room and was taken aback when the other angels turned to me and bowed. I wasn't sure how to react to their gesture. But I knew they were doing it with deep respect because of what we had accomplished so far. I bowed back, feeling my cheeks burning with embarrassment.

"Thank you," I said as I smiled at their bea-utiful faces.

As soon as they turned back to their consoles, I made my way to Christik's side while looking at the large, thick glass window screen ahead. We were obviously traveling at high speed again, but not yet the speed where I had to protect myself.

"Are the other ships behind us?" I asked Christik.

"No, they have gone ahead. They will stop before they reach Marilia, so they stay undetected until we arrive. We will heal as many Marilians as possible before the battle, and the other races are ready to come through the star passages when we give them the signal," she explained.

"How can you give them a signal when they are all on their home planets?" I asked with no idea what her answer would be.

"We only have to send a burst of power through the Marilian star passage back to our planet. Our angels will then signal the others," she said confidently. "Are you ready to kick some Marilian ass?"

I grinned at her choice of words, thinking to myself that we were definitely rubbing off on the angel.

"Born ready." I chuckled.

I moved between two of the consoles and positioned myself before letting my power encase and protect me.

"Let us go!" Christik declared.

The angels' craft shot forward at a tremendous speed, and just as before I felt every inch of my body being squeezed from the pressure, even with my powerful protection. I tried to focus on the angels in front of me, who annoyingly weren't affected by the high-speed travel at all.

When we finally began to slow down, we were next to the Marilian moon. As I held myself up with my hands on my knee, I swallowed hard, desperately trying to keep my last meal down. Christik glided to my side placing her soft hand on my back, letting her power soothe my space travel sickness. It was weird that space travel sickness was even a thing.

After a few moments and with Christik's help, I was back to normal and looking out the control rooms large window at the large grey moon and the Marilian ships, piloted by the Viziers. They were all waiting for action.

"I know we have a lot of Marilians to heal before we get down there," I told Christik, pointing at the Marilians planet in the distance, "but I want to change James and the others first."

I needed to be with the man I loved and hold him, especially as we didn't know how our invasion was going to go. I wasn't going to waste any precious time without him, and I knew he would feel the same way.

My heart was also pining for our kids, and every time I thought of Hope I felt a pang of guilt. Added to that was the uncomfortable feeling in my breasts as they filled with her milk. As I also thought of our encapsulated friends, I realized that Akhenaten was probably desperate to have Tracey released too. Christik nodded her head, her silvery red hair falling forward onto her slim shoulders.

"I understand," she said with a sympathetic smile. "We will go to them now."

She placed her hand on my shoulder and I felt my emotions calm at the same time as my aching breasts eased off. '*Thank goodness*,' I thought to myself. The last thing I needed was to feel like my breasts were heavy weights on my chest when we invaded the Marilian planet. As she turned to move, so did the elders, and I let her lead me to the holding room where our friends and my husband were being kept.

The elders followed behind, gliding in silence. My mind was on James, and before I knew it, we had arrived at the holding room without me remembering most of the walk there. Akhenaten was already there waiting patiently, although I could feel his longing for his love.

CHAPTER 21

James and our friends were in rows along the white walled holding room, frozen in their blue bubble capsules. Unlike the Marilians, James and our friends looked peaceful, their faces smooth and restful. I wa-lked towards them, and as I stopped feet away from James, Christik and the elders gathered around me, placing their hands on my upper body. I searched inside myself for my inner power and as soon as the angels let their power connect with mine, we released it.

James and our friends were instantly bathed

in the bright blue energy. It was still an amazing sight to see the capsules beginning to change. Once the capsules began to become turbulent, flowing around their still bodies, I knew it was time to take the power back.

I walked forward a little closer, letting the angels' hands slip from my body, heading for James and the others. I could feel my power reaching for me, and I instinctively raised my hands to receive it. Within moments, my body was absorbing the shimmering blue fluid from their bodies. By the time their bodies were barely covered, I could make out little moments of awakening. Unlike the aliens that I'd encapsulated and freed, none of my friends were naked, thank goodness. I don't think I could have looked them in the eyes again if they had been.

As soon as they were all released and their eyes fell on me and the angels, there were smiles and grins all around. The moment James was able, he strode over to me like a man on a personal mission, sweeping me up into his strong masculine arms.

It was the best reunion ever, and as I giggled while James buried his face in my neck to kiss me profusely. Our friends gathered around us with friendly pats on our backs. They all knew that being freed meant that we had been successful so far.

As everyone began to question Christik and

the elders about what had happened, James moved from my neck to my lips. His warm body and tender kisses soothed my soul and aching heart.

"I'm so fricking proud of you right now, hot stuff," he said, as he continued to kiss me.

"I can tell, husband of mine; now put me down before you wear my lips out." I giggled.

Reluctantly he placed me back on my feet, with one arm wrapped around my waist. Tracey was in Akhenaten's embrace and the look of love between them made me smile.

"Did you get all the Marilian ships? Did you have any trouble?" Derek asked one of the elders behind me.

There were questions from our friends in every direction and the angels did their best to answer everyone, before suggesting that they should all have some food and drinks in the canteen before doing anything else.

"Spend some time with your husband, and when you are ready, we can heal the captured Marilians," Christik said as she glided to our side.

I smiled in gratitude and we followed our friends who were still asking the angels questions, wanting to know all the details of what we had done. I think I smiled all the way to the canteen and possibly through our shared meal. I told James everything that had happened, and by the time we had all finished eating my voice was hoarse from talking.

"I need to help the angels heal the Marilians," I told James after taking a sip of the steamy, hot black coffee the angels had provided.

"I'll come with you," he said with a smile while reaching for my other hand, stroking the top of it with his thumb tenderly.

We excused ourselves from the table and waved goodbye to the rest of our friends. The Impa's and our human friends were all intermingled as if they had known each other forever.

The rest of the day and night was long. The angels took James and I from ship to ship so I could heal the Marilians or encapsulate them, depending on whether they could survive on the ships. There was no way I could have done any of it without the angels' help. Even then, by the time we had finished the last Marilian ship, I felt drained beyond measure. Christik and the elders were amazing, helping me heal the Marilians, then calming the newly changed aliens while explaining what was happening.

There wasn't one single race who didn't want to be part of stopping the Marilians once and for all. I started to wonder why no one had thought to stop them before, but then sometimes it just takes some to lead by example to others. I felt proud that my human race was going to be part of something that was going to affect the whole universe. Maybe it was going to help make amends for what we had done to our own world. Either way, I knew that what we were about to do would forever be in our human history. Someone could possibly write a book about it all one day. The thought made me smile.

"You are exhausted," Evest said, as he finished talking with an alien who looked like a cross between a rhino and a snake, but weirder.

The elder placed his hand on my arm and I felt nothing but gratitude as my body soaked up the power he was giving me.

"Go and sleep," he said sympathetically. "We will invade when you are fully rested.

James and I barely spoke on the way to our rooms. He could tell how tired I felt, even after a boost from Evest. I plonked my butt on the bed and without saying a word, James knelt before me and removed my boots, my combat pants and then my top. while he began to remove his own clothes, I slipped into the bed, savoring the feel of the silky sheets and the soft bed on my weary body. Within minutes of James sliding his arms around me and kissing the back of my neck, I was fast asleep.

I don't know how long I slept for, but it was a very deep sleep and by the time I woke, I was feeling as fresh as a daisy. James was no longer in our bed and when I looked around our room, I saw him dressed in combat gear and tucking into a tray of food at the small table near the round window.

"Good morning or good evening," he said with a smirk. "I don't actually know which it is, but you're looking very refreshed, my lady. I might have to get back into bed with you."

I slipped out of bed butt naked, instantly making my husband grin. Especially as my boobs were uncomfortably pert through not being able to feed Hope. '*That's how we ended up having so many kids*' I thought to myself.

"Keep your eyes and hands to yourself, husband of mine." I giggled. "We have an invasion to think about, not an insertion."

My handsome husband gave his best pouty face as I walked towards the bathroom to get ready. I was actually impressed when he refrained from following me. As much as I wanted him, the invasion came first, and I didn't want to waste precious time. I desperately wanted to be back with our kids, and I knew James felt the same way.

By the time I walked back into the room, James had finished eating and was standing by the circular window, looking out at the Marilians home world.

"It's crazy, being so close to their planet and them not knowing we're here," he said thoughtfully while watching me as I sat down to eat.

"You should have seen the look on the faces of the Marilians who actually saw us on their ships," I told him with a smile.

"What was it like on their ships?"

I shook my head at the images that popped into my mind.

"They were disgusting," I told him honestly. "You have never seen or smelt anything like it, honey."

I tried to not let the memories taint my appetite, especially because I knew that I needed my strength for the battle ahead.

"Christik wants us to meet her and the elders in the meeting room, so we'll go when you're ready," he said somberly.

I looked up from my food and our eyes connected. James's eyes were full of worry and unease. I could feel his concern over our kids and his trepidation for the invasion. Suddenly my appetite melted away. I left the tray of food, stood, and walked towards my husband, wrapping my arms around his waist, drawing him into me.

"After everything we've already been through-gh, do you honestly think we can't do this?" I asked him. "We have angels, dragons, and all kinds of aliens on our side this time, babe. The Marilians don't stand a chance."

James looked at me as if he had the weight of the world on his shoulders, and I wished I knew what to say to relieve his worries, but who was I kidding. I had all the same worries and concerns. The only difference was that James couldn't feel my emotions like I could feel his.

When we arrived at the meeting room, a few of the aliens I'd changed were just leaving. I smiled warmly at them and dipped my head in respect automatically, as did James. Christik and the elders were waiting for us and for once, I could feel a nervousness among them.

"I hope you are well rested, Mel and James," Christik said with a small smile. "We want to go over our plans for the invasion with you.

James and I sat down at the large wooden table between the elders so we could face her.

"Don't we need everyone else too?" I asked while wondering where everyone else was.

"We have already gone over the plans with them while you were sleeping, Mel. We wanted you to get as much rest as possible," Lindaz said kindly.

"Thank you, I appreciate it. God knows I needed the sleep," I told her. "So, what's our plan of action?"

Christik stood from her seat and she raised a hand to the center of the dark wooden table. As soon as her palm began to glow, an image started to form above the table. It was Marilia, the Marilians world that we were now so close to, swirls of hurricanes hiding most of the surface that we could see.

"All the races who are going to fight with us are ready for the battle," Christik said.

The image moved towards its surface, as if we were seeing camera footage from a drone. We watched as it showed the landscape of dark browns and burnt orange. I could tell that the Marilians used easily obtainable materials for their stone dwellings.

The image continued changing as the scene changed, until it began to slow at a large stone structure, similar to the Gate of the Gods we had visited. It had the familiar markings around its frame, but this star passage gate was made of the same stone that was surrounding it. I was starting to get the impression that the Marilians were lazy in all things, apart from their need to kill and destroy.

"Is that the star passage we need to activate?" James asked.

"Yes," Christik replied. "This is the gate that the races will have to pass through. They will come through, one race at a time, so we will need to be stealthy and quick.

"What if we cause a diversion, so the Marilians are all out of the area of the star passage?" James suggested.

Christik smiled broadly. "You humans have a natural skill for battle, James. Derek already suggested that idea. So that is part of our plan. We have already emptied one of their ships, and two of our remaining angels will crash it between the gate and the king's residence. They will flit from the ship before impact and meet us at the gate."

"It should cause one hell of an explosion," I told them. "Let's hope it attracts them like a moth to a flame. Hopefully they'll just assume it's crashed through pilot error, or that there's something wrong with it."

"I believe the Marilians are so arrogant and confident that they are unbeatable, I do not think it would occur to them that they could be under attack," Evest said with conviction.

"Then that will be their downfall and to our benefit." I grinned.

The image before us changed again. This time it zoomed to where the Marilian king resided.

"This will be our group's target," Christik stated.

The king was so confident that he had minimal guards outside the large stone building. I wouldn't have called it a palace, because it wasn't decorative or elegant by any stretch of the imagination. It was built in a very slapdash way and I could tell that they had built it themselves, without the angels' help. The fact that it had minimal guards was a definite plus for us.

"Does it look like Marilia has changed much since you were there?" I asked as the image moved back and away from the king's dwelling.

The image became a broader view of the area closest to the shabby palace, and I watched Christik and the elders as they studied the scene.

"Yes, there are definitely more structures than before," Evest said confidently. "Some are much larger than their normal dwellings, but I do not know what they could be using them for."

I looked at the large structures myself and Evest was right; they were a lot bigger than their usual homes, and they seemed more secure too, with large black metal doors at their entrances. They were still the same rough, stone domes, but they looked like the same size small aircrafts would be stored in. Nothing around them gave us any indication as to their use.

"I don't suppose you have any idea on their numbers either?" James asked as the image withdrew from the area completely, giving us only a glimpse of the Marilians on the surface before they could no longer be seen.

"I am afraid there is no way of knowing how many planets they invaded before we took their ships, James. Knowing the Marilians as we do, they would have wanted to replenish their numbers as quickly as possible," Evest stated.

"So, the plan is to activate the star passage and then take down the king and his court, while the others fight and secure the king's minions?" I asked, wanting to get it straight in my mind.

"Yes, exactly, as well as being prepared for anything," Christik answered.

"What about our friends and the others aboard the Marilian ships?" James inquired.

"And Qiu?" I added.

"Some will meet us in our hangar, the rest will meet us at the gate. Akhenaten, Tracey, and some of the Longs will be coming with us, including Qui. The others will fan out around the Marilian city with our angels to help them. From what we can tell, the Marilians still only have one city on their world. Their population never seems to grow enough to create any others," the angel replied.

We left the meeting room feeling fairly confident about our plan. All James and I had to do was to stick with Christik and the Elders and fight our way to the king's palace, with the dragon's help. Then we could stop King Drakron for good.

Christik and the elders flitted us down to the hangar and my body had already been through so much that I barely felt the cold shiver that usually occurred afterwards. As soon as we appeared, I glanced around at our friends, who were also dressed in their combat gear with guns and knives strapped to their bodies and ready for battle.

It was strange to think that not so long ago we were just average people with average lives, doing average jobs, but now we were alien ass kicking warriors. Even the way our friends stood was different, they now stood with a confidence battle hardened soldiers had. I felt a deep pride for our friends, old and new.

Qiu in his smaller form wandered over to us through the throng, everyone parting to let my fierce dragon friend through.

"Do you feel ready, young one?" he asked as he approached.

I walked forward as he lowered his head to mine, and I instantly felt our connection.

"I'm ready."

"I will fly down and meet you at the gate, young one," he said before turning and walking to the hangar exit.

I turned back to the angels and our friends, feeling my resolve strengthen.

"Let's thrash some Marilian ass!" I declared with a smile.

Everyone kicked into action and began to board the angels' small crafts. There were no them and us between any of the humans and the few various aliens who were coming with us. They streamed into the crafts as if it had been rehearsed.

James and I followed Christik and the elders, boarding a craft with Tracey and Akhenaten. I could feel Tracey's nervous determination as she took a seat next to me and James. I reached over and took Tracey's hand in mine, hoping it would remind her that we were all in it together. No sooner had I taken Tracey's hand, our other halves reached over and took hold of our free hands. It was such a small gesture, but I think it made us all feel a little more confident.

As soon as the crafts seats sucked us into place, I knew there was no turning back. Christik glided to the front of the craft and within seconds, she was touching the sides of the cockpit and connecting with the craft. As soon as the silver vines had finished snaking around her hands and forearms the craft began to rise off the hangar floor.

I could feel Christik's energy flowing through the craft, using her power to make it invisible to the naked eye. We began to glide towards the hangar exit and as I tried to peer past Christik's body, I thought I saw a glimpse of blood-red scales before disappearing. I knew it was Qiu leaving and I was looking forward to being back at his side. Just having my fierce dragon friend next to me made me feel ready for battle, and I knew he would protect James as much as he would protect me.

Christik followed Qiu out of the hangar, heading for the planet Marilia. It was a massive planet, and I started to feel that it was wasted on the Marilians, especially as they only occupied such a small part of it. Any other life on their planet probably kept a lot of distance between themselves and the Marilians.

During the rest of the flight to the Marilians' home world, I thought about our kids and how much safer their lives were going to be when it was all finished. We headed for the star passage gate and although I couldn't see them, I knew that the taken Marilian ships were following our smaller crafts, and one of them was getting ready to crash on the planet.

I started to feel everyone's anticipation on board our craft, including the angels. I shouldn't have been as surprised as I was; after all it was their first time invading a planet too, and everything was on the line.

When the small craft began to force its way through Marilia's turbulent atmosphere, I felt the vibration through my whole body and my nervousness really began to kick in. The force of the vibration grew stronger and just when I thought my teeth might start rattling inside my head, it suddenly stopped as we burst through. Christik straightened the craft slightly; steering towards our destination, and the butterflies in my stomach returned with a vengeance.

It didn't help that I was feeling everyone else's nervousness heighten as we got closer to the gate. By the time the craft began to slow and descend, I felt actually relieved. I wanted the whole thing to be over with as soon as possible, so we could return to our kids and finally begin our new lives.

The craft landed softly on the hard-rocky ground with a small thud and Christik immediately disconnected herself, turned, and then headed to the rear door as our seats released their hold. One by one we released each other's hand and stood to follow Christik and the elders as they started to disembark.

When the hot air hit my face and body, it reminded me of Peru, and I began to wish I was back there instead. We had landed close to the large stone gate, but with enough room for everyone else to land the small crafts, and for everyone to come through the gate. Just as I began to wonder where my dragon friend could be, I felt his hot breath down the back of my neck. In the time it took for me to turn around he had appeared in all his fierce glory.

After stroking his thick neck affectionately, I turned in a full one eighty to look around. There was nothing but dirt and the burnt-orange rocks that the Marilians used to build their dwellings and large structures.

"It was not always like this," Christik said, responding to my thoughts. "It was once a beautiful planet."

Before I had a chance to say anything to Christik's comments, the other crafts began to land. I felt the thuds of their landings, but it wasn't until their doors opened that I could see where they were.

Before any of our friends had a chance to disembark, the first of the defeated Marilian ships burst through the sky at speed. It was flying at such an angle that it would be clear to any Marilian that saw it, that it was going to crash unless the crew did something fast. I knew our friends were starting to disembark from the crafts, as I could see them in my peripheral vision, but I couldn't look away from the ship that I knew was going to crash in the distance. The sound of the high-speed ship plummeting to its demise was deafening, and I wasn't the only one to place their hands over their ears, knowing what was to come.

The ship flew out of sight behind the many large rock formations. Seconds later the explosion that followed burst into the sky as the shock wave rippled through the ground in a big shock wave, vibrating up my legs and body.

CHAPTER 22

The sky above the crash site, which was naturally fiery colors, was suddenly alight with dark red and orange flames from the exploding ship. Huge plumes of thick black smoke began to billow upwards and outwards. We could just about hear noises of commotion as the Marilians began to surge towards the crash. '*God, I hope this works,*' I thought to myself. Without wasting time, our friends rapidly disembarked their crafts and started to fan out either side of us.

I forced myself to stop looking in the distance at the smoke and flames. When I turned back to

James and the elders, I saw that two angels were now standing with them. I had been so busy looking where the crash was that I didn't even notice that the angels who had been flying it had appeared. The two angels didn't have a shimmering hair out of place. They did however have smiles on their angelic features, and I could feel their sense of achievement for a job well done.

"Let us signal the others," Evest stated.

The elder turned, gliding towards the dark orange stone gate with the other elders following him. I didn't know whether I should watch them or keep an eye out for any Marilians who might discover us, but as I glanced around at our friends, I knew there were many eyes looking and searching the area already.

I looked back at Evest just as he was raising both hands towards the center of the stone gate, while the other elders stood either side of him. I actually felt their power before their hands began to glow and it felt as though my new power was growing.

A wind began to pick up around us and my thoughts went back to our time in Peru. I began to wonder if the Marilian planet had gold within its surface, like our planet had had, while hoping that no Marilians close by would wonder where the strong wind was coming from.

"Turbulent weather is common here," Christik said calmly above the noise and picking up on my thoughts. "You saw the hurricanes from our main craft. The Marilians will not think twice about strong winds here."

The wind was getting stronger and stronger, whipping our hair around our faces. Either side of Evest, the elders held out their palms towards the barren land and the ground started to tremble. I was expecting gold specs to start appearing, but the metal specs that began to rise from the dust was black, just like the Marilians blood. Through the gusts of wind and our unruly hair, we watched as the elders began to direct the black metal flecks towards the star passage gate, the tiny particles collecting in the deep hieroglyphs.

Before long the hieroglyphs were filled with the black metal and they started to glow within the gate. The elders' power was strong and as they stopped filling the symbols with the metal, they directed all of their power to activating and opening the gate.

A small ball of bright shimming power started to form between Evest's outstretched palms, and I watched as it grew by the second. By the time it was the size of a basketball, I felt a large surge of power emanating from him. The void within the stones of the gate became a haze of orange as it opened.

Evest brought his arms back towards his body, so the ball of power between his hands was shimmering brightly in front of his face. With an "humph" sound leaving his lips, he pushed the power ball through the opened gate, giving the signal to our alien allies. The gusting wind began to dwindle, and lowering their hands the elders turned and started gliding back towards us. Now we just had to wait.

Everyone who arrived with us were already in position for our invasion. I was checking my weapons for the umpteenth time when the first aliens began to pour through the star passage. The Jeli arrived in a stream of tentacles, carrying long speared weapons. I was surprised that they were able to move along the dry dirt as efficiently as they did. I was also stunned that they were able to be out of the water. It wasn't until some of them drew closer to us, that I realized they had some kind of water filled film covering their heads, down to their shoulders.

Hundreds of them came through the gate, all carrying their deadly weapons. When I thought the last of them had passed through, something pointed started to pierce through the glowing barrier. It was some sort of transport and as it came through, I could feel a draft against my trouser legs. The Jeli craft was just big enough for one, a streamlined, light-gray craft emerging from the gate.

The top part of the craft was clear and inside was King Ardis. From the air current coming from the underside of the craft, I assumed it was similar to a hovercraft. There were no loud engine noises coming from it, as it glided across the ground. The king glided to a halt alongside Qiu, me, and James, while more of the Jeli crafts emerged, spreading themselves out along our lines.

Looking along the lines of different races, my confidence was already growing tremendously. Within moments of the final Jeli craft arriving, the gate pulsed with power and our next group of allies emerged.

The Impa's appeared every bit the warriors we knew them to be. Brightly colored war paint decorated their athletic bodies, stripes of reds, yellows, blues, and greens, in between the moss and flowers that already adorned their skin. The long dark feathers that grew from their backs, bristled proudly as they gracefully strode through the opened gate. They quickly glanced around before striding to their positions. I could sense that everyone was feeling bolstered by our growing numbers.

No sooner had the Impa's finished coming through the star passage, the next alien race emerged and then the next. We hadn't had a chance to meet most of the alien races that were streaming through the gate, but we all had one thing in common, the desire to defeat the Marilians.

When the dragons came through, they were quick to head straight towards the angels, elders, and our human friends. For our friends it was their first time, but without any hesitation they mounted the dragons, making themselves look like professionals.

The Jagu were the last to arrive, and they were just as fierce as any of the other races. Their speed through the gate was impressive and just like the others, they fanned themselves out in between everyone else. I suddenly felt like we were all in a weird alien version of the Braveheart movie. I glanced at the huge alien army around me, and as I watched them prepare and check their weapons and ready their natural defenses, goosebumps prickled on my skin.

Without even thinking, my hands felt for my own weapons again for the hundredth time, mentally reassuring myself on where they all were. James leaned in closely, brushing his lips against my ear.

"We can do this, baby," James said quietly. "Now go get on your dragon!"

As he pulled back our eyes connected and through everything that we had endured, our bond was stronger than ever. I had to trust that the elders and Christik would have his back, and he had to trust that Qiu had mine.

“I love you,” I told him before turning away.

‘*I love you more*,’ I heard in my mind.

I strode towards Qiu, who was waiting patiently for me, surrounded by our allies who weren’t fazed by his size by any means. Qiu lowered his large scaled head to mine and as soon as my forehead connected with his, I felt our ever-growing bond.

The power within me instantly reacted without me even thinking about it, reaching out to my dragon kindred spirit. I knew that Qiu and I were already glowing with our connected power because I could feel it. The aliens closest to us moved backwards as our glow brightened with our growing determination to kick the Marilians’ asses.

Qiu lifted his front leg and I stepped up, gracefully swinging onto his back. I didn’t feel like a battle leader, but it soon became apparent that all eyes were on me and Qiu, even the elders and angels were looking at us, as if waiting for the signal to surge forward. I forced myself to close my eyes and to remember what the Marilians had done. The slicing of our son's chest, murdering Christine's father, and so many other lives lost.

My rage began to grow as I went over in my mind all that they had destroyed. Gasps around us broke me from my thoughts and when I opened my eyes, Qiu and I were ablaze of purple power. I knew that he was feeling my rage, hearing my thoughts, and sharing my painful memories as much as I was feeling and sharing his. Looking at the alien army surrounding us, I raised my arms, flaming with our joint power.

"Today we fight and stop the Marilians forever!" I declared.

Our alien forces stamped the dusty ground in agreement, and I lowered my arms, gripping Qiu's blood red scales in my hand. 'Let's go."

Qiu raised himself up on his hind legs, letting out a blood chilling roar before surging forward, our allies charged into action, along with our mounted friends and angels. Sitting astride my dragon, I could only imagine the vibration from the aliens pounding feet, hooves and other strange appendages. The Marilians were definitely going to wonder what was going on. As Qiu raced forward, I glanced at either side of us and the sight of so many fierce and scary looking aliens made the hairs rise on the back of my neck. '*Thank god they're on our side*,' I thought.

We moved fast across the arid and lifeless ground, speeding away from the gate. There was no turning back, this was it.

Before too long the Marilian's dark-orange, stone dwellings and structures were visible in the distance, standing out against the pale dusty landscape. My pulse began to race as my body released its adrenaline. The stone buildings were close together so we couldn't see any Marilians who were outside, I knew we'd have to be ready for anything. The smaller dwellings were in circle arrangements with the larger structures just outside them. I didn't have to see them to know that in between each circle of dwellings were stone circle fighting rings, where they would fight each other to the death. The images that the angels had shown us of them fighting, was still fresh in my mind.

Drawing closer, our allies started to go in various directions, some going left of the dwellings and some going right, so they could flank the rest of us. Qiu and I knew what we had to do. We just had to get to king Drakron's palace and hope that our allies could handle the rest.

Christik and the elders were right. The Marilians were so arrogant, we didn't see any sentries or lookouts as we approached their city. An uneasy feeling in the pit of my stomach began to form and I touched my com at my neck.

'*Something feels off*,' I said to James, the angels, and our friends.

'*I feel it too*,' Tracey replied quickly, '*but I don't know what it could be*.'

I looked around to find Christik a few feet away. '*I do not know, Mel, but I trust your instincts.*'

I gave Christik a nod and then faced forward again. The adrenaline pumping through my body had me on high alert and I was ready for anything.

'*I sense something strange too, young one, there's something big in those larger buildings,*' Qiu said.

'*Let's be extra cautious when we get close,*' I replied.

We were approaching the building at speed when we heard some of our allies coming into co-ntact with our enemies. Roars and shouts started filling in the air with clashes of metal as our allies began to fight. I hoped that between us all, we could save and change as many Marilians as possible, but the Marilian changelings or true bloods just wanted to fight.

Pushing onwards, we began to pass through the first circle of dwellings, but as the fighting noises became louder, a loud, shrill horn noise sounded and that was when all hell broke loose.

Suddenly the large black metal doors to the larger structures were opened, and like a flood, hundreds of Marilians poured out in a tide of dirty, long-haired bodies, needle-sharp teeth, blood-red eyes, and talons like razors. It was as if the king had been storing Marilians for some reason. As soon as the Marilians were set free, their eyes darted around looking for prey. Their blood red, glowing eyes quickly fell on us and our alien warriors. None of us hesitated as we raced towards the oncoming Marilian force.

Qiu and I forced our way through the throng of Marilian bodies as they tried to attack. Our warriors quickly engaged, their weapons and natural defenses ready for action. All of a sudden, the noise around us was deafening, with the sounds of weapons and talon clashing, roars, and battle cries.

Qiu was quick to act, lashing out with his talons, while his deadly tail swiped from side to side. He wasn't trying to kill, but the Marilians weren't giving him much choice. While I held on with one hand, gripping Qiu's thick red scales, I quickly reached for the Glock that was strapped to my thigh. With one swift movement, the gun was in my hand and I was aiming at one of the Marilians, who appeared to be besting one of our Jeli warriors.

The Jeli wasn't as quick as the Marilian, and even though it was trying hard to defend itself with its spear, the Marilian was slashing at the Jeli's body effortlessly. Without any fear or hesitation, I aimed and fired.

My shot hit the Marilian right in the left eye, its head flinging back with the force of my shot, the back of its head opening in a burst of black blood and red brain matter. The Marilians went limp, releasing its talons from the Jeli's bloody body. When the Marilians body landed heavily on the dirt floor, the Jeli warrior turned to face me, its eyes widening with shock. Dark purple blood was trickling down from large open wounds on its torso and down its tentacles.

Just as I was about to jump off Qiu's back to help the Jeli warrior, one of the angels flitted to its side. The angel placed his hand on the Jeli's shoulder, and they vanished. I knew the warrior would be healed immediately, so without missing a beat, I turned my attention back to the battle.

We were inundated with Marilians and I thanked our lucky stars that we had so many fighting with us.

'*Push forward, Mel; if we get to the king, we can stop this*,' Christik said.

I looked around to try and spot her, only to find her, James, and Tracey completely surrounded. I knew that I needed them to help me at the palace.

'*We can't use my fire to help them, Mel; the Marilians will use it against us*,' Qiu said.

I knew he was right, and there didn't seem to be any water around that we could use to defend ourselves either.

'We're going to have to fly our way out of here to get to the palace, Qiu.'

Before I had a chance to say anything to James and the others, Qiu began to curl inwards, preparing himself for flight. I could feel his immense power building as I was being raised up high on his scaled, arching back. His head lowered the more he ached and just as we were about to take off, a Marilian decided to attack Qiu's vulnerability.

The vicious monster shot forward, leaping into the air with its razor-sharp talons raised ready to attack. I knew that if it stuck Qiu's eyes he would be defenseless. Changeling or not, I wasn't going to let the monster hurt my friend.

Raising my gun, I shot it, aiming for its eyes and missed. Hitting a moving target was a lot harder than one standing in place. I panicked and fired again and again, until luckily, I caught the monster right between the eyes. Their bodies were so tough that it didn't penetrate, but it was enough for him to miss Qiu's eyes.

The sound of the Marilian's metal talons scr-aping down Qiu's scaled face made my blood run cold. There was no time for me to check to see if the Marilian had caused any injuries. Qiu raised his head as he bent his legs and we launched into the air, leaving the battle behind us. I instantly felt guilty for having to leave our warriors on the ground fighting, but Christik was right. Drakron and the true bloods were our priority, and we had to get to them quickly.

As we ascended into the air, I gripped Qiu's scales tightly and turned to the scene below. Christik, James, and our other mounted friends had all seen us leave and they were trying to follow. James and Christik were already taking off, and I could see from the other dragons' postures that they were nearly ready. Turning back around I lowered my body, streamlining myself along Qiu's thick scaled back. I knew that Qiu would spot the palace before I would, so I took the short reprieve to catch my breath, calming my racing heart.

'*Are you hurt*?' I asked, worried for my friend.

'*Just a little scratch*,' Qiu replied with a little humor in his tone. I was relieved and I felt my body relax against him.

We flew over the circles of dwellings and I could still hear the fighting below us.

'*I can see the palace, young one*,' Qiu said, instantly making my heart pick up pace again.

Trying to hold on tightly, I leaned over slightly to take a look. Drakron's palace didn't look very grand from the air either. Only difference was that there were now guards surrounding the palace that we would have to deal with. Burning torches had been lit and were dotted between the sentries. I should have known the king wasn't stupid enough to not take action to protect himself as soon as he knew something was happening. I had hoped that his arrogance would make him sloppy.

I quickly looked to see if the others were following, relieved to see them close behind. None of them appeared to be injured at a glance.

'*Get ready to land, young one*' Qiu said as I felt his angle tilt forward.

I did as I was told, gripping his scales in my hands and clenching my thighs against his sides. With so much noise from the battle below us, I couldn't tell at first whether we'd been spotted. That was until a ball of fire flew through the air, hitting Qiu in his chest. '*Stupid Marilians,*' Qiu said, with humor in his tone.

Not only was the fire harmless to Qiu, but our combined power made it harmless too. We began to descend rapidly and just before we hit the ground in front of the guarded palace, Qiu tilted again to land on his back legs, while at the same time taking a huge breath. I knew what was coming, and so did some of the Marilians. However, not all of the closest guards defended themselves quickly enough. Qiu roared, blasting them with his fire as he turned his head.

The guards who didn't protect themselves were instantly standing pillars of burning hair and flesh. Qiu swiped at the unharmed guards with his talons as they surged forward to attack. Thuds behind us made it clear that James and the others were la-nding. '*Here we go*,' I thought.

CHAPTER 23

Looking at the entrance to the palace, there was no way that Qiu and I could get in there while I was on his back and he was so big. The entrance way was tall but very narrow, and the large black metal doors appeared to be securely close. Swinging my leg, I quickly dismounted. As my feet hit the floor, I reached for my gun and a new clip. Dropping my used clip, I loaded the new one, aiming it at the nearest Marilian who wanted to take me on. Adrenaline was coursing through me and so was my power. The Marilians were coming at us from all directions. '*The Marilian's have been busy*,' I thought.

Christik, James, the elders, and the others slid off their dragons and as the angels tapped into their power, the others reached for their various weapons of choice. The Marilians weren't giving us any option than to defend ourselves. They were rushing at us at such speed it was tough to slow them down, let alone stop them in their tracks. I fired at those closest to me, firing round after round. Qiu and the dragons began swiping at them as the angels tried to slow the monsters down.

There were bodies flying through the air, but as soon as they landed in a heap on the ground, they were instantly back up and attacking again. James was shooting with a pistol, Tracey had a Glock like me, and they were making a good team. As Akhenaten used his power to slow the Marilians, my husband and friend were picking them off one by one, while trying to edge their way to me and the palace.

There was no time to wonder where all the Marilians were coming from, but it was clear that the monsters had been on a mission to replenish their numbers and then some. We kept pushing forward through the throng, fireballs flying through the air, as they used the flaming torches against us.

The dragons were quick to intercept, batting them away as if it were a game, occasionally hitting our enemies. It was pure chaos, and my frustration and anger were building. The onslaught was constant, and no sooner had we put one of them down, another would take its place. We needed something to give us an advantage and then an idea popped into my head.

Touching my com, I reached out to all those around me, while trying to keep the Marilian's from slicing and dicing my body. One misjudgment and they were going to cut through my combat gear like it was made of jelly.

'*We need to try and blind them, so we can stop them long enough to get into the palace*,' I told them all. '*Can you all give off a big blast of white light*?'

I knew there was no way of knowing if it would work or not, but it was worth trying.

'*Yes, we can, Mel*,' Christik answered quickly.

'*What about the dragons? We don't want to blind them too, they'll be just as vulnerable*,' Tracey asked, her stress clear in her tone.

'*Do not worry young one, we will be unaffected by the light*,' Qiu told her.

'*Do it on the count of three*' I told them, as I saw their power beginning to emanate from their hands, while twisting and dodging yet another swipe of razor-talons. '*Three, two, one*!'

Trusting the angels completely, I raised an arm to cover my eyes, while closing them as tightly as I could. Even with them closed and covered I still saw some light, it was that bright.

'*Now, go!*' Christik said urgently through her com.

Quickly uncovering my eyes, I opened them to find all the Marilians around us stumbling blindly, lashing their talons through the air. They were desperately trying to slice something, anything, that could attack them now that they were defenseless. I bolted without a second thought, racing as fast as I possibly could for the palace doors. Stomping feet behind me let me know that James and the others were behind me.

I reached the thick, black, metal doors, looking and feeling for a way to open it with my free hand, unwilling to holster my gun.

"I can't fricking open it," I shouted as I started to panic.

We had no idea how long the Marilians were going to be blinded for or how much longer our advantage would last.

'*Move away young ones*,' Qiu said beside me in his smaller form.

Immediately we all backed away from the door, careful not to bump into the nearest Marilians, who were now roaring in anger and fear because they still couldn't see. Many were even blindly attacking each other in their panic.

Once we were all out of Qiu's way, he stepped back a couple of feet, sending the Marilians behind him toppling down like bowling pins. As they roared in shear rage, Qiu charged forward while lowering his head. The sound of the impact was as loud as a small explosion and the doors didn't stand a chance against the force.

The large, black, metal doors flew inwards, sending the Marilian guards on the inside flying across the stone floor. Qiu barged his way through, and I followed closely with James and the others. Three of the dragons followed behind in their smaller form while the rest blocked and defended the entrance.

We still didn't know how long we had until the Marilians were back to normal, and I wanted to try to make good use of what time we had. The thought of facing the king and the true bloods had my heart racing with nervousness, and my power was thrumming through my body, making my fingers tingle like the after-effects of pins and needles.

As soon as the knocked down Marilians got themselves back on their feet they were charging at us. There wasn't enough room in the palace foyer to fight, not with the dragon's bodies still being so big. When the first of the Marilians got to within striking distance, something in me snapped. I was pissed off that the monsters were so relentless, eating up our valuable time.

"Enough!" I bellowed in pure rage, holding out my free hand.

I was just as surprised as everyone else, when a pulse of blue lightning shot out of my hand, knocking the Marilian off his feet. It went flying through the air, only stopping when its body hit the wall. This time the monster didn't move. The rest of the Marilians kept coming at us and one after the other, I dropped them with more power bolts, one after another.

"Damn, woman, you're a bit freaking scary right now," James said from behind me.

I didn't turn around. We didn't know where the Marilians were going to come from next, but I smiled to myself.

"You'd better not piss her off in the future, James," Tracey joked. "If you do, you'd better run fast and zig zag."

James laughed at her remark, but it was short lived. Qiu was sniffing the air to locate the king. We were all assuming that he would have guards surrounding him by now, just in case.

When we turned a corner and into a corridor, there were more guards. Five Marilians were standing behind a line of fire on the ground, which was spreading up the palace walls. The moment they saw us around the corner, they pushed the red and orange flames towards us. There was no room and no way for Qiu and the other dragons to bat the flames away.

In one swift movement, Christik and Evest sprang from their positions, leaping through the air and over the top of the Longs. It all happened so fast. One second they were behind us and the next they were in front, using their power to deflect the flames from turning us to human fireballs.

I dropped my gun instantly as the Marilians tried to defend themselves against their own fire trap, sending a big blast of my own their way, through the gap between Christik and her father. Once they were down, I retrieved my Glock and we sped forward. Using their power, the angels extinguished the unconscious Marilians and the fire trap as soon as we were close enough. There weren't any more Marilians past the trap as far as we could see, and while catching my breath, I started to worry about those we'd left behind fighting.

"Do you know how the others are faring?" I asked Christik, who was now walking beside me.

"They are doing their best, Mel. The Marilians must have been stockpiling their captives."

Instantly, images appeared in my mind of the battle we'd left. Mental images from the angels who were trying to help our allies. There were so many hurt or dead, laying on the ground with devastating wounds. Then just as quickly they were gone.

"We need to step it up and get to the king," I blurted, the images of our injured warriors bringing home the urgency of our mission.

The palace was a maze of corridors and rooms with no organization, forcing us to back track a few times. It wasn't until we reached a wider corridor with stains on the walls that we realized we had reached the king's private area.

"What the hell is that?" Tracey asked, touching one of the dark brownish marks.

"That is blood," Akhenaten told her sadly. "This is the entrance to Drakron's trophy room; those marks are from the blood of his victims."

"He is one sick monster!" Tracey replied, wiping the blood off her fingers in disgust on her trouser leg.

There was another set of black, metal doors at the end of the corridor and what seemed to be a T-junction, with corridors leading off either side. With no guards in sight, it had to be a trap.

The angels were obviously thinking the same thing, I could feel their power building with every step we took. The hairs stood up on the back of my neck at the same time that we heard commotion behind us. They had flanked us, while we had been getting lost. I whipped around to find dozens of them at our rear, and I could hear more coming from the T-junction too.

Suddenly it was a frenzy. Bolts of fire and Marilians began flying through the air at us. They didn't care if they hit their own, as long as they were getting us in the process. Instantly we all leapt into action, dodging the fireballs and their razor talons while trying to take them down.

Qiu and the dragons tried to defend us again from the fireballs, while trying to knock the Marilians away with their own talons and spiked deadly tails. With my gun in hand, I aimed to kill, while trying to blast them with the other. One-minute James was fighting next to me, the next he was gone.

For a second, I thought I was going mad. I was sure I had seen a Marilian close in on James and then both vanished. Panic rose within me.

"James!" I screamed.

I turned wildly, trying to see him while defending myself. Tracey was fighting hard, her Glock in one hand and a knife in the other. I watched in horror as a Marilian leapt at her and they disappeared too.

"What the hell!" I screamed as my heart pounded in my chest.

"Tracey!"

Akhenaten's desperate cry made my blood run cold; I was beside myself.

Just as suddenly, the Marilians retreated. We were in the middle of the corridor panting, looking around wildly, while wondering how it could have happened. I was feeling frantic and so were the others.

We'd had no idea that some of the Marilians could flit like the angels, and now James and Tracey were God knows where. We now knew what the Marilian captive on Earth was hiding, but it was too late.

"Give me back my husband you evil scum bag! You've taken enough," I screamed, not actually knowing if any of them could hear me.

A loud clunk rang through the air, and we all turned in the direction of the large black, metal doors at the end of the corridor. The doors swung open towards us, and James walked out slowly with Tracey beside him.

They looked off as if they were under a trance, walking stiffly like they didn't have a choice.

When I realized that both of them had a sharp knife in one hand, my heart skipped a beat and my breath caught in my chest.

"James?" I called.

He looked at me with a completely blank expression, and as I started to walk towards them both, the others followed. I felt a gentle hand on the small of my back and I didn't have to see it, to know that it was Christik. Her power was seeping into my body, but rather than soothing my panic, she was feeding the power within me. James and Tracey halted a few feet from the doors, standing there like zombies, holding their knives downwards.

It wasn't until we were about ten feet from them that I spotted a black ring on James's middle finger and realized what was going on.

"That is close enough," someone roared from the darkness of the room beyond.

We stopped in our tracks.

"Drakron," Christik muttered under her breath, just loud enough for us to hear.

Emerging from the darkness was a hideous beast. The king was obviously a fierce Marilian once, but the monster before us now was a hunched over, shadow of his former self. Long, almost black, matted hair covered a worn out and withering body. His once needle-sharp teeth were black and overgrown, jutting from a severely scared face, but his blood red eyes still glowed with malevolence.

Drakron trudged forward slowly as if walking was painful, following behind him were at least ten old and battle worn Marilians.

I assumed that these were all the true bloods, but only one other walked close to the king, and she was just as hideous as he was. Drakron stopped when he reached James and Tracey, placing himself between them with his queen taking his side.

"I know why you are here," he drawled, as spittle dripped from his mouth.

"They think they can stop us." The evil bitch beside him sneered.

Just hearing them speak made my skin crawl, my anger building even more. My eyes flitted between James and Tracey's faces and the blades they were carrying.

"You've taken enough from us!" I declared, my emotions making my voice waver. "Release my husband and my friend, or so help me, I will fricking end you!"

My rage was building and building within me, and Christik's power that was still flowing into my body was only fueling it. I slid my gun in its sheath and touched my com, while making it look as if I was moving my hair away.

'*See the black rings on James and Tracey's fingers? They're the kings, get them off*," I told the angels.

"Do you honestly think any of you stand a chance of stopping us, earth woman?" Drakron sn-eered.

Christik's hands were glowing and so were her parents' hands. I glanced at James and Tracey, and I could see both rings were beginning to slip from their fingers.

"Nothing and no one can stop us. You are all feeble, but we will change that," the king promised.

His queen was just as vile, sneering and no-dding as her king spoke.

'*As soon as the rings are off, flit them both out of here and take the others*,' I calmly told the angels.

'*We are not leaving you, Mel*,' Lindaz stated.

'*You'd better protect them all then, Lindaz*.'

"You aren't going to take any more lives, you piece of shit," I shouted, as my hands started to shake with my fury.

"Really?"

With a click of his talons, James and Tracey instantly raised the blades they held to their own exposed necks. Drakron was getting them ready to slit their own throats, and my heart skipped a beat in fear. My eyes were darting from the black metal rings on their free hands that were nearly off, to the sharp blades that were causing trickles of blood to run down their bare skin.

'*Be ready,*' I urged the angels.

"You don't have to do this, Drakron," I said as I raised my tingling palms. I was holding in so much power, I felt like I was going to explode any second.

"I think I do," he drawled, spittle seeping from between his rotting teeth.

Before I could even blink my eyes, there was another click of the king's talons and James's blade sliced across his own throat. The scream that came out of my mouth didn't sound like me, but rather a badly wounded animal.

Evest and Lindaz vanished instantly, the moment Tracey and James's black rings dropped to the cold stone floor, just before James began to crumple. In less than a second, Evest grabbed Tracey and Lindaz was catching James. Her glowing hand clutched his open throat, before they vanished again only to appear beside us.

"Now!" I yelled, holding my hands in the true blood's direction. Everyone one of the angels released their power, protecting everyone behind me, as I released everything I had. A blast of dark blue power exploded from my body like a tidal wave; the king's blood-red eyes glowing with instant fear. The true bloods and the queen held up their thick arms to protect themselves, but as the wave of my power hit them, fueled by my rage and horror, they disintegrated before our eyes. I fell to my knees, suddenly exhausted, panting from the exertion.

There was nothing but black ash where the king, queen and true bloods had been standing, and I felt nothing but relief. Relief that they were no more. I hastened to get up, wanting to get to James. Qiu raised his leg a little, allowing me to use him to steady myself. My hands were shaking badly, and my legs wobbled as I straightened myself up.

As soon as I was upright, I could see Lindaz and Evest kneeling beside my husband, their hands glowing bright white as they tried to heal him. Bright red blood was pumping from his deep open wound, streaming off his neck and pooling to the stone floor. Panic was building in my chest and my heart actually hurt.

"Please save him," I gasped as tears sprang to my eyes.

Everyone was watching as the elders worked on James. Tracey was wrapped in Akhenaten's arms protectively, and she looked at me with total confusion, not knowing or understanding what had just happened. Christik glided to my side, feeling my pain and anguish.

"Please tell me it's not too late to heal him, Christik," I sobbed, not caring that I was crying in front of our friends.

Her arm wrapped around my shoulder, partly to comfort me and partly to stop me falling apart in a heap of anguish. I lowered my head, covering my face with my hands, letting my pain and tears flow freely.

"Mel, look," Christik urged softly.

My hands slid down my face to my mouth, and my uncovered eyes widened as I witnessed my husband's deep neck wound beginning to close. I sobbed in utter relief as everyone started to hug each other in celebration.

"Oh my God, don't think I can fricking take any more excitement," Tracey told Akhenaten as she began to cry into his muscular chest.

Stumbling on still shaky legs, I made my way to James, kneeling on the floor beside him and holding his blood-soaked hand as Lindaz and Evest continued to make him whole again. Tracey joined me, wiping her tear stained face before kneeling and stroking my sweat soaked back. It was a while before James's eyes started to flicker, showing real signs of life. When his eyes fully opened, my heart flipped in my chest.

“What’s going on?” he croaked.

“Sssh, don’t try to talk yet baby,” I said softly, placing my fingers over his lips. “You’ve been badly hurt, let Evest and Lindaz heal you.”

His eyes were still trying to focus properly as he tried to look around. My heart began to slow to a more normal rate as I watched the elders use their gift. I was feeling so many emotions. Gratitude that James was alive, relief that the king, queen, and his council were dead, and a desperate need to get off the god forsaken planet and get back to our kids.

As soon as Lindaz and Evest reined in their power and their hands stopped glowing, I knew that James was fully healed. My poor husband didn’t even get a chance to thank them. The moment that they straightened themselves, I flung my arms around him and holding him so tightly, it was a miracle he could still breathe.

“It’s ok, baby, I’m good now,” James soothed as I held him for dear life.

By the time I had collected myself and helped James up off the floor, the others were ready to go. I could feel that they were all ready to get off Marilia as much as I was.

“Did it work?” I asked Christik and the elders.

Their resounding smiles spoke volumes. "Yes, it did," Christik beamed.

CHAPTER 24

Qiu began to lead us out of the palace. We walked down the long corridors, finding newly changed aliens everywhere. Our allies rushing in to aid them alongside the angels. The aliens who were struggling to survive out of their normal environments were helped first.

"I know you are exhausted, Mel, but we will need your help to contain them," Christik said with regret.

"Don't worry, my friend. I knew that already." I smiled.

As we headed through the battlefield, there were bodies everywhere. We had lost many of our allies because the Marilians had had such large numbers. The angels were actively healing those who could be saved, while respectfully removing our fallen friends.

While the angels and our surviving allies organized the transport for the Marilians' victims through the star passage, the elders and I encapsulated all the others who needed help. James wasn't going to let me out of his sight and to be honest, I was glad, and I felt the same way.

Working tirelessly through the rest of the day and night, we were beyond exhausted and feeling dead on our feet by the time it was our turn to leave. As we boarded our craft to fly back to the angels' main craft, I felt a wave of euphoric relief wash over me, thrilled that we wouldn't have to step foot on Marilia ever again and that one day, the Marilians would just be a bad faded memory. I could only imagine the celebrations on each of the planets when their loved ones and friends returned home.

We had one day and one night of rest and catching up before I had to encapsulate James and the others for the journey back to Anunaki. It still didn't seem real that the Marilians were gone, even though I killed the king, queen, and true bloods myself. All I could think about was getting back to our kids and our new baby.

When we finally arrived back in Anunaki's

atmosphere, I was elated to be out of my protective power bubble. Even the after-effects of the journey felt like nothing compared to everything we had just done. Once my body was feeling back to normal, I went down to the holding room with the elders to release James and our friends.

We all made our way back to the control room and gathered at the front so we could look out of the large window. The angels' planet had never looked so beautiful and as we got closer to its surface, heading to the landing area, I could see angels, dragons, and humans had gathered to greet us. Suddenly, flares of bright white power began shooting into the air and I realized it was the angels celebrating.

We landed with the other large crafts, and it was wonderful to smell the fresh scent of a world that was alive and thriving. Holding James's hand, I stopped to take a moment to appreciate everything.

"Mom, Dad," a young female voice shrieked.

It was Abigail running towards us, with April chasing after her. We could see the rest of our kids following behind, and Holly was cradling Hope in her arms with Nalik beside her. My heart swelled in my chest as I gazed at our beautiful children.

Abigail launched herself into our waiting arms and as April reached us, she wrapped her slender arms around as far as she could reach. By the time our boys, Holly, Nalik, and Christine got to us, we were finally being released from the loving hold and the girls were in tears of relief.

"It's so good to see you all, my darlings," I told them as I took hold of my waking baby.

Hope's tiny wings began to flutter at the sound of my voice.

We hugged each one of our kids in turn, and it was medicine for our souls.

"So, you did it then? You all stopped them?" Holly asked with a huge grin.

"Honey, your mom wiped them off the face of their planet," James told them proudly.

Their eyes widened, and I wasn't sure if it was because they were impressed or sickened that their mom had killed. We were all so full of emotions it was overwhelming.

"I had no other choice," I said quietly while starting to feel ashamed.

"Mom you're amazing and I know if there had been another way, you'd have done it. We are so proud of both of you, you're fricking heroes," Anthony said in awe.

"Yay, our parents are bad-asses!" Abigail yelled, startling poor Hope.

Let's go celebrate and you can tell us what

happened," Holly added, just as Zanika began to approach with Tracey and Akhenaten's little girls.

The celebrations carried on deep into the night outside the angels' dwelling with the dragons, Impa's, and Jagu all sharing their stories of their own personal fight during the big battle. I lost count of how many of them hugged me, patted me on the back, or shook my hand and thanked me. There was no judgement on my actions, only gratitude that the Marilians were finally no more.

The kids finally said goodnight, taking Hope with them, and our warrior friends began to drift off to bed too, leaving just our usual group. We sat around the firepit soaking in the peace and quiet.

"I wonder what will become of us all now?" Mimi said quietly.

"We wanted to talk to you all about that, but we were going to wait." Christik smiled. "We would like you to stay and live with us permanently."

"We would also like to offer our world as your new home!" White Wolf stated.

"Us too," Orchi added. "We have a home for any of you who would like to live with us."

We must have looked ridiculous, looking from the angels to both chieftain's and each other. It was overwhelming to have such a gesture from all of them.

"Thank you, all of you," I said, in awe of their kindness. "We'll have to all think about it, but we're truly grateful."

That night James and I fell asleep feeling astonished that we suddenly had three possible homes for our race.

Over the next few weeks, there was much talk between ourselves as to what everyone wanted. Many of our human survivors had grown close to the Impa's, while others had bonded with the Jagu and angels. We were all thrilled at actually having choices, but it didn't make the decision any easier. What was clear was that our race was going to be spread across the universe on three different planets, and it made me wonder how each human colony would evolve over time.

James and I had a nerve-wracking conservation in the angels' gathering room with our kids, Nalik, and Christine. Neither of us felt we had the right to tell them what to do. They'd been through a battle for their lives and the end of our world. If that hadn't made them strong, independent people, we didn't know what would.

"Your dad and I think we would like to stay here with the angels," I told them. "I really don't want to leave, especially as Hope has so much angel in her. Plus, I don't want to leave Qiu either."

"It's not like we can't visit our friends if they decide to go with the Impa's or Jagu. We have the star passages, and we can visit them whenever we want," James added, "What are your thoughts?"

April looked at Abigail, who gave her an encouraging nod.

"I want to help dad re-establish all the animals we saved."

James smiled broadly, clearly very happy to have one of his girls working with him. Anthony sat up straight on the hanging day bed next to Christine.

"We're going to help the angels rebuild the homes of the Marilians victims, but this will be our new home too."

Harrison looked thoughtful as he listened, but he didn't say a word.

"What about you, Nalik and Holly?" I asked.

Nalik smiled at Holly with sheer adoration, and it was clear he would do anything for her.

"We're staying here as well. I think I want to record everything that's happened, so our future generations don't make the same mistakes as we did. I don't think people will need my help to organize new colonies now, as they're going to join existing ones."

"What are you thinking, Harrison?" James asked our youngest son.

"I honestly don't know what I want to do, so I'm going to help where I can here, until I can figure it out," he said honestly.

Abigail hadn't said anything, and even though I couldn't filter her emotions, I could tell by her lowered eyes and clenched hands that she was feeling nervous.

"Abigail, what do you want to do?" I asked gently.

"I'm going to live with the Jagu and train to be a warrior," she said as she looked up to face us.

My heart sank, but I could tell she'd made her mind up.

"Are you sure, darling?"

"Yes, I don't want to feel like a victim ever again. I want to be able to protect myself, friends, and my family," she said confidently, "Orchi's tribe are willing to train me."

The next few days were very tough and emotional as we said goodbye to our friends. Many left with the Impa's, including our body painting friend Ann, as well as Beccy and Derek. Next to leave were the Jagu and that meant Abigail too. I was relieved to discover that Mimi and Andrew had decided to go with them also. It was reassuring to know that Abigail would have familiar company, as and when she needed it.

Standing at the opened star passage gate, I was fighting back the tears. The Jagu and our friends had passed through, and now our youngest daughter was about to leave. She already looked every bit a warrior, dressed in combat gear with a large bag of clothes and supplies.

"You come back whenever you want, okay," James told her as she hugged him.

Hope was trying to flutter her wings in distress as she reacted to our heartbreak. Holly had tears streaming down her young face while Nalik tried to comfort her, while our boys and Christine were trying to keep it together like I was. When it was my time to hug her, I fell apart.

"Please come back if you need us, baby girl, okay," I said through my tears.

"I will, Mom, I promise," she replied, releaseing me to hug everyone else.

Holly struggled to let her little sister go and as Abigail walked towards the star passage gate, I honestly thought my heart was going to shatter into a million pieces. Abigail turned one last time. She smiled, and then she was gone. We walked away comforting each other, but we knew that we had a future now, on a new world with a new extended family.

By Beth Worsdell

The End

ABOUT BETH WORSDELL

Beth Worsdell is an English born author, who has lived in America since 2011 with her husband and four children. Beth loves to spend time with her family and their two golden doodles.

Writing is something Beth has always had a passion for. Beth began to write poetry as a child into adulthood, which turned into songwriting in 2007 when Beth was writing a poem, and the melody began to form in her mind.

Beth has written many songs over the years, writing about love, life and all the shenanigans in between. However, for the last couple of years, her focus has been on completing the Earth's Angels Trilogy.

Don't forget to follow Beth on her author pages, social media pages and join her angels on her website. Beth has regular giveaways, so keep up-dated.

Want to get featured on Beth's website? Send Beth a photo of yourself with your copy of her book, ebook or paperback, and send it to her via her social media or website.

Don't forget to tag Beth in your Earth's Angels, The Marilians or Destination Unknown posts, as it makes her smile, and she loves to share.

Leave your Earth's Angels and The Marilians book reviews on Amazon and Goodreads today. Let other bookworms read your feedback

Links

https://www.bethworsdellauthor.com/

https://www.facebook.com/BethWorsdellAuthorFantasyFiction/

https://www.facebook.com/EarthsAngelsTrilogy/

https://twitter.com/bethworsdell

https://twitter.com/EarthsAngelsNo1

https://www.instagram.com/bethworsdell/

https://www.instagram.com/earthsangelsbookno1/

https://www.youtube.com/channel/UCspTifrWrB3jsieleiN3-bw

Author Pages

www.amazon.com/Beth-Worsdell/e/B07JG9RYGN

www.goodreads.com/author/show/18523294.Beth_Worsdell

www.allauthor.com/author/bethworsdell/

www.booksprout.co/author/7141/beth-worsdell

www.bookbub.com/authors/beth-worsdell

Destination Unknown

Thank you ever so much for reading my Earth's Angels trilogy. I hope you thoroughly enjoyed my story. I can't wait to read your amazon review and if you share it on your social media pages, tagging me, I will send you a signed bookmark as a thank you.

If you would like to be featured as one of my Earth's Angels, send me a book selfie with one of my eBook's or paperbacks. Check out my other Earth's Angels at www.bethworsdellauthor.com

You can also become a member on my website, giving you up to date news, giveaway details and more. Plus, follow me on Facebook, Twitter, and Instagram.

Thank you again for your support.

Endangered Animals

African Elephant
African Wild Dog
Albacore Tuna
Amazon River Dolphin
Amur Leopard
Arctic Fox
Arctic Wolf
Asian Elephant
Beluga
Bigeye Tuna
Black Rhino
Black Spider Monkey
Black-footed Ferret
Blue Whale
Bluefin Tuna
Bonobo
Bornean Orangutan
Borneo Pygmy Elephant
Bowhead Whale
Brown Bear
Chimpanzee
Common Bottlenose Dolphin
Continental Tiger
Cross River Gorilla

Dolphins and Porpoises
Dugong
Eastern Lowland Gorilla
Elephant
Fin Whale
Forest Elephant
Galápagos Penguin
Ganges River Dolphin
Giant Panda
Giant Tortoise
Gorilla
Gray Whale
Great White Shark
Greater One-Horned Rhino
Greater Sage-Grouse
Green Turtle
Hawksbill Turtle
Hector's Dolphin
Hippopotamus
Humphead Wrasse
Indian Elephant
Indus River Dolphin
Irrawaddy Dolphin
Jaguar
Javan Rhino
Leatherback Turtle
Macaw

By Beth Worsdell

Marine Iguana
Monarch Butterfly
Mountain Gorilla
Mountain Plover
Narwhal
North Atlantic Right Whale
Olive Ridley Turtle
Orangutan
Pacific Salmon
Pangolin
Penguin
Plains Bison
Poison Dart Frog
Polar Bear
Pronghorn Concern
Red Panda
Rhino
Saola
Savanna Elephant
Sea Lions
Sea Turtle families
Seals
Sei Whale
Shark
Skipjack Tuna
Sloth
Snow Leopard

Southern rockhopper penguin
Sri Lankan Elephant
Sumatran Elephant
Sumatran Orangutan
Sumatran Rhino
Sunda Tiger
Swift Fox
Tiger
Tree Kangaroo
Tuna
Vaquita
Western Lowland Gorilla
Whale Balaenoptera
Whale Shark
White Rhino
Yangtze Finless Porpoise
Yellowfin Tuna

Printed in Great Britain
by Amazon

58421168R00239